COSMIC EGG RAPTURE

ROBB HOFF

Hydra Publications

ISBN: 978-1-940466-65-1

Hydra Publications
Goshen, Kentucky 40026
www.hydrapublications.com

For all those who embraced that fateful offer they just couldn't refuse:
to live the life of lovers like no other lovers have ever lived this life.

Collaboration 1
Brown Egg Resurrection

March 20th, 2010
White Stone, Virginia

"WE CAN NEVER REALLY KNOW WOMEN," the recently deceased author of the *Resurrection Gospel* told me. "We may think we do, but we don't."

At the time he said this, I was far more curious about the reel-to-reel film projector that he wheeled into the middle of his living room than his announcement about the mysterious nature of women. He shot a knowing smile at me before he pulled down the blank white projector screen attached to a tripod stand.

"And think about how treacherously women are portrayed to us in the chronicles of the Judeo-Christian tradition," he resumed as he reached for the projector's electrical cord.

"Consider the event at the Mount of Olives temple when a woman caught in the act of adultery was brought before Jesus. Was she stoned to death for breaking the seventh commandment or was she forgiven for her transgression?"

He stooped to plug the projector cord into the outlet strip on the floor. He then knelt on one knee, facing me as he awaited my answer.

"You know, that one sounds familiar," I began. "But please refresh my memory."

"Jesus refused to condemn the adulteress according to the Law of Moses," my friend smiled then stood to prepare the projector. "He simply told her not to sin again."

"So, Jesus ordered a slap on the wrist instead of a proper stoning?" I surmised.

"Indeed," he confirmed with his back toward me. "But first, Jesus told the throng to let he who was without sin be the first to cast a stone at her."

"Yeah, that's right, the whole 'he who casts the first stone' lesson," I said to my friend as I watched him try to pry open the metal film case with his fingernail.

"That statement by Jesus certainly was the memorable moment of the whole exchange," he remarked before the film case popped open and he turned the bottom half of the case upside down for the reel to drop into his hand. "But there was another facet of this event that seems far more intriguing to me.

"And what would that be?" I asked.

"Jesus bent down to write in the dirt with his finger two separate times while the crowd demanded that he mete out the appropriate justice for the adulteress."

"What did Jesus write in the dirt?" I blurted my question before my friend could continue.

"The first time," he began his answer before he undertook the task of attaching the reel to the projector, "maybe he wrote that we never really do know women."

"And the second time?" I posed to him on cue.

"We may think we know women, but we don't."

This preamble about women and adultery suddenly made me anxious.

"What does all of this adultery talk have to do with your film?" I finally asked him. "I mean, I'm really not interested in watching some kind of antique stag film if that's what you have there."

"I will halt all talk of adultery now," he said as he stepped toward the light switch on the wall beside the screen. "And you can chew upon another frame of reference before we start."

"And what would that juicy morsel be?" I tried to joke.

"The biblical account claims that eternal life without death on earth was forsaken because of the original sin of Eve," he replied. "But always remember this: without woman and her affinity for temptation and pleasure, there would be no cause of death.

"Without the necessity of death in this world for all of us, the most important facet of human spiritual life on this planet would never be known."

"Oh my God, what kind of film is this going to be?" I nervously half-laughed.

"This is all I'll add," his voice boomed as he placed his fingertip on the light switch. "Without woman and her seduction there would be no opportunity for humanity to ever know the one miracle even greater than creation itself – resurrection. Without woman, we cannot know our own souls or truly divine nature because we would never know of the power of resurrection released by human death."

THE ROOM IS dark before the black and white film starts across the projection screen. The grainy image of the face of a person lying supine appears from a close-up horizontal camera angle. As the camera zoom pulls back, the face assumes the features of a man. An egg teeters between his nose and his bloated bottom lip. Single corners of a few dollar bills are stuck to his face, and the traces of thinly twisted and curling mustache strands punctuate his cheeks. A hand emerges into view then the index finger of the hand pokes into the egg before the thumb and fingers spread open the broken shell of the egg.

Several ants scurry out of the egg across the man's rising face.

When the camera draws farther back, the man struggles to stand within a rectangular enclosure suggestive of a coffin. Coins and dollar bills fall from him as he uses a wand to gain footing in the false coffin. Once he does fully stand, he makes a sequence of hand gestures before pointing to the unseen ceiling with his wand.

The screen then fills with the poster-sized photograph of a woman's portrait. She appears middle-aged with full, shoulder-length streaked hair and smiles as she holds an egg between the thumb and fingertip of her extended hand.

A smattering of applause ensues before the camera view wildly spins away from the image of the woman on the ceiling to a pair of grayish eyes directly in front of the camera lens. The grayed, speckled eyes stare slightly off at an angle away from the lens itself. The camera then backs away from the eyes before the unblemished face of the same middle-aged woman revealed in the ceiling poster sharpens into focus.

High cheekbones hoist her lustrous skin. Her thick, wavy coiffure cascades in a stream of shades that shift between dark and gray before her hair silkily fans against her shoulders.

She wears an Op art printed top that shimmers from the lit projector screen. The checkered squares of the print pulsate within overlapped circles as the waist of the top clings to the curve of her high hips. The long sleeve of the top tightens against her wrist as she lifts her hand to reveal an egg of shaded contrast.

"Alpha and Omega," her silvery voice resonates as she holds the egg tip-to-tip between her thumb and index finger. "Your transfiguration awaits you, my love."

Her gleaming smile spreads above her succulent bottom lip to dimple the corners of her mouth, then her smiling face warps, her eyes bubble to show only white and a haloesque ring flashes around the crown of her head before her face instantly corrodes from the glare of exposure.

"WHAT DO YOU THINK?" my friend asked me once the screen went completely white.

"I'm definitely relieved that what you showed me was not debauched cinema," I answered as my racing pulse began to slow. "I'm not sure what I just saw at the end there with that alluring temptress and her egg, but as for the rest of it, I think I just watched the artist Salvador Dali get out of some kind of bathtub after an egg hatched spiders across his face."

"That most definitely was Salvador Dali," he confirmed as he turned on the light. "Those were ants not spiders, though.

"That was Dali in New York shot in 1965 as part of publicity performances in the city. I was there. The footage you see taken was mine. That's not the footage that was eventually used, however. There were two of us there shooting the event."

"That must've been some sight," I said with my heartbeat steadied.

"Indeed," he confirmed. "Never seen anything like it before and never have seen anything like it since.

"I was working in corporation film development at the time and living in Manhattan. I was hired to shoot just this one scene and then edit the film. I've mentioned this to you before but not in such detail."

"Nice gig to get, eh?" I remarked. "I guess you were credited for it?"

"Nice gig, yes, but credited, no," he replied. "Very good money for 1965.

"But if I had to do it all over again, I'd curse myself to Hell and back before I'd agree to take the camera for that performance. You see, the *woman* in this film has tormented me ever since I saw her face and heard her voice."

"Why's that?" I questioned him once he started to rewind the film onto the reel.

"That stunning creature who is filmed at the end of *my* footage apparently didn't really exist in human form as we know it," my friend bluntly claimed. "This is the last I saw of her or heard from her.

"To compound matters, this woman is nowhere to be seen or heard anywhere in the room at any time in the other footage that was actually used for this event. She just vanished like she was never really there to begin with. I've never been able to explain her presence, and it doesn't look like I ever will."

"Just because you don't see her on the other film doesn't mean she wasn't really there," I countered. "And she was pictured on the ceiling poster at the end, wasn't she?"

"That makes me even more convinced that she wasn't human as we understand it," he said. "The funny thing about that poster of her is that it only appears on my film version, not the one that was ultimately used, which featured a poster of Albert Einstein that I didn't even notice until I worked with the other footage.

"The *woman* filmed here seems more accurately described to me as a spirit in human form that has realized resurrection before death, almost like what was historically referred to as a doppelganger – a double of an actual person somewhere else at the time of the appearance – and, even more accurately described, an angelic human Nephilim who will eventually return to live on earth again once complete in her transfiguration."

I incredulously studied his face as I glared at him and could see there was an unusual edginess about him now that was accelerated beyond his customary energetic self.

"You got to be kidding me?" I shot back at him. "You're trying to tell me there's two different filmed performances and yours features this woman who wasn't really there while the other one does not?

"That's it? That woman is a paranormal entity – a doppelganger – trying to transform into a full-fledged angelic human who will live life on earth?"

"A Nephilim Siren who will live *eternally* on earth," he clarified. "But a woman who can astral travel and transcend time in her pursuit of consummation with a soulmate perhaps."

My friend then paced back and forth in front of me, rubbing his chin all the while. I could tell he was searching much harder than he normally did to find the right words to explain his theory.

"There is no way around this one," he muttered in an uncharacteristic loss for refined detail. "I've never been able to understand this ever since I discovered it."

"I'm really not sure how to follow what you're saying," I replied with mustered calm. "She had to be real. There's just no way she wasn't real. Maybe you added her to the film after the event happened."

"No," my friend somewhat snapped at me. "This entity clearly manifested before me as a direct result of the performance by Dali. It was as though Dali opened a portal for her to travel through time and the material dimension for the sole purpose of her interaction with me."

"Say I'm willing to go a little ways out there on your limb with this," I offered through a sigh. "Why and how would the Dali performance open some paranormal portal for this otherworldly actress of yours?"

"Dali's rise from the coffin-like structure was a resurrection of homeopathic magic," my friend began his explanation. "He reenacted an astral flight from a sarcophagus to the celestial dimension where resurrection renews being, much like the transfiguration an initiate would experience within the empty sarcophagus of the Great Pyramid of Ancient Egypt."

"So, you saw this as a reenactment of initiation into the practice of resurrection?" I asked him.

"More or less," he continued with his explanation. "I believe Dali's performance represented the astral flight that the initiate experiences once immersed within the capsule of the sarcophagus. It illustrates hermetical practice as the means of ascension from the constraints of physical being. This doesn't represent an entombment because of death: it is the pathway for resurrection achieved through enlightenment and separation from the body."

"You really think this reenactment shows and explains a pathway to resurrection through astral flight?" I asked him for further confirmation.

"Yes," he replied. "But that's not the aspect of this performance that effectively changed my life forever. There's one thing about this film that I just can't shake."

"What's that?" I asked.

"That non-existent woman is holding a real brown egg," his voice now boomed. "Not only did I see the brown egg with my own eyes, she more or less gave the egg to me when she flipped it up into the air for me either to catch or let fall to the floor while filming.

"I chose to catch the egg, and I still have that very same brown egg."

"You still have the same egg from fifty years ago?"

"Yes, I do still have the egg," he nodded. "I waited forever it seemed after I lowered my camera with the egg in my other hand, wondering if she might return from wherever she vanished. She never did return, though, so I wrapped the egg in a cloth and secured it in my camera bag.

"After I had kept it in my refrigerator for a week or so, the idea of preserving it for the long term somehow entered into my mind. I talked with a Chinese cook about the process and he actually found suitable materials for me to do it. I used a preservation technique derived from preparation of the Chinese century egg."

"What on earth did you do to the egg?" I probed in disbelief.

"Well," he began, "I had eaten century eggs before as they are considered quite the delicacy. Essentially, the egg is preserved in a way to force flavors to emerge that didn't exist before by virtue of the egg inside the shell slowly transforming instead of quickly spoiling like a normal egg would do.

"The name *century egg* really isn't accurate, though. In the traditional Chinese method dating back several centuries, the eggs are basically encased in a clay, lime and rice husk mixture for about a month or so that keeps the egg from spoiling and preserves it while it undergoes its change within the shell."

"Sounds like a glorified rotten egg to me," I commented, shaking my head.

"Actually, it's quite appetizing once you get past the kind of burnt-flame, ammonia scent," he countered. "It's somewhat unsightly though. The white of the egg becomes this clear brown jelly, almost an amber color. The yolk of the egg becomes a corroded-looking dark bluish-green like certain types of algae bloom."

"Did you ever think about eating your egg?" I blurted to my own surprise.

"Yes," he admitted. "Even more so recently, now that I've kept it for nearly a full half-century.

"But I'm not sure why any sane person would actually ever decide to eat it. I still do have to wonder, though, what it would taste like, how sick it would make whoever ate it, and whether or not it contains some secret from another realm that can only be conveyed by ingesting it. I just never have quite mustered the courage to indulge."

"Do you have it here?" I asked him.

"I do," he said. "Would you like to see it?"

"Of course, I would!" I blared. "How could you have kept this from me for all of these years?"

"I'll be right back," he laughed as he walked across the room. "It's in my deep freezer in the garage."

As he left the room, I remember thinking just how impossibly bizarre everything he was telling me seemed. From his version of the Salvador Dali footage to his womanly earth angel of Nephilim descent and a fifty-year-old frozen brown egg, nothing about his abrupt disclosure was particularly adding up for me, but it all seemed quite otherworldly exquisite just the same. Still, I just couldn't fathom how any of what he was saying was possible to the point where I once again had to question his motive.

Nothing in my dealings with him over the course of nearly a decade suggested that he would concoct deceit to such scale that he would stage some stunt with a phony angel-woman and an absurdly mummified egg. Besides, his body of work on the supernatural subject of spiritual manifestation into bodily form was well documented. Likewise, his literary affinity for Nephilim in some of his theories was no mystery to me either.

In the context of his oeuvre throughout his decades of production, there was nothing inconsistent with his explanation of the film and his beliefs. In fact, I could see why he found validation of his life's work through the presence of this haunting woman and her phantom brown egg in such an intriguing milieu.

I suddenly appreciated how the sheer presence and then disappearance of the woman on his film could challenge everything that exists in this world on the level we understand it if my friend were taken at face value with his claim. That inexplicable mystery for him would embody the closest manifestation of living proof that he could ever have of spiritual genesis into human form. Even if that were the case, however, he still hadn't explained her ultimate purpose beyond the message of initiation and resurrection associated with the performance by Salvador Dali.

While he was fetching his marvelous egg, I was beginning to comprehend just how serious he was about the whole intrigue conjured by the presence of the woman in the film. He had enjoyed a rather weird writing career that provided him with a decent living for nearly three decades. His four primary books all focused upon alternate history, especially his theory about the extraterrestrial or angelic origin of humanity through spiritual manifestation into bodily form. He initially called his theory of human origins from a strictly spiritual existence *psychogenesis*, but later dropped the term due to confusion about its meaning and stigma associated with the word in a formally psychological context.

His use of the term *psychogenesis* did not refer to the mainstream definition of the word in the field of psychology today – the psychological cause from which a mental illness or behavioral disturbance may be attributed. His use of the word *psychogenesis* may have been more aptly named *Psycho Genesis* with reference to the biblical account of human origins in the Book of Genesis.

"Here is the phantom object, shall we say," my friend's sonorous voice snapped me from my reverie as he reentered the room. "It is undoubtedly coated in the alkaline equivalent of the philosopher's stone, or maybe philosopher's soap. I really don't know what to say about this surreal shellac in all seriousness."

"Phantom object definitely is a fascinating description of it, especially in a literal context" I commented as I stood. "In the surrealist sense, that's exactly what you have there: it's materialized from some other dimension if you truly believe a vanishing angelic-like human creature or doppelganger gave the egg to you. Plus, clearly it no longer looks anything like an egg. That would have to be the most compelling phantom object ever considered in the catalog of surrealism, I should think."

"Very apt," he concurred. "But I've always fancied it more along the lines of a Cosmic Egg for some reason. I like to imagine that this egg represents the creation myth of ancient cultures in that the two halves that exist incomplete without each other are once again whole and together in this form, thanks to a little divine intervention from our ethereal leading lady."

I met him in the middle of the room and leaned toward the object as he held it in his hands. It was the size of a grapefruit. Its casing was a chalky conglomeration of clumped fragments. It resembled a cocoon of some sort much more than it looked at all like any kind of an egg. I shuddered at the thought of the potential chrysalis involved.

"What is covering it?" I asked as I touched it with my index finger.

"Well, not long after I applied the coating over the egg," he started to explain, "I decided to freeze it. The clay, lime mix that was originally used lasted until I eventually moved here, then it started to crack and deteriorate. I then decided to improvise by crushing oyster shells and lime-burning them before I mixed that with a mortar of Rappahannock River sand and mud right here from Mosquito Point Beach.

"I decided to continue to freeze the egg after I did that, but about twenty-five years had passed from the time I was given the egg to the time I reapplied the casing."

"This has to be the strangest story I've ever had anyone tell me," I said to him. "And I've heard quite a few, including several from you before this whopper."

"Truth may be stranger than fiction in this case," he replied. "But I still can't ascertain the exact purpose behind all of this. I really don't want to ever open the egg. In some respects, I don't feel like the egg or even the being who gave it to me were meant for me to ultimately receive."

I remember waiting for him to continue his account of the encased brown egg and the woman he thought could be either angelic or perhaps even a phantom object herself, but he remained silent instead. I finally lifted my gaze from his phantom object in front of me. He was staring at me with a smirk on his face.

"It has also crossed my mind," he finally said once I noticed his stare, "that this phantom object is like a statue that has encased the soul of some angelic source for the release of prophecy. All that is needed is the opportunity for that release to happen. Maybe you can find some inspiration in this. Who knows, you could even turn this into some kind of literary project one day if you discover that all of this was really meant just for you."

"If I can't," I responded, shifting my eyes from him to the transformed egg, "then it's certainly not for a lack of material. But that one day you speak of might be a long ways off because I'm really not too enthused about doing anything right now that requires any kind of extended creative undertaking or intellectual exertion of the paranormal variety."

"I understand," he replied before he carefully placed the encased egg on the center of his coffee table. "Few people understand the kind of commitment of mind and energy it takes to produce a lengthy literary project of distinguished quality.

"Even among other authors, the immersion into an otherworldly dimension is not something that most ever encounter, so a project like this would be asking a lot for someone to accept. You would almost have to be ordained, so to speak, and even then, there's no guarantee you would survive the onslaught such a project might unleash upon your senses."

"Now, I'd probably be more willing to take at least the egg off your hands," I remember saying uneasily, "if it were a turn-of-the-19th century Faberge egg."

His subsequent cackle alarmed me for how shrill and mistimed it was. All of these years later –now that I know what I know – his uncharacteristic outburst at that time didn't seem like a laugh to me at all. I'm really not sure what to call it now, but in retrospect I'm afraid it was more like a call to some agency within another dimension to let that entity know I was becoming his heir apparent. He was passing his torch to me, or the egg, rather, in this case.

"One day when all questions are answered for me one way or another," he resumed. "I will make sure the film and this egg find their way to you. That's all I can really do, I guess. The rest will be up to you and whoever or whatever you channel to assist you in such an enterprise."

"Well, don't worry about it too much," I replied with a surge of dread spiking through me. "Like I say, I'm looking forward to living sheer life without any complications due to literary or supernatural agencies. If you feel the need to leave this particular legacy to somebody else other than me, I sure will understand and probably be grateful you didn't give it to me."

"I understand," he said as he peered down at the egg on the table. "But time has a way of making saints and angels of us all if we live long enough and become sufficiently aware that such transfiguration is even possible, especially when we start to consider the truly transformative possibilities of the likes of Nephilim, Ancient Egypt, Atlantis and the Hall of Records."

"I've pretty much had my fill with all of that," I told him as I patted my stomach. "The last year we've spent working on the whole paranormal smorgasbord along those lines has bloated me to the point where I just can't take another bite."

"I really do understand," my friend remarked before he took the egg from the table and started back across the floor to return the egg to his garage.

As I watched him leave the room, I remember thinking how a Bahaman Atlantis and its potential Yucatan Hall of Records site became a topic that significantly motivated much of my friend's literary endeavors during the time that I knew him, but his forte remained the mythical Hall of Records of Ancient Egypt. I had done everything I could think of to try to effectively market his work on these subjects while I served as his literary agent but couldn't sell enough to financially justify my work for him in that capacity.

The synergy between these Nephilim, Ancient Egypt, Atlantis, and Hall of Records quadrants of his literary halo, if you will, compelled him to write *Resurrection Gospel*, which was his work in progress when I became his agent. While I shopped his new book elsewhere, I convinced him to excerpt parts of his unpublished work for the basis of another separate angle about Ancient Egypt and the Great Pyramid. This angle would essentially serve as an updated version of the seminal book he wrote in the mid-1970's about the Ancient Egyptian pyramids.

Based on the development of this analogous work, I found a magazine editor interested in a piece about why there were no mummies ever found in any of the sarcophagi of the Ancient Egyptian pyramids. The reason was the same as one that permeated his work dating back to his literary odyssey about the pyramids – the sarcophagi were not designed to be tombs but rather initiation capsules for spiritual enlightenment in the mysteries of astral travel and eventually resurrection.

Central to this piece was his hypothesis that Jesus Christ was initiated into the mastery of the resurrection religion within the Great Pyramid itself during the years of his life not detailed in the New Testament. According to my friend, Jesus had mastered the psychogenesis behind the act of resurrection by learning how to transport his astral body through the passages of the Great Pyramid until he physically appeared in the empty sarcophagi of the Kings' Chamber.

Those so-called "Lost Years" of Jesus were a rich resource of speculation for my friend and provided another foundation for *Resurrection Gospel*. The entire purpose of *Resurrection Gospel* was to provide the framework for resurrection as an art and science in which the participant was initiated in order not only to experience the precursory astral travel for resurrection but also attain awareness of the perfected union of body, mind, and soul while still very much bodily alive.

"Perhaps this "Lost Egg" and the "Lost Years" share the same yolk," I had mumbled to myself at the time while I awaited his return to the living room.

I knew that the actual biblical Gospel had become for him more of a handbook about how to achieve resurrection than the teaching of all other Christian messages combined. All of these other messages behind the teachings of Christ and the miracles performed emanated from this one basic truth about the life and death of Jesus for my friend – Jesus experienced resurrection both while alive as evidenced by such feats as walking on water and physical transfiguration, as well as after death through apparitional reemergence then permanent departure from physical form.

The magazine article he wrote about the absence of mummies in the tombs of Ancient Egyptian pyramids so impressed the magazine editor that he opened up dialogue about a potential collaboration between the two of them that could be serialized through the magazine. The editor was already deeply influenced by the previous works of my friend, so the idea seemed plausible enough to me as an agent. This proposed collaboration gained some traction once the central concept was agreed upon by both of them – the Ancient Egyptian location of that mythical Hall of Records espoused by the renowned "Sleeping Prophet" Edgar Cayce.

"You know," my friend blurted once he had returned the preserved egg to the freezer in his garage and re-entered the room, "I

would think that if there really were an Atlantis that did boast a superior or at least giant race of humans or hybridized human-angels like
Nephilim, any prospective Hall of Records would assuredly revolve
around their existence and their essence."

"That could very well be," was all I cared to say in regard to his
comment.

"I would think," my friend continued, "that of all the more
profound and ultimately transformative knowledge that any such
depository as a Hall of Records could reveal, it would most certainly
convey the true nature of human origins and the purpose behind
shamanic spirit flight and resurrection."

My familiarity with the subject helped me anticipate the direction my friend was headed. The Hall of Records is a supposed library
of knowledge about human origins and the lost civilization that
predated pre-dynastic Egypt, including the dubious Atlantis. This
would likely date the existence of any undiscovered Hall of Records
– if such a wonder exists – back to at least 3,500 B.C. and perhaps
even considerably more ancient than that.

I more or less knew what my friend was about to say next.

"Perhaps our lovely vixen on our humble version of a silver
screen here is a courier sent with the truth about the Hall of
Records," he said.

"That's it!" I nearly yelled. "Either you open a bottle of single-
malt Scotch or I'm leaving because that's what it's going to take to
keep me here to listen to you expound further on this mercilessly
vicious cycle of a subject!"

My friend laughed heartily at my eruption before he informed
me he was all out of single-malt Scotch. He might not have had a
bottle of his preferred liquid delicacy but did suspend his pending
oration long enough to pour two tumblers full of ice and blended
Scotch for us. I knew this would in all likelihood be our final drink
together, and I believed by the look on his face that he knew it, too.

"I guess this will suffice," I said before I inhaled the fumes from
the glass he handed to me. "Much obliged."

My friend wordlessly smiled in return before he clinked his glass with mine and we sipped.

"I have to admit to you," he managed through his Scotch-induced grimace, "I was looking quite forward to the collaboration you had arranged with our editor friend who bought the sarcophagi article."

I, too, had thought the collaboration arranged between my friend and the magazine editor had the potential for stunning revelation and some monetary success. Both held the Hall of Records in quite high esteem within their respective pantheon of unsolved mysteries from antiquity.

Quite simply, the collaboration between these two proposed to use different approaches to find some common ground about the existence of the Hall of Records and its location buried beneath the Giza Plateau or elsewhere in the region. This endeavor had been pursued before by countless others and remains on the radar of some actively involved in this fringe aspect of Egyptology.

"I thought so, too," I finally added after gulping another swig of Scotch that drained nearly half the glass.

For my friend, Edgar Cayce was the only real mouthpiece for the Hall of Records. The very phrase 'Hall of Records' likely originated with Cayce himself during one of his entranced psychic readings. Cayce also pinpointed through trance that the history of the lost civilization of Atlantis was contained in a second related Hall of Records somewhere within the Yucatan peninsula from which the Mayan civilization eventually sprang. This second depository of ancient wisdom in the Yucatan became almost as important for my friend in his later years of research and writing as the Hall of Records purportedly covered by Egyptian sand.

"I wish somebody would find some kind of Hall of Records in my lifetime," my friend bellowed before he sipped more Scotch from his tumbler. "Then I would know if my theory was true."

His theory was that the discovery of the Hall of Records would induce such a transformation of collective consciousness that humanity would be transfigured by the rapture of omniscience for a

whole new and different level of existence. It could amount to
paradise regained and death overcome for eternity with the purity
and power of Adam and Eve restored for all to experience as a revital-
ized Garden of Eden. At least that was my friend's predisposition to
consider discovery of the Hall of Records in this light, as though the
discovery itself could precipitate the actual Rapture and Second
Coming of the Christian Messiah.

Despite his paranormal bent, my friend most definitely was a
practicing and, for all functional purposes, devout Episcopalian. His
beliefs about Adam and Eve, Nephilim, resurrection, transfiguration,
and the like were all steeped in his Christian faith, much like these
beliefs were engrained in the Christian mysticism of Cayce.

"Verily," I belched in return once I had drunk the rest of the
Scotch from my glass.

My friend and his magazine-editor collaborator both had agreed
in principle upon this Jubilee revelation of an unearthed Hall of
Records, which was also intimated by Cayce. The structure of their
collaboration would allow them to develop their own respective
expectations about the particulars of knowledge revealed by any
speculative Hall of Records discovery. Both agreed that the location
should be confined within Egypt for that more storied and culturally
recognizable Hall of Records.

But even though the two agreed to limit the scope of their respective Hall of Records quest to Egypt and not include the Yucatan, the
two greatly diverged in the Egyptian aspect of their proposed collaboration.

For one, the possible spring equinox alignment of the constella-
tion of Leo between the paws of the Sphinx in the year 10,500 B.C.
was the starting point from which to find the "X" that marked the
spot to the buried Hall of Records.

For the other, a mathematical model was used to calculate a
proposed location for the Hall of Records outside of the Giza Plateau
where time itself perhaps originated through the agency of the
Ancient Egyptian deity Thoth in his psychogenesis from the Duat

realm of dead and supernatural beings. This spot was further delin-
eated by the presence of figurine votives unearthed in a previous
cursory excavation of the site identified.

Unfortunately, the two sites depicted were too vastly different
from each other. Neither collaborator was able to convince the other
of the ultimate merits of the other's theory. The two sides couldn't
find enough common ground to merge both of their theories into one
project.

They were as far apart as the Yucatan peninsula and the Giza
Plateau, and there was nothing more I could do about it.

This stalled collaboration marked the end of my journey in
actively working with my friend as his literary agent. My efforts to
market his work ended after about a year in large part because I
would be moving soon and intended to drop all of my literary
endeavors for the future.

"You know," my friend cheerily began as he grabbed the bottle of
Scotch to pour another drink for me, "I thought of contacting The
Institute about the Hall of Records idea again to see if they might be
able to use their resources to help me find the woman in the
Dali film."

By *The Institute,* I knew the group to which he referred. He had
affiliated himself with this alternate history research group for more
than two decades, but I wanted nothing to do with them due to
their arcane mission of paranormal research and their questionable
tactics when it came to acquiring information and actualizing
events.

"What was it that lovely egg lady said again?" I asked him to
repeat for me without mentioning The Institute in reply.

He immediately stepped to the projector then forwarded the
film. He stepped to the light switch, turned off the light, and returned
to the projector. He then replayed the film from the point right before
her eyes overtook the lens:

"Alpha and Omega: Your transfiguration awaits you, my love."

My friend stopped the reel before her image completely warped on the frame. He stood there silently looking at her again, shaking his head.

"That certainly does sound like something an earth angel in the trappings of a human woman would say," I sniped at him before I pressed the tumbler rim against my bottom lip.

Once I swallowed my sip of Scotch, I resumed my line of inquiry with him:

"So, you honestly believe that this rather attractive, forty-year-oldish woman in your film is holding up that egg and saying *Alpha and Omega. Your transfiguration awaits you, my love* just to demonstrate that she's an incarnation of an immortal Nephilim hybridized from the loins of a human mother and an angelic father?"

"I will continue to maintain that she is the progeny of the human-angelic hybrid race of Nephilim," my friend declared. "To be more precise, even, she is a primordial *Siren* who I believe is the incarnation of one of the original hybrid women who were begat through intercourse between human women and the angels that first manifested themselves into human form on earth by means of psycho-genesis.

"There is no evidence that you see here now to suggest that she is what I have hypothesized for you, but later in time, you might also come to feel the same way as I do."

"Why are you just showing this to me now?" I asked somewhat gruffly to voice my slight annoyance by the timing of all of this.

"You're permanently leaving the area soon," he answered, turning toward me now with the smiling face of the woman still visible on the projection screen in the unlit room. "I wanted you to know this so that you may one day pick up this thread if you so choose. You may never discover anything more about her than what I've told you, but I have to know that I at least tried to have someone else who trusts my intelligence and sanity know about this."

"What is it exactly that you want me to do?" I snapped him, suddenly more agitated now that he seemed to be conferring some directive upon me that I did not want to accept.

"I don't know," he replied. "But if you ever see the face of this woman, you need to know that you're no longer only dealing with just a woman. You're in the midst of a presence from an altogether different dimension of existence – an earth angel descended from Nephilim or perhaps the prototype Siren who is the most ancient and archetypical of all Nephilim. Who knows for sure?"

He finally turned off the projector. The woman was gone for good. He stepped to the wall switch to turn on the light then returned to the projector to rewind the film and return it to its case.

"Well," he announced as he stooped to unplug the projector from the outlet strip on the floor, "I guess that's all a wrap then, isn't it?"

"I'd say so," I replied as I leaned toward him with my hand extended. "It sure has been real. Well, for the most part."

I bid farewell to him. Both of us knew that this meeting could very well be our last. As intriguing as his literary enterprise had proven to be for me, I was glad to be leaving that behind with my imminent move.

When it came to writing and literary projects, I had quite simply had enough at that time. My new life with my growing family in a new place held such an appeal of normalcy for me that I just couldn't wait to get started by shedding my old literary skin.

But despite my determination to shirk the written word, I still felt some jarring sense of wonder about the film footage and the fantastical phantom object of the century egg that my friend had shown to me the last time I saw him before I moved. I admit I was both intrigued and skeptical for a week or so but had too many other earthly matters at hand for the film footage, the enchanting woman, or her otherworldly egg to remain relevant in my mind for too much longer after that.

I just didn't have enough time, energy, or desire to put too much thought into trying to wrap my mind around something that promised nothing more than another frustrated search for answers that probably didn't exist or, even if they did, were beyond any real purpose to understand or care too much about at that point in my life.

Now, I know better. All I had done was shed skin. The same creature I harbored remained beneath the discarded vestige. Once I decided to start writing again a few years after the move, I discovered that not only was my literary identity preserved intact but that I had grown stronger, sharper, and more resolute to resume the purpose that I had abandoned.

I was writing again for different publications, and although I hadn't pursued any book-length projects up to this point, I felt like my literary renewal was vocational redemption. If I had known then what I just discovered before chronicling this collaboration to this point, I would've done an about-face and ran for my life. It is now too unfortunately clear that no one should think what I think and no one should know what I now know.

If I had listened to what my friend was really trying to tell me and heeded what he had shown me before I had moved, I would've never left and moreover probably would've become obsessed with what I now realize I've only delayed. Maybe then he would have told me the full story about the film and the scene that I didn't see at that time. Maybe then I could have convinced him to tell me the whole story so that I could have proceeded from there. Maybe that's all he was really trying to do anyway was to help me like no one else on the face of the earth could help me because no one else knew what he knew about what was going to happen to me.

But all of that will have to flesh out with the rest of this story, which I must write by living out as resolutely and fearlessly as I can. There is no other recourse for me now. I write for my sheer survival, and I am sad to report that I fear I am losing the battle.

Had I known then what I know now, I would have pursued the woman in the film to the ends of the earth with all of my resources and might. Instead, as it turned out, she's the one who found me, and with her discovery of me came my own earthly undoing. I've come to understand that my place in this world is far more fluid than I ever imagined and that the world that seems to be relatively normal is far more mysterious and miraculous than it ever appears during the course of our earthly life.

I have to preface this undertaking this way so that it is clear that what follows from here is the only real will and testament that I can possibly leave now because I have come to gain a sense of acquaintance with the unfathomable omniscience at the heart of us all. I understand more now what I am than who I am, and that will be the closest manifestation of a legacy that I shall ever be able to bequeath to anyone even remotely interested enough to consider that or this worth anything at all to them.

That day when my friend played the film was the last time I saw him until it was too late to delve into his mind with his full wits about him. I only communicated via mail and phone twice over the six years after I moved. About a year before the writing of this preface, I talked with him over the phone when a mutual friend called me with him in the car. My friend had been walking along a back road a few miles from his house when he was picked up. He had little idea who he was or why he was wandering where he was.

The onset of dementia had rendered him seemingly lost forever. Even though he could speak quite clearly, he had no idea who I was. Not only had we worked together for six years for an employer and worked closely on his literary projects, but we had also watched football games just about every Sunday during football season for almost the whole time I lived in the same area as him. That was in part how I knew how far gone he was at that time and how much of him still remained despite his condition.

You see, my friend was a lifelong Green Bay Packers fan. On different occasions, he had recounted some of his trips during his youth to the "Frozen Tundra" of Lambeau Field to watch his beloved Packers play. When I talked with him that time he was picked up in the car, I asked him questions about the Packers. He still remembered the Packers' Hall of Fame quarterback Bart Starr quite well but couldn't locate any memory of the more recent Packers' Hall of Fame quarterback

Brett Favre. He said Favre must've been before his time of being a Pack-ers' fan, even though he was with me watching a televised game played in Cincinnati when a fan ran onto the field and snatched the ball away from Favre before running away downfield in the other direction.

I knew at that time my friend was off on his own journey into a world of unfamiliarity and confusion. I later found out that he even-tually lost his home during the fallout of the Great Recession of 2008. He apparently was wandering around within a couple of miles from his former home, sometimes taking shelter in an abandoned outbuilding not too far from his former residence and other times seeking private beaches or woods in the area to find sleep. Some of his friends and neighbors were helping to take care of him by making sure he had food. He would also go to their houses in the area when he needed things.

His itinerant sustenance eventually came to an end when he was finally admitted to a long-term care facility. Once I discovered this, I decided that I should reverse my course of separation from my previous life and visit my friend once again. Some time passed before I gained permission to visit him at the facility that housed him, but I eventually was able to clear my schedule for a few days and fly down to meet with him.

December 22nd, 2015
Tappahannock, Virginia

"I'M RETIRED NOW," my friend said through a beaming smile as he stood thin in his Santa Claus suit that included a red Santa hat with white pompom at its end.

"Must be nice," I said while we vigorously shook hands.

"It's fantastic!" he exclaimed. "Three squares a day and plenty of running water! Only downside is the people here. Too much going on upstairs for me to want to deal with, if you know what I mean."

Although my friend did look appreciably older than the last time I saw him, he proved to be in great spirits and possessed that same dynamic enthusiasm that I remembered so well. His wiry, full head of hair and beard were hoary white now and his face bore the wrinkles and cracks from his seventy-five years. When I asked him his age, he replied that he was only thirty-three-years old.

"Same age as Jesus probably was when he died," he whispered and winked once he leaned toward me.

"Jesus, eh?" I prodded.

"That's right," he resumed with normal voice. "The savior of all mankind and the master practitioner of the art and science of resurrection. The only one of the masters of the resurrection religion to ever find their way to the empty sarcophagus in the Great Pyramid King's Chamber from the pit at the bottom of the Descending Passage."

"That's right!" I exclaimed, snapping my fingers as I spoke. "Weren't you working on a book called *Resurrection Gospel?*"

"Not that I recall," he said after pausing to rub his chin. "Sounds like a fine book project, though. Definitely something I would like to read if I had the patience to sit down that long."

"Were you working on any kind of book project recently?" I asked him.

"Yes, I was," he admitted to me with outspread hands. "But they all thought I was out of my mind again."

"What kind of book is it?" I asked.

"Well, I've given up on it now," he replied. "Like I said, I'm retired."

"Can you tell me about what you were doing with the project before you retired?" I entreated him. "I'd be interested to know."

"Who are you again?" he snapped at me.

"I'm with a research institute studying the Sleeping Prophet, Edgar Cayce," I lied to him. "We're very much interested in what you might be working on now, even if you're only thinking thoughts that you're not writing down."

"Finally," he leaned forward again and whispered. "Where have you been? I've been waiting for someone to come back. It seems like forever, I think, unless I'm stuck in some kind of time warp."

"We couldn't get here until now," I continued with my lie. "You know how it is when you get busy."

"Indeed," he concurred with his tone still subdued. "The police pulled me off the site, not that I had actually reached the Yucatan Hall of Records from there. But still, I think I know how its message is being conveyed audibly. It's quite a fantastic transmission."

"But you were not in the Yucatan." I politely pointed out.

"I know that," he replied with vexed tone. "The site is not actually in the Yucatan. It's about two miles inland from Mosquito Point Beach. What I'm saying is that the knowledge contained in the Yucatan Hall of Records is transmitted to this site."

"How do you know that?" I asked, nearly laughing.

"I heard the earth angel Siren singing the hymns of lost knowledge at the site of an unused aquifer well tap," his voice grew increasingly louder as he continued. "The voice was the glowing light of the very same earth angel Siren I saw once. She was transfigured alive with the glory of light, singing the truth of eternity and revealing all secrets of the universe to me in a tongue I did not need to speak to understand."

His voice was now booming. I noticed a couple of attendants across the spacious meeting area glance toward us. I tried to calm him down and convince him to lower his voice.

But it was to no avail.

"She sings of the resurrection that ends all suffering, all mystery," he was now yelling and strutting about the room, waving his hands and pumping his arms in his Santa Claus suit. "She sings of the next Ascension and its time when the way is cleared through the Tribulation for Heaven on earth to open up to us again, and we live our new life with all knowledge in our minds, all the love in the world and beyond in our hearts, and all the bliss in Heaven in our souls! Her melody courses through my veins like the Pyramid Texts of Unas, telling me the time is coming for me to step out of my body to join her and the others. The revelation she unveils for me makes me feel weightless and electric like my soul is engorged from the expectation of the Rapture that will deliver me to my own resurrection!"

By the time the two attendants reached him, I understood there was nothing I could physically do to intervene between him and the two large men now beside him. I yelled in a voice louder than his with the hopes that my reaction might help him subdue his fervor.

"Remember you're retired!" I shouted. "We'll take it from here!"

Fortunately, my exclamation stopped him from continuing his otherworldly inspired rant. Each of the attendants took him by an arm and began to walk him away from me. He managed to turn back to look at me one last time.

"Thanks for the visit," he said to me as his Santa Claus hat fell from his head.

Watching him whisked away like that brought tears to my eyes in more ways than one. It was sad to see my longtime friend in the throes of such crushing memory loss. At the same time, tears of joy were mixed with those of sadness. I was elated to know he could still wholeheartedly launch his beliefs through the voice of his former self with the utmost conviction, even if he no longer had any idea who I was.

He might have lost much of his memory, but he hadn't yet lost the most meaningful part of his identity. He still was the inhabitant of his own understanding of his human soul. His possession of his mind blurred into this realm that now seemed oriented toward one location alone – the celestial end to his earthly means through the miracle of resurrection, whether it be the Resurrection through the agency of Jesus Christ or his own self-actualized resurrection enabled by his earthly mastery of resurrection religion.

I really thought that would be the final time I ever saw him. I would've been somewhat content if that was our last encounter, knowing that the vestige of his former self still lurked within the depths of his infirmity. He still recognized himself floating above the murk of memory sunk and stuck in the bog of his mind.

Little did I know then that there were forces lining up that would help him come out of his 'retirement' to resurrect his bizarre career before there would be any actuality of death and promise of final resurrection fulfilled. It was almost as if he were ordained to survive not only his condition but thrive like he hadn't in quite some time because he was summoned for an encore to refine the literary legacy he would bequeath to those few who could competently decipher the essence of his quest.

I had returned home to Kentucky the next day after my friend's rant in the long-term care facility. Only a couple of months had passed before I was contacted by a mutual friend of ours and apprised that he was actually returning to the house he had called home for the quarter of a century prior to his admission to the long-term care facility.

Friends and advocates of his through his church and The Institute where he had frequently spoken about Edgar Cayce had decided to buy his house then provide the necessary care assistance to ensure that he could return there to live without incurring the constant vigilance of authorities.

I was told by an attendant of his affairs that the visit I had made to him at the care facility had helped him tap into some inner dimension that gave him stream-of-consciousness access to a font of prophetic mysticism, like he was some kind of shaman now spouting divine insight instead of an aging elderly man who was losing his mind. It might have proven to be just a short-lived reprieve, but he was out of the woods for a while with as much of a chance for a new lease on life that his condition would permit.

I was invited by his attendants to visit him at his familiar home. I gladly accepted. I had to see for myself what had happened to him, so I returned to visit him again for what I truly believed would be the last time.

March 20th, 2016
White Stone, Virginia

DRIVING down the dusty macadamized road to the neighborhood where my friend's house stood brought back memories of my visits with him when we would discuss some topic related to his fields of study in depth over bourbon or Scotch. Many times, we had convened our meetings of the minds for hours on end to delve into the details of a project or theory. Often times those meetings concluded with a walk along the white sand of Mosquito Beach across the road from his house.

The road to his house cut through the forest of this Tidewater place – loblolly pines scattered among the poplars, walnuts, and oaks that flourish in the usual absence of tropical storm winds. The inland character of the area complements the aquatic beauty that carves through the terrain by virtue of so many brackish creeks flushed from the ebb and flow of the two tidal rivers – the Rappahannock and the Potomac – that form the Northern Neck peninsula.

The lay of land and water that struck the English explorer Captain John Smith when he sailed into the region in the first decade of the 17th century still remains largely traceable despite the passage of so much time and the presence of inhabitants who used the environs for their own purposes. Smith wrote that heaven and earth had never so agreeably framed a place for human habitation, almost like the place somehow radiated with the promise of a resurrected Eden itself.

The area was also the birthplace of America in many respects with three of the country's first five presidents born on the peninsula. The mother of George Washington and the first American president himself were born in the midst of this storied Northern Neck.

And now here I was again back within all of this history and natural splendor with just a single-minded purpose to my return. I hoped my friend would be up for the visit. I had to clear it with the network of caretakers who had taken his charge. I was advised that there would be others present with me during my visit with him but wasn't told exactly who these people would be.

When I turned past the pink-flowering camellia to pull into his driveway, his presence alongside the gravel startled me. He was facing me, and it seemed to me like he was expecting my arrival. I didn't doubt that he might be told I would visit, but I didn't expect him to be standing halfway out in his front yard waiting for me.

As I braked to a stop, the front door of his house opened and three men filed outside. My friend turned to them as he pointed toward me and said something to them that I couldn't discern. I shifted into park and dismounted from my rental SUV.

My hearty greeting induced a toothy smile from him. I stepped toward him with my hand extended for him to shake. He leapt toward me, vigorously clasping my hand and strongly shaking it.

I smiled as I introduced myself, then we released our handshake.

"Who exactly are you?" he asked me.

"I used to live around these parts and thought I'd stop by for a visit," I said. "Some friends of mine said I ought to look you up and stop by for a chat."

"Excellent!" he beamed. "What would you like to converse about?"

"Whatever you would like," I smiled in return, pleased to see him back at his homestead with access to the community private beach that he loved so much.

"You are the one who the earth angel Siren in the well foretold would come," he blurted to me before he turned to face the three men. "You see, there is a wheel of fate spun throughout all of this world that makes the golden mean unravel its threads of faith. Without this splendid silk of time, we have no basis for judging our way through mortal existence. Only the extraordinary departure into the dimension of these earth angels makes us fully realize the promise of our everlasting resurrection."

The three men stood attentively while my friend spoke, nodding at times. My friend then returned his attention to me once he finished addressing them.

"Who are you again?"

"I am just another humble servant of the Alpha and the Omega," I answered him once we released our handshake. "The steward of revelation from the past and future for this present time."

"I knew it!" his voice boomed. "You are the one whose consummation with the earth angel Siren I met will beget the egg from which salvation will hatch for those who cannot receive it in any other way. They will eat the light and shine from all of God's glory, transfigured within until all of the unknown colors of the universe burst through their skins and shoot to heaven. They will all be transfigured!"

"The *Resurrection Gospel*," I said.

"Exactly!" he shrieked, his eyes bulging and his finger pointing at me. "The consummation between you and the Siren will finish one chapter of that book so that you can write the last chapter about the origin of time and the defeat of death."

"I did not realize that I was a collaborator," I said.

"We are all collaborators in this ancient mystery religion," he said with a wink. "Some are asked to play much bigger parts than others, though, and those whose roles change the course of history and transform the spiritual realm within this earthly corridor find that their ability to channel the convergence of minds is truly the charge of saints and angels.

"This is ordained and actualized by the genesis of spirit into flesh. All we have to do is take advantage of the opportunities that present themselves to us for us to remember who we truly are."

"The psychogenesis," I added.

My friend then turned from me to address the three men still standing at some distance from us.

"Yes, I believe a shaman of the wisdom tradition once called it such," he resumed before he squatted to scrawl something in the gravel driveway with his index finger. "And once we understand their presence through our own earthly and eternal salvation, we can then strive to practice the art and science of resurrection to find out if we are one of these blessed saints or heaven-sent angels."

"We can't become either if it's not already within us to become one or the other," I pursued his reasoning. "But we can learn how to fulfill our own fates if we are saved and realize that such entities as saints and angels even exist?"

"You sound like me now," he remarked before he sprang to a stance and turned toward me, grinning. "I'm afraid not everyone gets to go."

"But there's one thing that caught my attention that I don't quite understand," I said. "The idea of consummation with this Siren earth angel you speak of, is that a physical consummation?"

"I suppose it could be," he answered. "But I've only seen one angel who seemed to know she was an earth angel or a Nephilim Siren, rather. That would be quite an extraordinary experience to consummate with an earth angel who knew she was an angel already. You would be one lucky guy to find yourself in that situation!"

"How can you know if you're with an angel who doesn't know she can be an angel?" I asked in return. "I mean is there some way to tell if a woman can become an angel before there's any thought of consummation like you're suggesting?"

"Good questions," he said rubbing his chin. "That might require an entranced communion of some sort within the astral realm to divulge the truth. Or maybe some type of reenactment could enlighten us if we could just locate a suitable earth angel."

"You mean a trance like Edgar Cayce underwent?" I asked him before he could communicate his train of thought about his concept for reenactment.

"Perhaps," he said with a wave of his hand then squatted to scrawl with his finger in the gravel of the driveway once again. "I would have to go back to hear the Siren earth angel sing at the well for that, and they've said I can't return there for now. Every day I wake up, I'm told about the angel and the well where the Yucatan Hall of Records is broadcast for me to hear. And each and every day they tell me that I can't go back there today. Maybe tomorrow will be different, but I believe the longer that I'm kept from returning, the likelier it is that she'll leave for good."

"That is correct," the shortest of the three men came forward and addressed me as he held out a business card for me to take. "My name is Thoth, and I'm the director of external affairs for the research institute named on the card.

"We have been the primary caretakers for your friend in his return to his home for the past couple of months. The Institute has functioned as guardian for your friend to ensure he can spend as much of the rest of his life as possible in these comfortable and familiar surroundings."

"Thoth," I uttered as I read the card. "So, your namesake is the Word, the Logos, the highest manifest god of Ancient Egypt who might just be the Lord of the ever-elusive Hall of Records."

"Very impressive," Thoth replied. "But unfortunately for your friend, there can be no trance at the Hall of Records well site in this locale today due to certain trespass issues that our legal team is trying to resolve, but we have arranged for a reenactment in the meantime that you might find interesting."

"What's that?" I asked. "What reenactment?"

"Our friend here once witnessed a peculiar piece of performance art in New York City in 1965," Thoth said. "It was Salvador Dali rising from a coffin-like state. He had an egg on his face and broke its shell to release several ants from the egg before the artist stood up."

"I know this," I interjected but stopped short of telling the man about the existence of the film and the oddly preserved egg that my friend had once shown to me. "And he was covered with dollar bills and coins. Then he stood up and pointed with his wand at a poster of a rather lovely middle-aged woman."

"No," Thoth contradicted. "The poster was of Albert Einstein. There was no woman involved in that performance."

My friend had wandered to a magnolia tree in the front yard and was rubbing one of the trees glossy green leaves. I watched him but peripherally noticed the tallest of the three men approaching me.

"We realize this may seem a little outside the bounds of normal decorum," the tallest man said to me. "But this reenactment was negotiated as part of your friend's release from institutional admission. Without our intervention, he unfortunately would have remained in that facility where you previously visited him."

"And who are you?" I asked.

"My name is Horace," the tallest of the three men introduced himself. "I am a technical-assistance attaché for the same institute as Thoth."

"Horus?" I blurted. "Really? The institute's director of...what was it...external affairs is named Thoth, and now we have a specialized attaché from The Institute who is named after the immaculately-conceived son of Isis and Osiris."

"I can assure you that I was not named after the Horus of Ancient Egypt," this second man stated, "but, rather, after my maternal grandfather, whose named was spelled H...O...R... A...C...E.

"Part of the reason why we're doing this today is that we were told you would be here. We know who you are and also know about your unique background involving Egyptology in relation to your friend's literary endeavors, even if he doesn't remember you. We appreciate the impact that you've had upon his literary development during his later years."

"What was that you said about a poster of a lovely middle-aged woman on the ceiling of the Salvador Dali reenactment?" the third man blurted. "Do you know who this woman is and her potential whereabouts if she is still alive?"

"Why do I all the sudden feel like I'm being carted in here like a prop," I remarked without answering the question about the poster of the woman in my friend's film. "I mean, this just doesn't sound or feel right."

"Please don't be flustered," this third man tried to allay my concerns. "We're just trying to live up to your friend's expectations regarding the details about these sorts of things."

"And who might you be, Sokar perhaps?" I mockingly guessed. "Or maybe you are Ra or Unas or a transgendered version of Thoth's syzygy Nehe-maut?"

"Ha!" scoffed the man. "All clever guesses but none of the above. My name is O. Cyrus."

"But, of course it is!" I laughed in reply. "I should have guessed that right off the bat! Since we have Horus here, we certainly need to have his neutered father Osiris back live from his resurrection!"

"No, not that Osiris," the man corrected. "O...C...Y...R...U...S. My mother loved the short-story writer O. Henry but changed the 'Henry' part of the name to 'Cyrus' in honor of her paternal grandfather."

"Unbelievable," I muttered. "With names like that, how can I view your collective presence here as anything but ulterior."

"I can assure you that there's nothing ulterior or otherwise unseemly about our presence here or our enterprise specific to your friend," rebuffed O. Cyrus. "But do understand that, although neither you nor he are under any kind of surveillance per se, we will be capturing the Dali reenactment on video.

"We don't usually have him do out-of-the-ordinary things like this. We do try to arrange for him to be taken care of as normally as possible and well enough to safeguard him and the others in the neighborhood in exchange for some of this research that we conduct."

"You plan to reenact the Salvador Dali performance with him?" I asked. "For what God's earthly reason?"

"We believe there's an untapped resource of spiritual energy available to us from this reenactment," Horace said. "What he witnessed during the original performance forever changed his life and altered the way he viewed the world. We're not sure exactly how or why yet, but much of his lifetime's worth of written material seemed to be validated by what he experienced at that time."

"I don't know how that experience transformed him, either," I lied. "But how are you going to reenact the Dali performance? Surely, you can't put him in the position of Dali, and I'm quite certain it won't be me on your center stage."

"He will assume the role of Dali in the reenactment," Horace told me. "We rehearsed with him some, but he doesn't always remember what to do."

"He doesn't even know who on earth he is," I replied. "How can you expect him to do anything meaningful? Does he even remember any of the original event?"

"Why don't you ask him?" suggested Thoth.

I turned toward the magnolia tree to voice the question but was startled to find my friend standing beside me. I then asked him what memory he had, if any, of the unusual Salvador Dali performance art he said he had witnessed nearly fifty years ago.

"You know, of course I do somewhere remember something about it if I indeed saw that to which you refer," my friend began. "And I'm sure my memories are quite vivid.

"But this is such a delicate subject. We're not dealing in normal temporal bearings now. I remember what has happened in the future, for instance, so how could I possibly be expected to predict what will happen in the past."

"That's very clever," I said, grinning at him. "But I know you know better than that. Either you were there or you weren't. Why you were there and what you were doing if you really were there is a completely different question that is all but irrelevant for our purposes here."

"Nonsense!" he rebuked me. "Why I was there is all that matters. I was summoned there to film you and the Siren earth angel. Salvador Dali's presence there and all of the theatrics involved were exclusively ritual to open your otherworldly portal!"

"What do you mean, film me?" I fired back. "How could you possibly film me fifty years ago?"

"You will see, my friend," he glared at me at first but then a look of confusion spread across his face before he grinned tentatively and held out his hand for me to shake. "Who are you again?"

I realized then that he may have very well been stuck in a vicious cycle in which his memories were arbitrarily erased at any moment, but I also understood that he was the one who had mentioned filming the original Salvador Dali event in New York City. I slowly shook my downward cast head as I walked toward the three men.

"He has no idea what he's talking about," I whispered. "His mind is completely blown, but if you are intent upon this degrading reenactment, I suppose I'll stay to supervise it in my own way"

"We think he unconsciously knows exactly what he's talking about even if he no longer consciously understands what he is saying or doing," said O. Cyrus. "And we think what he is saying may prove to be of great value to the future of humanity."

"We would like for you to film the reenactment for us," Horace requested of me. "It will only take two or three minutes for the entire performance."

"Why do you want me to film whatever it is that's going to take place?" I nearly yelled.

"It was your friend's request when we arranged for all of this to transpire," Horace replied. "Believe it or not, there are times when he really does remember you."

"Now I do find that hard to believe," I said as I glowered at Horace. "There's no possible way he would've asked for me to film this."

"He did specifically ask for you," confirmed Thoth. "Not by name exactly, but by face. We showed a picture of you to him after he said he wanted the person who had helped him write the *Resurrection Gospel* to film him here.

"I will also be shooting the reenactment with another camera from a different angle. We also have someone else coming with an additional prop for the reenactment."

"Who else is coming?" I wanted to know. "And what kind of additional prop are they bringing?"

"A young woman is bringing a brown egg," disclosed O. Cyrus. "Your friend was insistent that we included a brown egg for his performance, and he also had requested that the egg be brought by a specific person from this area."

For a moment, I couldn't believe what I was hearing. But then I understood with such lucidity that the shudder that streaked through every fiber of my being made me instantly twitch all over. I knew what was about to happen. I just didn't know if the three men also understood the dynamic of what was about to materialize.

These men were arranging an exact reenactment of the version of Dali's 1965 performance in New York that my friend said he had filmed, which was the same footage that he showed to me the last time I had visited him before I moved.

The timing of the other participant's arrival couldn't have been scripted any more on cue than it was. No sooner had the prop and person bearing it been mentioned than a car paused on the road at the edge of the driveway before turning onto the gravel and easing forward until it reached my SUV.

Once the car stopped, the passenger door flung open and a young woman stepped out of the car. My friend ambled over to her with a grin plied across his face and his hand extended.

The young woman wore a black and white optical-art printed top that sparkled in the equinox sunlight. The checkered squares of the print pulsated within overlapped circles as the waist of the top clung to the curve of her high hips. The long sleeve of the top tightened against her wrist as she tugged at her shoulder. She then pulled at her black knee-length skirt as she stood in her black riding boots in the gravel driveway.

"And who are you, young lady?" my friend bellowed with his smile flashing.

"I'm here for the ceremony," she said, shifting away from him and not extending her hand for him to shake.

"Ceremony?" my friend asked even louder with his hand still extended toward her. "What kind of ceremony is that?"

"The one with the egg," she answered, looking at me and then the three other men. "A brown egg ceremony of some sort."

"A brown egg ceremony!" my friend blared before he clasped his own hands together. "That's sounds delightful! We'll all have such a scrambled good time! Where is this ceremony being held?"

"This was the address I was given," she said before she peered past the open car door to look at the driver.

"This is the right place," the male voice of the unseen driver confirmed for her.

"Quite right," Thoth said as he stepped forward. "This is the place where we will hold the event that you'll be participating in."

"It's actually more along the lines of performance art," clarified Horace as he also stepped toward the young woman and held out his hand for her to give him the egg that she held in her closed hand.

"Performance art?" she probed as she placed the egg in the palm of Horace's hand. "What kind of performance exactly do you guys want me to do with this egg?"

"Nothing dangerous or unseemly, I can assure you," O. Cyrus said as Horace immediately left with the egg to re-enter the house. "We just want to recreate a scene of performance art by the artist Salvador Dali."

"Ever hear of him?" I asked the young woman before I allowed myself to indulge in the shifting optical illusion of her black and white top then searched for the name to place upon her familiar pretty face.

"I have seen some of his paintings," she said as she too studied my face. "Hey, I know you! You were my mom's friend, Jam! I played soccer with your daughter!"

"Oh my God, child!" I yelped once I recognized the grown young woman in the girl I remembered.

I had grown quite close to the young woman's mother before leaving Virginia. My children had become good friends with the young woman and her two brothers. Sadly, the girl's mother had died suddenly not long after I moved my family from Virginia.

"I am so sorry about what happened to your mom! I feel so bad for you and your brothers! I had no idea she was so sick until it was far too late!"

I lunged to her and embraced her, wedging my chin on the top of her head. She nestled her head against my chest and hugged me around my waist before my sobs wrenched free with such force that they smacked her forehead against me. She pulled the top of her head away from my chin to look at me. The tears cascaded down my face as I met her gaze. I clenched my face tight in the attempt to suppress my sobs, but my chest heaved with each cry that escaped.

Her mother had died unexpectedly – to me anyway – not too long after I had moved. During the last two years that I had lived in the area, I would take my two children to meet with her mother – Brown Eggs, as I nicknamed her – and her three children a few times a week before my family and I moved away for good. Her mother and I grew fond of each other during that time, and we frequently engaged in lengthy conversations together at a nearby community center.

I didn't even realize she was terminally ill until she had been admitted into hospice care at the regional hospital. Within two weeks of hearing about how gravely ill she was, she died. I felt devastated by the news. Even though she wasn't part of my immediate family, her death was as sad and shocking to me as any I've ever experienced within my own family.

As I stood there hugging her daughter, I relived the surge of guilt that had exacerbated my grief over the death of Brown Eggs. I had decided to forego any further contact with Brown Eggs or anyone from the area after my family and I moved. The rationale for making a clean break may have seemed good in theory, but once I learned of her illness and then her death shortly after that, my grief was compounded by the fact that I had put her in a position where she would've thought I didn't care about her at all.

"I'm just so sorry for not being there," I continued sobbing. "I let all of you down."

"Even though you weren't physically there with her," the young woman said as she shifted her hands to my shoulders and looked into my eyes, "you were there for her in her mind. Near the end when she was most out of it, she talked to you like you were right there in the room with her. I sat and listened to her talk to you at least three times and once went on for a really long time."

"What did she say?" my friend intervened.

"She was talking a lot about angels and saints and Jesus in the water, I think," she turned to my friend in answering him before she brought her attention back to me. "I really couldn't make total sense out of it but she kept calling you by the name she always called you – Jam."

I took her hands from my shoulders and held them as I lowered them between us. The rear passenger door of the car opened and her younger brother stepped from the car. The driver's door then opened and her older brother emerged.

"We loved your mother so much," I manage to tell her through another sob. "She was my friend, and I'm sorry we didn't do anything for you kids."

"But you did," she replied. "We all saw her talking to you. You were the one who was finally able to help her find peace from every-thing unfair and awful that was happening to her and us."

"You did," the older brother concurred as he stepped toward me. "You helped her cope with what was happening. You helped us all just because you meant so much to her."

"You were her friend," the younger brother added. "She loved you for that."

"The grace of God is with us right now!" my friend suddenly yelled before spreading his arms, arching his back and tilting his back to face the cloudless blue sky. "We implore you, Heavenly Father, the

Djed of circumpolar flight, that you bestow comfort in our hearts and peace in our minds! This great miracle you have performed here today is cause for us to rejoice in the glory of your mercy!"

"Wow!" the older brother half-laughed. "Is this guy some kind of preacher or just a nut?"

"Preacher," O. Cyrus quickly clarified. "He does have sufficient credentials to qualify him as such, including a doctorate of divinity conferred upon him."

"He sounds a whole lot better than the preacher that spoke at mom's funeral," the younger brother remarked. "That guy was a jerk the way he bad-mouthed mom during her service."

Once my friend decided to amble back to the magnolia tree, the two boys returned their attention to their sister and me.

"I'm so sorry for everything else that happened after your mom died," I said to them as I motioned for them all to hug me together. "You kids have been through more than anyone your age should ever have to go through."

"We're all right, now," the older brother said as we maintained our hug. "It's been hard, but we've had a lot of people here help us deal with all that has happened."

"I'm so glad," I said, feeling the urge to sob return but stifling it long enough to finish what I wanted to say. "Your mother would be so proud of how strong you three are."

As shocked as I still was to see the three children of my dear deceased friend and then learn that somehow their mother had been comforted by some imagined presence of me, I began to realize that none of this could possibly be coincidental. I turned toward the three men.

"Was this arranged by you three?" I asked them.

"Only the logistics of it," Thoth answered. "The rest of it was your friend's idea. He wrote all of the instructions down for us."

I turned toward my friend, finding him back at the magnolia tree once again stroking one of the tree's glossy leaves.

"How could he?" I asked. "He is out of his mind."

"We really don't understand it either," Thoth admitted. "But he communicated all of this to us while he was in a trance-like state. He had just sort of drifted off in his mind one afternoon and started to make a motion like he was writing something down in the dirt. We handed a piece of paper and pen to him and he wrote the young woman's name down.

"He then acted like he was writing something down in the dirt again before we gave the paper back to him, then he also drew a picture of a womanly hand holding a colored-in egg between the thumb and the fingertip. It had the words *Brown Egg* underlined."

"Here," O. Cyrus said, divulging a folded piece of paper from his shirt pocket and extending it toward me.

I took the paper and unfolded it. I couldn't believe what I thought I was seeing. Sometimes the passage of time sabotages the mind with details that either didn't exist or otherwise mutate in some variation from actuality. But the hand with the shaded egg immediately evoked the woman from the filmed Dali performance. So much of that was coming back to me now that I started to feel light-headed and wobbly.

"Turn over the paper," Thoth said, "and tell us if that means anything to you at all."

On the back of the paper read the following in quotation marks:

Alpha and Omega: Your transfiguration awaits you, my love.

I had to conceal both my knowledge of what the phrase meant and also my excitement about what this transcription entailed about my friend's true state of mind. He may have lost the ability to control his memory, but he still clearly remembered details and events, like his filming of Salvador Dali and the woman to whom he still referred as the Siren earth angel.

"Can't say this means anything to me," I lied, knowing I still had to conceal my knowledge about the film as I handed the paper back to Thoth. "But it sounds kind of religious to me."

"Another detail about this message," O. Cyrus said to me as Horace stepped out of the house in his return to the front yard. "Your friend told us that he wanted the young woman named on the front of the paper to read the message on the back. He also detailed her attire verbally, which is why she is wearing this optical art designed shirt right now."

"Plus, "added Horace. "He told us that, once he concludes his reenactment, he would like for you to film her reading those words while she holds the egg as shown in the picture."

I looked around to find my friend so that I could gauge his perception of the scene in his front yard, but he was gone.

"He's ready for us," Horace announced. "You are all invited to join us inside at this time."

"And all I have to do is hold the egg up at the end of this and say my line," the young woman asked Thoth, "then you'll give me two-thousand dollars?"

"That is correct," confirmed Thoth. "That is the wish of our associate."

"Let us proceed then," Horace said. "Our artist awaits us."

O. Cyrus stepped to the front door and pushed it open. He extended his arm and signaled for the rest of us to enter the house.

"This is the way," O. Cyrus announced. "Step inside."

Horace stood behind O. Cyrus, and Thoth stood behind Horace. The trio deferred to the four of us. We entered the house first.

"Is there an admission for this?" the young woman asked as she stepped into the house followed by her two brothers.

"Most certainly not," O. Cyrus replied.

"Maybe there should be," I whispered to the three men. "Leave your soul at the door."

All three men heard me and laughed simultaneously. Horace had the highest-pitched laugh of the three and, Thoth had the lowest tone to his laugh. They all stopped laughing at the same instant then followed me into the interior of my friend's house.

The narrow entry hallway bore the dingy residue of years of nicotine that had wafted from cigarette smoke to the plastered walls. The hardwood floor creaked beneath our steps until our procession stopped. The young woman had paused at the threshold to the living room adjacent to the hallway.

"What in the world is this?" she gasped then covered her mouth.

Her two brothers squeezed past her to step into the room. They both stopped and the older one laughed.

"This is straight up crazy," he murmured then left his mouth agape.

"No doubt," the younger brother agreed.

I reached the three of them then peered around the group. My friend was lying within what appeared to be a black sarcophagus. He had dollar bills stuck to his face and hair and also had a quarter covering each eye. Dollar bills and coins also covered his body within the sarcophagus-like vessel.

My peripheral vision detected something anomalous above me. I shifted my eyes from my friend to the vaulted ceiling. Blue and red stars were painted on the steeply sloped sides of the ceiling.

I then lowered my eyes to the wall behind my friend. Pictures that appeared to be hieroglyphs were rendered upon the yellowed wall behind him.

"Step into the chamber, please," Thoth instructed. "What you are about to witness is a spectacle for the ages. A legendary performance by a master illusionist steeped in the arcane wisdom of the resurrection religion."

"I do wish that I had natron softened water in here with me instead of all of this money so that I could float," my friend said as he slightly tilted his head forward without forcing the quarters from his eyes. "That would have been the solution used by shamans in antiquity to practice astral flight and resurrection from a sarcophagus like this."

"How much money is in there with you?" the younger brother asked.

"Exactly two-thousand dollars. "Horace answered on behalf of my friend.

"You mean you're giving me that money?" the young woman pointed and said with her face scrunched in disgust.

"Indeed," confirmed Thoth.

"Jeez," she muttered. "Guess it will spend just the same."

"What exactly do you want me to do?" I asked Thoth, just as my friend lowered the back of his head to the level of the coins in the sarcophagus and allowed the two quarters to drop from his eyes.

"As we've already mentioned, we would like for you to film what is going to happen," Thoth answered. "And we ask that the young lady play her part for the filming, too, once the staged resurrection is complete."

"I'll get the egg," Horace said before he walked out of the living room to the unseen kitchen.

"There is the camcorder we would like for you to use," O. Cyrus informed me as he pointed to the camera mounted atop the tripod positioned at the foot of the sarcophagus.

"What is all of this, for real?" the younger brother asked.

"Well," began Thoth, "the coffin-like vessel our artist is lying within is a replica of the basalt sarcophagus at the Pyramid of Unas in Saqqara, Egypt that was constructed during the Fifth Dynasty. The stars above us are fashioned after the stars that were depicted on the ceiling within the chamber where the actual sarcophagus is located. And the symbols and pictures on the wall behind him are derived from the actual pyramid texts that are also present in the chamber. This is all designed to recreate the incantation of the Pyramid Texts of Unas about astral flight and resurrection, or at least the version of it projected by our artist here."

"But why?" the older brother asked.

"To advise him about how to perform his own resurrection so that he may travel the stars to wait for his next incarnation," I answered. "You see, this is partly a reenactment of an event my friend witnessed in New York City in 1965 when Salvador Dali performed something similar to this.

"But my friend has his own ideas about what that performance actually represented based upon his study of the prominence of resurrection in Ancient Egypt among the ruling and educated classes."

"That is a fair synopsis," replied O. Cyrus. "You may hear us chanting utterances that correspond to the symbols depicted in the hieroglyphic scenes, so don't be alarmed by us."

I stepped to the camera to familiarize myself with its operation.

"The tilt and pan are manual," O. Cyrus explained. "We only ask that you do not use the zoom."

"I suppose I can figure it out," I said. "Mind if I practice shooting footage for a bit?"

"By all means do," replied Thoth. "And when the time comes to detach the camcorder from the tripod, we will tell you so you can film the young woman with the brown egg."

"I think I see how to detach it," I said. "It looks easy enough, but I'll wait until the time comes to try it. This angle with this degree of zoom makes his face look unnaturally bloated."

"All right everyone," Horace announced as he returned to the living room. "We are about to begin our event tribute. Cameramen, please take your positions. To our guests, please feel free to enjoy these proceedings, but we do ask that you remain in one area and not move about the room so as to allow us to focus upon our performance artist."

Horace then showed us the egg he held in his hand. The egg, however, was not a brown one. It was white. He stepped to my friend and bent over him with the egg held in front of his face. I viewed the egg through the viewfinder but saw nothing unusual about it.

"You might have to pucker your lips," Horace told my friend. "Otherwise, the egg will slide down your chin, and what good would that do?"

"I have no idea," my friend managed to say through his puckered lips.

Horace balanced the egg between the puckered upper lip of my friend and the end of his nose then momentarily held his hands above the egg before he officially began the proceedings.

"Action!" Horace announced before I pressed the record button of the camcorder to capture my friend's contorted face and the egg in camera view. "Welcome to this event of fascination and wonder as we give tribute to a similar proceeding that took place more than fifty years ago when the artist Salvador Dali performed this very rite of passage to recapture the art and science of resurrection."

O. Cyrus clapped robustly, alone at first, until the children joined him in applause. He then stopped clapping and stepped to my friend. He placed one index fingertip on top of the egg then visibly shook as he pressed the tip of his other index finger against the side of the eggshell. Finally, the egg cracked then crushed at the point of his fingertip.

"Make sure you're getting this," O. Cyrus turned to me and said.

His fingertip wedged into the egg, but when he stepped aside and removed the finger, fluid spilled to my friend's closed mouth. A small translucent creature wriggled from the eggshell puncture and slapped itself across the top of the egg until it gained enough grip to pull itself through the opening. The creature then squirmed on top of the egg as another one just like it also freed itself from the eggshell.

"Oh, my God!" the young woman shrieked. "What are those things?"

As another and then another of the slithering creatures emerged from the egg, the first then the second dropped from the egg to my friend's closed mouth.

"These are glass eel elvers," O. Cyrus announced. "American Eel young recently arrived and caught in the Rappahnnock River at Tapphannock after their larval journey from the Sargasso Sea where they hatched."

I suspected what would happen next. I prepared to tilt the camera in anticipation of my friend's reaction to the creatures on his lips, but before I could shift the angle, my friend opened his mouth and slurped down the baby eels.

"These elver glass eels are a delicacy often poached from Tide-water brackish creeks for their value in Asia," O. Cyrus explained. "But I can assure you we obtained the proper permits for their use here in our performance tonight."

Once the water level within the egg dipped below the puncture, my friend swatted the egg away. He then gripped the walking stick that was propped against the side of the sarcophagus. He trembled as he applied downward pressure on the cane in his attempt to stand but finally managed to pry himself upwards as the dollar bills and coins dropped from him to the sarcophagus. I tilted the camera upwards to keep him in lens view as he stood.

I could hear the men start with their chants and utterances as though they were speaking in tongues to the unversed ear, but I kept my focus upon my friend in his struggle to maintain his stance in his awkward position within the faux sarcophagus.

Once standing, my friend surveyed the room, making a sweeping gesture back and forth with his left hand and his arm extended as if to point out the hieroglyphic messages depicted upon the walls behind him and to his sides. My friend then dropped his left arm as he yanked the hidden end of the walking stick from the bottom of the sarcophagus and thrust it into the air toward the star-painted ceiling. He pointed at different spots along the ceiling until he reached a ring suspended several feet down from the peak of the ceiling. He stuck the end of his walking stick into the ring and pulled down.

Instantly, a poster of Albert Einstein unfurled and straightened before us at eye level. I wondered why this was a poster of Einstein instead of a poster of the woman holding the egg that I had seen in my friend's film version, but my contemplation was cut short once the two men not filming the event began to heartily applaud. Almost immediately, the children joined with applause of their own.

I wanted to pull my eyes from the camera and applaud too, but instead I kept filming him as he bowed then waved his walking stick through the air like he possessed some type of magic wand that was tracing and transcribing the secrets of the universe and the formula for resurrection for all to witness.

I had to smile at my friend in his last stand of glory. Clearly, he wasn't completely lost in a world that made no sense to him. How he had managed to participate in such a reenactment while being in such a condition of deteriorating memory loss was beyond me.

But my admiration for him was soon interrupted by a tug at my shoulder. I turned to see Thoth standing next to me and motioning for me to stand so he could speak discretely to me. I stood, allowing the camera to continue to run, but he stopped me and motioned with his hand for me to power off the camera. I did so, but once again Thoth pointed to the camera.

"Go ahead and detach so you can film the next part of the tribute," he directed me. "Horace has just retrieved the brown egg."

Once I held the camcorder in my hand, Horace approached the young woman. He motioned for her to move toward me. She smiled as she stepped my way. Once she reached me, Horace stopped to her side and extended the brown egg for her to take.

"We would now like for you to conclude our event here today," Horace said as she took the egg from him.

She straightened herself as I raised the camera to prepare shooting the footage. As I positioned my eye against the viewfinder and pressed the record button, I glimpsed the flash of what appeared to be the face of a man who seemed different than Horace. I briefly lifted my eye from the viewfinder but immediately returned it before I could see whose face appeared because the young woman started to speak.

"Alpha and Omega," she said as she raised her hand to reveal the brown egg that she held from tip-to-tip between her thumb and index finger. "Your transfiguration awaits you, my love."

She had the sweetest smile when she said her part. I couldn't help but wonder what her mother would think of this bizarre performance. It would be hard to imagine that she would approve, but it was done without any physical harm to her or excessive anxiety for her, I suppose. How the scene she witnessed would affect her in her life afterwards remained to be seen.

Her brothers joined her at her side. O. Cyrus stepped to me and told me that I didn't need to record further. I lowered the camera to my side as I watched her brothers and her laugh together at what had just taken place.

I then turned my attention to my friend standing in the sarcophagus. The walking stick was at his side now. He still had a couple of dollar bills stuck to his face, but I could see beneath those remnant props that he bore some semblance of satisfaction as he surveyed the handiwork rendered on his living room walls and ceiling.

Horace came to me with his hand extended and asked me for the camcorder, which I gave to him. He thanked me for my participation in the event before he and the other two men converged with the siblings in the center of the room.

As the group interacted, I turned my attention toward my friend, who was still standing in the faux sarcophagus. Now, he was looking straight at me with a half-smile on his face. He proceeded to shift his weight in the attempt to dismount from the sarcophagus. Seeing he needed assistance in this task, I stepped across the room to help him.

When he took my hand, he stopped his attempt to remove himself from the sarcophagus. He looked at me wide-eyed with his mouth open. I felt the pressure from his hand increase as his whole arm visibly trembled.

"Now I know who you are!" he virtually screamed. "You are Uriel, the most powerful of the seven archangels who watched over the world from the time of Adam and Eve!"

"Lucky me," I said as I remained steadfast in my grip of his hand.

"You are the patron saint of the sacrament of confirmation!" he began his loud rant. "You were the angel who warned Noah of the coming flood! You were the one who revealed the power of the constellations to Enoch!"

The volume of my friend's voice stopped the rest of the conversation in the room. All eyes were now upon the two of us.

"You beseeched God on behalf of humankind during the reign of the fallen angels who watched over the world, imparted celestial wisdom to humans, and took human women as wives! You were the one with the blood of the earth angels on your hands! You let the Nephilim – those children of woman and angels – be destroyed for all eternity in favor of humans!"

His face skewered with anger at this point. I pulled his hand toward me as I stepped back, forcing him to lift his leg from the sarcophagus or else be toppled. He did lift his leg and brought his foot to the floor once it cleared the side of the sarcophagus.

Once he freed his other leg from the sarcophagus, he shook his hand free from mine and pointed directly at me before resuming his diatribe against who he thought I was.

"You are Uriel, and you let God murder the children of Atlantis!" he raged at me as his spittle spattered against my face. "You, Uriel, let your own angel cousins be judged for defiling mankind and sentenced to a fate worse than damnation for the false charge of leading humans astray into a realm where sacrifices were made to demons glorified as gods!"

"I'm sorry," I calmly said to him. "But I think you have me confused with someone else."

"Perhaps he is right," Horace said to my friend. "It's easy enough to confuse somebody for someone else. It happens all the time."

"I am not confused," my friend declared less loudly. "This is Uriel, the archangel of God's light and the most powerful of the seven angels who watched over the earth until he betrayed all but himself and two others – two women who were half divine."

"Say I did what you say I did," I supposed aloud for him to distract him from further ire. "Why would I appear to you now?"

"Don't try to entangle me in your deception, Uriel," my friend raged as more spittle flew from him. "I know the whole story about you and your plans for this world. Yes. The female children born from the union of your fellow angels and human women were cast out of their earthly homes to live as Sirens cursed to haunt this world in a form neither truly all the way here in this world nor all the way there in the other realm of existence. But I know what you told Noah before the Great Flood. You instructed him to create compartments for the only two surviving Sirens who you wanted to keep for yourself, didn't you?"

"Why would I want Sirens for myself?" I asked him, now hoping he would continue to elucidate the entire mythology wrapped around his mind because his rambling had started to pique my interest.

"You wanted them so that you could do what your damned angel cousins did," began his accusation. "You wanted them so that you could create your own race of Nephilim. And the children from celestial loins would once again mingle with the humans descended from Noah."

When I turned to scoff at this and tell the trio of men that all of what my friend was saying was preposterous, I saw that all three were writing in their notepads. I also noticed that the three children were now looking at me in anticipation of my rebuttal to these outlandish claims.

But instead, I decided not to feign any indignation. I opted instead to follow his thread and ask the questions that would further his explanation of the possibly historical events he believed somehow involved me.

"That would mean that my progeny now populates the earth in great numbers," I surmised aloud. "And that these half-angel, half-human Nephilim hybrid creatures that you have accused me of exterminating are now restored to their rightful earthly habitat."

"Not so fast!" he snapped back at me. "I know why you waited. You have let these two half-bred women beget their own human progeny first over all of these centuries since the Flood. You know that neither of them can die because both have been cursed to live forever caught in between worlds. They just keep resurrecting as new incarnations."

"That's really quite fascinating," I said, now admittedly somewhat alarmed by what he actually was implying. "But why would I wait?"

"You needed to make sure that the ancient knowledge of Atlantis was so diluted over the course of millennia that there would be no way for that wisdom to convey through the offspring of the Nephilim Sirens themselves," he glared at me as he spoke.

I tried to laugh at that point, but I'm sure it sounded forced and perhaps even suggested my guilt somehow. At least, I know I felt that way at that time, even though I had no earthly idea why my friend would think I was an archangel named Uriel or why I would be so involved in some angelic conspiracy of biblical proportions.

"Look," I began. "I'm not an angel. I'm just a man."

"That's the true genius of your design," my friend now seethed. "You are just a man right now. But once you experience your transfiguration, you too will be restored to your former self and will join the Siren that you hope to have for your eternal wife – your earth angel soulmate."

"What if all of what you say is true," I said to him, "but, in the end, it is actually God's will and not the will of an angel to partake of some cosmic tryst with a woman who was only part woman and the rest angel?"

The look of confusion that passed across his face was sudden and complete. He withdrew his eyes from me to look at his own hands. He turned his hands palms upward and stared vacantly at them until he broke his gaze from them and returned his attention to me.

"And who are you again?" he asked, smiling as he extended his hand for me to shake.

At that time, it dawned upon me for the first time that his frequent return to the question about who I was wasn't as much of a matter of his vanishing memory as it was a rhetorical question for me to truly ponder beyond what I previously had conceived of myself. I realized then that there might not be a right answer to his question beyond my offering of a name to associate with me as a sentient being beyond the realm of ordinary description.

I turned to the trio of men who were now intently watching the interaction between my friend and me. All I could do was smile at them for their efforts to stage this reunion and recreated event. I understood that this had to be the final time I would see my friend alive.

"I am Uriel," I answered my friend as I took his hand. "An archangel so in love with two angelic Nephilim women that I was willing to betray the race of Atlantis for their eternal affection."

"That's fantastic!" my friend squealed with delight, as he began pumping my hand. "I've never met any angels before or any human that went by the name of Uriel!"

My friend then drew me close to him so that he could whisper into my ear.

"But you are only in love with one of the women," he said so that only I could hear. "The other woman serves another purpose beyond this world. You will understand all when your time has arrived. I will let you know then, and you will see the proof of eternity. It will jump out right in front of you like a reflection of your own face across the sun and her face across the moon. You will launch in your transfiguration beyond the concerns of this human world forever."

As he was saying this, I realized that I would have to try hard to remember his words the best that I could because there did not seem to be any frame of reference that I could really understand them by. As nonsensical as his verbal confusion may have seemed, I do have to admit that my friend's outburst and then his bizarre clarification about the women did set me on a course later to research the entity he called Uriel.

Much of what seemed most relevant about his accusations against this supposed archangel were clearly rooted in the belief my friend had about the lost civilization of Atlantis. If one is willing to suspend disbelief long enough to consider Atlantis anything other than a fictional creation by Plato, then the nexus between the 'betrayal' by Uriel before God – as my friend implied – and the demise of Atlantis was a fairly obvious one: Uriel made the call to God to destroy the Atlantis built by the giant Nephilim race.

The notion that Uriel petitioned God on behalf of humanity for humans to be restored their rightful place upon planet earth seemed most striking to me in connection with the supposedly lost status of a superior civilization preceding the onset of the strictly human civilization that is understood today. I mean, how could a race of half-angels, half-humans guided and taught in all arts and sciences by the fallen angels not be superior to a race of merely humans?

Well, apparently the hybrid half-breeding didn't fare too well. The debauchery that ensued became a scourge that forced the removal of the fallen angels and the decimation of the half-breeds through The Great Flood. The cursed and banished half-women Sirens were also eradicated except for the pair that my friend contended were saved by Uriel.

I am not one to discount notions or beliefs so readily, even those that at first blush seem ludicrous for their want of even the most basic infusion of common sense. If I were prepared to believe even theoretically in the existence of Atlantis and by extension, the Hall of Records, then I really did not have any other recourse than to take my friend's communication about the destruction of Atlantis at this implied face value: Atlantis was destroyed by God because Uriel along with three of the other seven archangels – Michael, Raphael and Gabriel – appealed to God to seize the fallen angels and destroy the Nephilim race of half-angels and half-humans.

I came to understand later that most of the basis for the Judeo-Christian picture of Uriel came from *The Books of Enoch*. Whereas my friend was one to pursue all manner of esoteric wisdom whether it is contained within apocrypha or canonized bodies of work, I am not so inclined.

Frankly, I was not so inclined to spend any more time than absolutely necessary to unearth the information I sought. My priority for research was to obtain information that corroborated other information. I was less interested in research for research's sake to form my own theories or opinions than I was to understand someone else's theories – like those of my friend.

Once again, I found myself in a situation with my friend where I couldn't possibly expect myself to wholeheartedly embrace his intent, be it conscious on his part or the raving of a lunatic who had lost his mind.

I had a schedule to keep after all. I had deadlines to meet, and a home and wife – a one-hundred-percent human woman of a wife as far as I knew – to which to return. Unlike my friend, I wasn't going to get hopelessly immersed in an unused water tap where a half-human, half-angel woman sang from the Hall of Records about the divinity of an untold resurrection.

No, I just wasn't going to bear that cross. I had come to the same conclusion that I had come to before when I packed my family up and left the area for good the first time: leave me out of all the insane bluster.

Of course, that's not what would happen.

Until that next pull from the stars beyond the dimension of possibility and experience drew me back into the vortex of eternity, I had to fumble my way through this world.

My friend would depart this world (at least I'm fairly convinced that is what happened) within three months after his Salvador Dali reenactment. Thoth from The Institute called me with the news and also told me that the condition of my friend had deteriorated from the time of his Dali reenactment but that he had eventually died peacefully in his sleep.

I would make one last trip to see him in his earthly repose. He seemed serene in death as he rested with his full head of white hair and wiry beard in his coffin. All of his questions were surely answered by that time, and the quest he was so convinced awaited his soul would have to be in full swing while his prepared corpse awaited its final destination in the hard ground.

June 20, 2016
White Stone, Virginia

BEFORE THE VIEWING formally started with the procession of visitors, the Episcopalian priest announced that there would be two hymns played at the request of my friend. I can't say that I can recall my friend ever playing the two songs he selected. In fact, he never seemed very interested in music at all and never revealed any kind of affinity for music perhaps best described as gospel.

But in any event, his first selection played was "Zion's Hill" and the second was "Beulah Land". I'm not sure that either song could be characterized as particularly Episcopalian hymnal fare. Still, both seemed favorably apt selections by my friend for the journey that he thought awaited him after death.

Once the viewing was complete and the casket closed, the service proceeded as a rather muted tribute to my friend. Muted, I say, because anyone who knew his flair for the dramatic understood that a service full of fervor and volume would have been more suited for a man of his talents and temperament.

The Episcopalian priest delivered the eulogy for my friend. His message focused on some of the good works my friend achieved while he was alive: how he helped several charitable organizations in the region with their public relations efforts, how he was an important member of the church whose clarifications about technical aspects of theological interpretations were always welcome, and how his inspired editing of posthumous tributes to newly deceased members of the community were quite touching and ever poignant.

I can't say that I was particularly surprised to see the trio of men who had coordinated the Salvador Dali and brown egg reenactment on behalf of The Institute. There they were again, this time much more subdued in their dark-colored suits and ties, nodding and gesturing solemnly toward me as if hoping to convey some measure of muffled despair in all of this.

But I couldn't help but audibly laugh at them when I thought of their ludicrous Egyptian deity names. To my embarrassment, my unintentional laugh drew a couple critical glances from others in front of me who turned around to glare. I fought hard to reshape my persistent smile into something more solemn.

Still, this balding trinity dispatched by The Institute seemed posed there in their pew like the Hermetic Three Stooges. The tallest man was "Horace," whose name clearly evoked the Ancient Egyptian "Horus" and his mythically immaculate conception through Isis. We had discussed the distinction when we initially met, but he reassured me he was named "Horace."

Then there was the middle-sized man "O. Cyrus," who had told me when we first met that his own mother was so found of short-story writer O. Henry that she named her son after the writer only to change the middle name from "Henry" to "Cyrus" in honor of some paternal relative. He also had been quick to reassure me that the name had nothing to do with "Osiris," the resurrected Ancient Egyptian god who was put back together by his wife Isis after his mutilation, only to be reassembled without the one part that he would have needed to be considered the biological father of the immaculately-conceived Horus.

And last but certainly not least, there was the shortest man, Thoth. He was quick to tell me that he was in fact named after the Ancient Egyptian god Thoth, who myth would have it provided the incantations and knowledge that enabled Isis to resurrect Osiris and, of course, was also the root of the Hermes Trismegistic literature uncovered at Nag Hammadi, Egypt and elsewhere. It seemed fitting to me that this most diminutive of the trio should be named after the most powerful of all the deities for the embodiment of Thoth as the god of revelation and resurrection through alchemy, magic, and the wisdom tradition.

How could I not but laugh at the transparent attempt by the trio to mirror the Hermeticism that clearly motivated them and The Institute in their unending thirst for the Hall of Records, Atlantis, Edgar Cayce, Nephilim, and all of the rest of the outlandish alternate history that had also consumed my friend?

Despite the death of my friend and the deterioration of my own unnerving personal situation, how could I not help but laugh at the lunacy surrounding me?

I was somewhat surprised that the trio had not contacted me until my friend neared death in the three months that had elapsed since the Dali reenactment. I still had to wonder whether any of them even knew of the existence of the original Dali film that my friend had shown to me. I was curious about whether they knew anything at all about the first woman who held the brown egg while she delivered her message of transfiguration on black and white film some fifty years ago.

After the church service, I soon realized that I was among many people I knew from the Northern Neck community in the past. Most still remembered me well and knew of the connection between my friend and myself. Word of the Dali reenactment had spread among a few of them, and they wanted to know more about it from me. I told them it was just an addendum to the *Book of Life* that my friend wanted to perform in honor of Edgar Cayce before he left this world to the rest of us. The reference to the cryptic Cayce backed them off from further inquiry quite effectively.

The trio of men approached me after most of the people had left the sanctuary. I greeted and shook the hand of each one before it dawned upon me that I had not seen the young woman and her brothers.

"That was quite a subdued service," the tallest man, Horace, said to me. "I sort of expected something like sound effects and flashing lights, especially for someone with such a spectacular oeuvre as your friend's."

"Your friend bequeathed items to you from the trust The Institute held for him," the shortest man Thoth said to me. "These items will be distributed to you expeditiously now that your friend has passed."

"What exactly will I be receiving?" I asked with some apprehension.

"We do not know," O. Cyrus informed me. "And The Institute is prohibited by the terms of your friend's willed directives from opening the packages he left for the different people he knew. But we would appreciate any information you might be able to share with us about your items at some later date once you learn of their nature."

"I most certainly will," I lied as O. Cyrus handed his institute business card to me. "When do you think I'll be receiving those items?"

"I would expect that they'll be available for release within the week," Horace said. "Our research about your friend is still very much ongoing. Incidents have occurred and are still occurring, frankly, that we just haven't been able to satisfactorily explain yet."

"Oh," I rolled my eyes as I slid the business card into one of the pockets of my wallet, "Like what?"

"Did you notice anything unusual when you were filming the brown egg footage with the young woman?" Thoth asked me.

"I did sense a presence," I acknowledged. "I even looked up from the viewfinder, but the girl started to recite her lines. I had to look back down after that and didn't notice anything unusual in the room when I did finally stop filming."

"That still wouldn't explain the flashing presence of what appears to be the footage of a man's face and body," Horace said. "The footage you took shows the presence of what appears to be an unknown figure moving through the room."

"Can you show me the footage?" I asked. "Maybe I know who it was."

"Unfortunately, no, and you shouldn't have even been told that much," Thoth replied as he glared at Horace. "We're obligated to terms requested by The Institute not to share any materials that may be deemed proprietary or have ramifications beyond the intended scope of a project."

"What about the egg?" I asked. "The brown egg?"

"Oh, dear," Thoth blurted. "We still don't know why your friend summoned the young woman for the purpose of holding the brown egg and reciting her lines. Can you shed any further light on that for us now?"

"Who knows what he was thinking," I dodged the question. "He wasn't in his right mind at the end. He could've conjured some half-baked scheme out of nowhere."

"Again," O. Cyrus started, "we cannot specifically show the egg to you, but I will tell over my colleague's undoubted objections that we did prepare a mixture to coat the egg the girl held. In fact, we used your friend's recipe, which he insisted would preserve it indefinitely."

"We're not exactly sure how long to preserve it or under what type of environmental conditions," Horace added. "But we've done as he asked. All he wanted us to do was coat the egg with a sand, mud and crushed oyster shell mixture."

"Fascinating," I breathed, knowing that either my friend or these men were intentionally duplicating the Dali reenactment to the fullest extent.

"Why fascinating?" Thoth asked me. "Does that process for egg preservation mean something to you? If so, please tell us."

"It doesn't mean anything in particular for me," I lied once again. "I just know that the mixture you described is one employed in China for the preservation of a delicacy called the 'Century Egg'."

"We are aware of that purpose behind the century-egg process," Horace said. "But that is only a temporary means for preservation. He left us nothing more to go by for the prolonged preservation of the egg."

"What about the girl?" I asked. "Has she gotten involved in any of this beyond that day?"

The men looked at one another without answering me.

"What is it?" I demanded to know once their silence extended. "What happened to the girl?"

"Nothing has happened to her, per se," Horace answered. "But there has been a change with her, I guess you could say."

"What change?" I snapped back at him.

"Well," O. Cyrus began, "she has discovered an affinity for the spot that your friend described as the angel well leading to the Yucatan peninsula Hall of Records. She has visited the site a couple of times now with her brothers. In fact, she is there right now."

"We were able to clear up the trespass issues with the site," Thoth explained. "Apparently, only certain – perhaps select – individuals can actually hear anything out of the ordinary there, but the young woman is one who does seem to be able to hear something."

"We don't know exactly what she is hearing, though," Horace added. "She won't talk to us directly about it, and her brothers won't let us question her by herself."

"Take me to her now if she really is there," I demanded of them.

"Most certainly," O. Cyrus said smiling. "You can follow us to the site right now if you like."

I wanted to make sure Brown Egg's daughter was not in some predicament that could jeopardize her mental health, but I also wanted to know what she was hearing at this so-called Yucatan Hall of Records site.

During the funeral service while the Episcopalian priest spoke, I can remember thinking my own thoughts about the passage of my friend from his incarnation in this life. As Christian as he was in many respects, he clearly believed in transmigration of the soul for successive incarnations on earth. What he came to write about as a resurrection was significantly different than the Resurrection of a crucified Jesus promised with the Second Coming of the Christ.

I wondered if perhaps it was my resurrected friend who the girl was hearing at the well site. The sojourn remaining on earth for my friend may have concluded some three months after I saw him last, but his purpose in this world perhaps outlived him on this planet if he was indeed communicating to her from the realm of the dead.

Perhaps he was now within his elusive Hall of Records relaying its secrets even while the answer to all of his prayers and his belief in resurrection awaited him like an angel in the guise of a beautiful middle-aged woman holding a brown egg in front of his suddenly shapeless face. That last part of my internal monologue – the woman holding the brown egg – was the secret that I just couldn't share with anyone yet, except for maybe the young woman since she had now unwittingly found herself as a potential heiress apparent to that rather bizarre brown egg legacy.

With the funeral service concluded, I followed the trio of men in my rental SUV. We would all miss my friend's burial, but I'm quite sure my friend would most wholeheartedly approve of my absence in lieu of this intriguing development. The destination we reached wasn't far from where my friend had lived. I followed them along a soft dirt road to the site of an orange outbuilding where another car was parked. I recognized that the car was the same car driven by the young woman's older brother on the night of the Dali reenactment.

The door of the orange outbuilding was flung open once the trio of men got out of their car. The girl's younger brother emerged alone. He looked toward me once the tallest man of the trio, Horace, pointed in my direction. The younger brother smiled and waved as he trotted toward me.

I instantly dismounted my SUV and jogged toward him to greet him.

"You won't believe what's happening, Jam!" the younger brother joyfully beamed once he reached earshot. "Mom is speaking through our sister! She says she's in Heaven or Atlantis, maybe. She's not exactly sure where she is, but it's her!"

"How do you know it's your mother?" I asked.

"Because she's speaking to my sister," he answered. "Or more like, she's speaking *through* my sister. She's done this for the last two days. It's awesome!"

"Please hurry," Thoth advised him. "Follow us to her."

I quickly shook hands with the younger brother before Horace placed his hand on my shoulder to nudge me forward.

"We don't know how long this transmission will last," Horace said before he dropped his hand from my shoulder. "We've seen her do this twice before, and this might help explain why your friend wanted the young woman to be involved in his reenactment."

Just then, a scream erupted from inside the building. We all sprinted toward it. The younger brother was the first to reach the open door. I reached the threshold in time to see him join his older brother at the bottom of the steps leading to the bare floor of the subterranean room. The older brother held the limp body of his sister in his arms. They were pleading for her to regain consciousness, but her pasty skin and barely audible breathing suggested she was still in the grip of the oblivion that overcame her.

It took her awhile to slowly revive, and when she did, her energy still seemed sapped. Her eyes fluttered in her attempt to keep them open, and her voice was initially a slur of soft moans.

"What's wrong?" the older brother asked as he gripped his sister by her shoulder.

"Mom was taken away," she managed to mumble once she started to revive. "She said an angel was coming...with one foot on land and one foot in the sea...then another woman's voice said she had to take Mom away before the angel came."

The trio of men and both brothers looked at me. I turned from them to study the girl's reawakening face to make sure she was all right but also to look for some sign of clarification about the connection she had made.

"Why did the woman say your mother had to leave because of an angel?" I asked her.

"Mom didn't say," she answered, now speaking slightly louder as her cheeks started to regain their color "But it really is you, isn't it, Jam? "

"What do you mean, sweetie?" I asked her.

"Just like your friend was ranting and raving about," she resumed with more strength in her voice now. "You are that angel. She said it was Uriel. I mean, Mom said she had to leave because Uriel was coming, and here you are."

"I really don't see how it's possible for me to be some kind of angel," I laughed to help ease the bewildered look of disbelief on the young woman's face. "If I'm an archangel or even just a run-of-the-mill lesser angel type, I believe we're all in deep trouble."

"But you really are Uriel," the young woman declared. "I know you are. You must be."

"Well, I don't believe that," I countered just as I realized I needed to speak to her and her brothers in a way that would reinforce their mother's fundamentally Christian beliefs. "But I do believe there is some connection at this place between my friend and your mother that tells us to be glad and rejoice that they might live not only in our hearts and minds but also eternally so that we may all cherish the life that God has granted us in this world and the next."

"I don't hear anything anymore," she said as her brow knotted like she was about to cry. "I only want to hear my mom some more."

"What else did your mom say when she was talking to you?" I asked her.

"Sis told me that Mom wanted us to know that she was alive in her resurrection," the older brother relayed. "And we would all be together again one day, but she had to continue to make her way back through that Hall of Records of Atlantis."

"What about that?" I pursued. "What else did she say about the Hall of Records?"

"I don't think she explained anything more about it this time," said the older brother.

"Mom wants us to know that everything about Jesus and God is true," the younger brother interjected. "And that we should dedicate our lives to Christ and help others who may lose their way to find themselves again."

"Resurrection," her daughter stammered through her sob. "And Rapture."

"That's beautiful," I breathed, hoping I could sooth her jangled state of mind. "Did she say anything at all about the other woman who was there with her?"

"No, but I heard the other woman speak," she said. "She had the high voice of an angel with some kind of ringing echo."

"We should probably help her out of here," Horace said. "I think she's had enough for the day."

"I'd say you're right," I replied.

Her two brothers helped her to a stance. She wobbled at first at her knees but soon regained her balance.

"I'm fine," she said as she looked at me and smiled from one side of her mouth.

"They can exit," Thoth said in his approach of me. "But we'd like for you to stay here for a moment longer while we discuss something about this event with you."

"That's fine," I answered. "Kids, I'll catch up with you in a little bit. Get your sister a drink. I have bottled water in the cooler in the backseat of my car. The door's open, but wait for me outside if you don't mind."

"Ok," the two brothers both said as they each gave an arm to their sister to help her walk toward the door of the building.

Horace escorted the children outside. The door smacked shut behind them. The other two men who remained inside approached me.

"This site seems to be some kind of hallowed ground," Thoth declared. "We plan to do some further sonar testing of the subterranean landscape here with ground penetrating radar."

"I think we might have just stumbled across the Yucatan Hall of Records," O. Cyrus smiled at me. "Or at least the passage that leads to it."

"That would be incredible," I remarked. "Perhaps too incredible to believe, especially since you do realize that we're not currently located anywhere near the Yucatan."

The lighting in the building flickered off and then on twice.

"Oh, dear," Thoth said. "I'm afraid we might be having another problem with the circuits. Can you join me by the breaker box, O. Cyrus?

"Please, feel free to look around the building while we see if we can correct the lighting issue again."

"Sure thing," I said.

The lights flickered one more time after the two men walked away from me toward the far end of the building. No sooner had they reached the circuit breaker box than a garbled voice seemed to burst from the ground and race across the ceiling of exposed trusses within the building. The voice clarified as it zoomed back and forth above me until it suddenly seemed to resonate uniformly within the subterranean interior of the building.

"Well, hello there!" boomed the familiar voice of my recently deceased author friend. "Sorry I had to leave your planet, but I'm quite sure you'll be able to take over from here."

"Yeah, right." I muttered as I looked toward the two men, but both had their backs toward me as they faced the open breaker box. Neither acknowledged the emergence of the voice in the building.

"I know this is probably quite overwhelming at this stage of the game," my friend's voice resumed. "I just want to make sure you know that some of those elusive eternal questions are already answered for me."

"Like what?" I laughed, still staring at the men with their backs to me.

"I have regained all of my memory," my friend's voice boomed. "And now I know that my transition from bodily trapped spirit to resurrected soul has marked my passage to the Hall of Records where I now await my next incarnation."

"Congratulations," I said as I stepped in the direction of the men.

"The other thing that may be most interesting to you," my friend

began, "is that I have our leading lady from the Salvador Dali performance here with me."

I stopped in my tracks.

"I suspected she and her egg never were intended for me to
receive," came my friend's thunderous voice. "Now I know for sure
that she and her phantom object were really only meant for you all of
this time. You are about to remember not only who you are but also
what you are. The true odyssey of your everlasting life is about
to begin."

"I don't want any of this!" I hollered as loud as I could as I spun
away from the direction of the men. "I want to be left alone!"

"Alpha and Omega," the voice seemingly amplified to my disbelief if not dismay. "Your transfiguration awaits you, my love."

Hers was the voice of an angel. Her message careened within my
soul, crippling my senses. I knew with every exposed fiber of my
tenuous existence that the haunting voice belonged to the hypothesized earth angel from my friend's film of the 1965 Salvador Dali
performance.

"Who are you?" I yelled into the room before frantically
surveying the inside surroundings for speakers or some other source
of sound amplification. "And what do you want with me?"

After a significant pause, the angelic voice of my friend's
ordained Nephilim Siren returned.

"I want you to remember who and what you are so that you can
join me in paradise regained for our union in eternal ecstasy," the
voice melodiously spilled into me before breaking into song.

I turned and noticed the other two men in the building were no
longer looking into the circuit breaker box. Now, they were both
facing me and writing furiously into their notepads.

The disembodied singing voice I heard was throaty, ranging from
a low rumbling contralto to a sweetly, high pitched reverberation. I
could feel the notes attach to me viscerally and pull me like a gravita-
tional field toward the source of the tap in the center of the building:

"Someday, I'll hear the angels sing

Beyond the shadows of the tomb,
And all the bells of Heaven ringing
While saints are singing, 'Home, sweet, home.'"

Then I recognized that this was the hymn "Zion's Hill" that had just played at my friend's funeral. I must've mouthed some intonation of astonishment because I heard Thoth shout if something were wrong with me.

"I hear the song I just heard at the funeral service," I yelled in reply. "The Nephilim Siren is singing "Zion's Hill", don't you hear it?"

Thoth shook his head from side to side, indicating that he hadn't heard whatever I was hearing. He then resumed writing frantically in his notepad. I tried to grab his attention again but started to wobble within the unearthly range of the voice singing the hymn that now seemed to be sung for my ears alone.

"Do I know you in this world or can you tell me your name?" I trembled aloud once her voice faded with the hymn's conclusion.

The pause before she spoke again was even longer than the first time, as if there were some delay in the transmission of my voice before it could reach her.

"You already know me in real life but you don't remember yet," her soothing resonance finally came. "I am your soulmate with whom you'll spend eternity full of the promise of everlasting bliss."

"But how can I find you in the flesh?" I asked. "You're a Nephilim Siren who travels time, aren't you?"

The pause before she spoke lasted so long this time that I wasn't sure if she would speak again. I almost repeated my question but finally her voice did revive from the void surrounding me.

"You already have found me in the flesh," her voice returned. "You will continue to see more of me to come. You can write it down. Once the time is heralded for you to remember our future together, you will be ready for our souls to unite again. The consummation between you and I is why I am here to sing my songs to you, my love. You will know me for certain once you have eaten the scroll of the seventh angel and the mystery of God shall be fulfilled within you."

"What do you mean once I eat the scroll of the seventh angel?" I implored her to explain.

"The scroll conveys the revelation that circulates through the Hall of Records from both the Giza Plateau in Ancient Egypt and underwater in the cenote sanctuary of the Yucatan discovery," her voice finally returned after yet another prolonged pause. "This is the conduit for the truth to ring forth at this sacred place here for you and those who can hear and speak the truth in their hearts and souls."

"So, we're in some kind of vortex here?" I asked. "This is some kind of release point for the spirit world to materialize?"

"This is the temple for you to ordain yourself within my transmission of the oracle for all eternity," the crescendo of her voice finally cascaded through the empty space after the longest pause yet. "You are both recipient and deliverer of the words made flesh. You are the one who is prophesized in this place to lead the exodus for all of those who are born of angels and those who are angels and saints at their essence."

The inundation that came over me was so palpable that my face clenched from the forming tears. Before I could stop the urge to weep, the angelic voice rang out in another song. It was the second hymn sung at my friend's funeral, "Beulah Land":

"I'm looking now, just across the river,

To where my faith shall end in sight.

There's just a few more days to labor

Then I shall take my heavenly flight."

The vocal somehow trilled with reverberation of the last note before her voice imploded into a seemingly rising echo that rang like multiple voices until the celestial chorus split into ringing tones that tapered steadily down in volume before quickly fading into silence. I waited for a few moments for her to resume speaking or sing another hymn, but there was only prolonged silence.

"Hello?" I finally ventured. "Are you still there somewhere?"

But soon it was clear she was gone. I knew her voice from somewhere but could not place where I had heard its haunting timbre anywhere other than at the end of my friend's Salvador Dali film. If I only had more time to convince her to disclose who she was and how I could find her, I would've not felt so empty.

But she had vanished back into the depths of that otherworldly passage to whatever vestige there is or was of such an elusively mythical place as a Hall of Records.

I had always wondered if some illumination forthcoming from the discovery of any such a thing as a Hall of Records would be one that imparted such culturally transformative knowledge on a scientific scale that it really could somehow enable humanity to realize the bliss on earth of a paradise regained.

Now, the voice of this timeless angel-woman inside of the building was more or less telling me that I *myself* would be the revelation of the Hall of Records once I reenacted the consumption of text brought by an angel.

I had lost much of my biblical knowledge over time, but this eating of the scroll was one canonized episode that I had never forgot. I recognized that this description was rendered in the biblical Book of Revelation, in which an angel delivered a divine scroll to the Apostle John for him to eat in order to receive divine insight and internalize the prophecy he would broadcast.

As lucky as that made me feel to receive such a charge perhaps similar to that received by the alleged author of the Book of Revelation, I just didn't want to have to deal with all of the distortion that emanated from such a supernatural convergence with my life regardless of how full of fascination and dramatic consequence the whole intrigue seemed.

I did have to swallow my careening heart first before settling down somewhat because the experience in the well was so transcendent that I was truly shaken by it. That exhilaration, however, soon irked me. I didn't want to be part of anything other than the version of normalcy that awaited me.

Besides, there was no way what I was experiencing was real. It had to be some kind of ploy or hoax perpetrated by these minions of The Institute. There was no other logical explanation for what I heard.

The side of my personality that sought normalcy – or at least a life that was not ruled by insanity of such supernatural ilk as this – had evolved to the point that this sensibility had usurped the affinity I once had for the mystical, paranormal, or otherwise dubiously spiritual. I felt like if I were going to imbue myself in something risky and complicated it would be more personally direct, like a developing relationship with a married woman, Sirena, with whom I had started to mentor in creative writing back in Kentucky just a week before my friend died.

But I had to admit at that point, there didn't seem to be much choice for me now but to go down this path of demented wilderness bequeathed to me by my friend, even if I were at the mercy of group of lunatics masquerading as researchers on behalf of some wicked organization.

After that exchange with the Nephilim Siren in her Hall of Records passageway, I remained numb with silence for a while inside of the building. The other men had long since stopped writing in their notepads but deferred to me to make the first move.

Finally, I did decide that enough was enough. Clearly there would be no more voices from the dearly departed or angelic variety wafting upwards and onwards from the depths of the hallowed aquifer below us. I was ready to leave my friend and all of the mystery and complications that surrounded him behind for good despite the effort of the angelic voice to seduce me further into the mystery. The one thing that I couldn't shake, however, was how familiar her voice sounded, and yet I still just couldn't place who belonged to the voice outside of the phantom lady on my friend's film, which I now craved to watch again.

The two men finally escorted me out of the building. When I reached the light of day, I saw Horace leading the three children toward the building from a trail that cut through loblolly pines. Apparently, they had not been anywhere nearby while I conversed with my audible angel. The group scrambled toward me with Horace behind the rest in pursuit. They all stopped once they neared me and panted to catch their breath.

"This was a tremendous experience for everyone all around," Horace then managed to say. "The Institute will be fascinated by the details we will communicate with the principals there."

"That's great, but speak for yourself about how great all of this was," I griped to him. "While you're at it, let everybody at The Institute or whoever it is who executes my friend's will, that they can just go right ahead and keep whatever it is he wanted me to have because I just don't want anything from him that has anything to do with whatever all of this Christ-forsaken noise is, and I just can't imagine that he'd want to give me anything that didn't have everything to do with whatever this accursed mess is."

"I'm sorry you feel that way," Thoth said as he stepped toward me. "Please don't be overwhelmed by all of this. I know so much of what has happened recently has to be very difficult to process."

"I've seen and done so much crazy..." I started to rather vehemently spew before I paused and motioned for the trio of men to approach me closer so I could speak lower without the children hearing me. "I've been in the middle of so many crazy messes that I dread the thought of any more. Life is so hard as it is without making it an absolute nightmare.

"Whatever my friend had in mind and whatever all of this is here, I'm quite content to just live my life out as peacefully as possible, and if I die and that's all there is to it – you know what – I hope that's all there is to this life at this point because anything else sounds too much like work to me. I've had it with too much work. All of the eternal questions are nothing but anathema to me because I just want to be a normal human being on the face of this earth who doesn't have to trouble himself over any questions more involved than figuring out what to eat for breakfast."

"I understand," O. Cyrus tried to console me. "We really don't mean to trouble you."

"And for God's sake," I seethed through a whisper, "please leave these children alone, especially the daughter. They've all been through absolute hell with the death of their mother."

"We do appreciate all of your time and trouble," Horace added.

"Godspeed," Thoth said as he stuck out his hand for me to shake.

I shook his hand first then the hands of the other two. I can honestly say I hoped to never see any of the three of them again. Cordial though they all three were, their very presence smacked of occult nonsense replete with bells on their fingers and séance moans, even though I since realized that the angelic voice of my friend's filmed Nephilim Siren was something that not even The Institute probably could have concocted due to the impossibility of the logistics required.

Still, I just wanted to free my mind of all of this hysteria as soon as possible and perhaps not have it invade my thoughts ever again, especially the part about whether what I experienced was real and true.

Meanwhile, it became clear to me that I might have some work to do with the children of my other deceased friend. Before I ultimately decided to perform any final gesture of goodwill for the children in honor of the memory of their dear, sweet mother, I first had to quickly assess my own situation to determine if I even wanted to offer my help because the more entangled I became in their lives, the more time and energy I might have to commit later to the whole intrigue sparked by my friend and his death.

In fact, I was starting to reach the point where I can say I really didn't want anything to do with anyone else who wasn't a part of my immediate and small little world, namely my own wife and children and my newfound literary friend Sirena, who had very much stirred such dormant vitality within me that I am unsure exactly how our connection will ultimately develop.

So above all else, I wanted to return home to be free from the chaos caused by my friend's death, but even more viscerally, I wanted to be with Sirena before it was too late to meet with her any more. There is guilt swirling within me about how Sirena is becoming more important to me than my own wife, but the conflict this causes me is no match for the thrill I feel when I think about Sirena.

Not even the intrusion of the apparent supernatural world between my ears could deter me for very long from entertaining notions about Sirena once again.

With my thoughts as such desperately veering toward my return home to relative normalcy on one hand and the tantalizing pull of Sirena on the other, I nevertheless caved into my altruistic side and opted to perform one final good deed in Virginia by gathering the children of Brown Eggs one last time.

Clearly, Brown Eggs' daughter believed she heard her mother just like I thought I had heard the spellbinding resonance of the angelic Nephilim woman. I suspected that the experience would run deep and last a long time for her daughter. I had to try to figure out a way to both minimize the meaning of the encounter while simultaneously extolling the whole cacophonous debacle as a blessing of divine intervention somehow.

And I'd have to do that before leaving for my flight back to my home, which gave me all of about two hours to resolve. Once I did my part in trying to make some sense of what was happening for the children, I can't say that I particularly wanted to see any of them ever again either.

I motioned for Brown Eggs' brood to approach me.

"Let's go eat," I said to them once they reached me. "All this talking to folks in some other dimension has made be hungry."

We reached the restaurant in separate cars within ten minutes. Once seated in the restaurant, I made sure Brown Eggs' daughter understood that hearing her mother's voice at the well site was a miracle that should be embraced as such.

"Be joyful for what you've heard," I said to her, trying my best to convey her mother's religious belief and spiritual values. "Know in your heart that you mother rests with God and you will join her there one day to be with her again so you both can be resurrected by Jesus."

Then I tried to help her brace for the confusion she would undoubtedly face in the future.

"You have to understand that sometimes we experience things," I calmly began. "Things that change our lives for the better but are so extraordinary that if we try to share those experiences with others, they may view us very differently to a fault."

"You mean like we're nuts," she blurted.

"Exactly," I confirmed. "We all need to make sure we can go about our lives in peace without the wrong kind of intervention by others, who may mean well enough, but really don't know enough to have our best interests at heart."

"We understand," the older brother said. "We kind of ran into that when we told people about Mom talking to you before she died even though you weren't in the room."

This mention again of the conversation between their mother and me on her deathbed arrested my attention, especially since I knew I was not there with their mother at that time.

"Tell me more about the conversation between your mother and me," I urged. "We really didn't get to discuss any of that the last time I was in town."

We talked throughout dinner and dessert about their mother speaking from some other dimension beyond this ordinary earthly one while she was nearing death in the hospice care ward of the hospital. I did not visit Brown Eggs while she was there, in part because I only found out about the degree of her terminal illness when it was far too late for me to even arrange a visit. But the children related to me that I really was there in an important way for their mother, even though I never physically appeared.

Parts of what they told me about their mother's perception of my presence baffled me, but on the whole, their descriptions of their mother conversing with me seemed to me to be a highly hallucinatory interaction with her projection of me as she neared death. This most likely was induced by medication, but the more I listened to their telling of the story, the more I wondered about just how much of a possibility it is for someone to perhaps transport through astral travel to meet someone, even when such a meeting is unbeknownst or otherwise remembered by the person who undertook the out-of-body travel.

By far, the most peculiar scene the children related to me was her last remaining minutes alive before she died laughing. I thought I misheard the older brother when he told me that his mother died laughing.

"What do you mean 'laughing'?" I myself snorted in disbelief despite the gravity of the subject of his mother's death.

Based upon the cause of death she endured and her relatively young age as a mother of three pre-teen children, there couldn't have been much in the way of humor available to her at that awful time. Perhaps the pain medication that most likely induced her hallucination of me had also prompted her incongruous laughter.

I had read once about a person who died laughing. The account came from literature of the *Ars Moriendi* about the art of dying in Europe during the ravaging clutches of the bubonic plague. One historian who had chronicled the physical states of plague victims as they died listed the account as a category by itself even though there were no others beside the one person who had died laughing.

That fifteenth century historical account aside, the final minutes of their mother's life was certainly more palpable to me. The older brother made his mother's death even more immediate for me by producing an audio recording of her during her final moments. He first played a part of the tape in which his mother sang a song with a choppy, quavering voice. I couldn't quite decipher the song she was singing at first because it sounded like she was partly laughing while she sang it.

But when I thought I did recognize the song, I instantly asked her son to play the audio again from the beginning. To my shock, I heard lyrics that she couldn't have possibly known well enough to sing because they were my own and were never distributed in any format:

'Shaken up, but it's OK.
It don't matter much anyway
If the stars all fade away
Or if the earth convulses today.
Go to the finish line
As fast as you can fly
And if tomorrow arrives
With more than enough to get by
Let's flop and die from laughing
Let's flop and die from laughing.'

I remember that during the time I knew their mother I did share with her a few board-mixed songs with lyrics that I co-wrote with a musician. That "Die Laughing" song was among them. But I don't remember ever giving a copy to her or writing any of the lyrics down for her. I believe I played the music for her more than just once, but still, the idea that she could remember the lyrics word-for-word after a couple of years had passed and at a time when she was medicated near death seemed impossible to me.

'Or if it winds up electrified,
Horrible and worthlessly aligned,
Absorb the shock and do not cry.
And if it seems like too much as it eats you alive,
Have a fit and die from laughing
Have a fit and die from laughing
Have a fit and die from laughing.'

Their mother continued to sing at the same volume throughout the recording. Her voice mimicked the half-laughter, half-vocalizing of the song itself. I couldn't believe what I was hearing in the restaurant to the point where I asked them to copy the audio for me so I could keep it for myself and listen to it more closely later.

'If you seem trapped
And your mind is crapping

And all you see are hands clapping,
Wake the kids up from their napping,
Take your arms and start them flapping,
Spook the dog and start it yapping.
Die
Die laughing.
I don't know about you,
But I do know about me.
I don't know what you'll do,
But I know I want to die
Laughing.'

The original recording featured me laughing harder and louder once the lyrics stopped but the music continued. It was real laughter that I was able to force myself to sustain throughout the final flourish of guitars at the end of the song.

She had mimicked the exact same laughter, but in her case, she died with the last gasped laugh. It almost seems to me that perhaps she was repeating the lyrics as if someone else unseen in the room sang or said the words first before she did.

Then with "Die Laughing" concluded, Brown Eggs died. The cries of her children followed on the recording, but the older brother immediately stopped the playback.

I was dumbfounded by the fact that Brown Eggs had passed away like this after enduring such hardship in life. Her daughter had beamed at me when she told me that her mother also had talked with me for several minutes prior to singing my song and dying in laughter.

The children had detailed other parts of phantom conversation their mother had with me during her near-death delirium. Apparently, a couple of instances had been recorded, but most of them had not. One of her talks that seemed more important than the others for all three of her children was a series of questions that she asked about how to proceed after her death. Her younger son said it was like I provided instructions for her about how to resurrect herself in her flight to find rest in Heaven.

This species of resurrection apparently first entailed her rebirth through baptism by immersion within an underwater dream. All three children agreed that she asked about whether she could breathe underwater in her dream with me. They said that their mother coughed at first for several seconds after she asked her question, then she spoke with a soft voice full of wonder at the sights she mentioned as she thought she was traveling underwater.

"So now I am born again?" her children remembered her asking aloud. "I am finally baptized so that my soul can really be saved?"

The children said she shrieked and breathed fast at one point during her bizarre journey underwater before she started to remark about how fast the current moved her through the liquid dimension and how the flashes of creatures – eels – seemed to explode all around her. Soon she was swimming in laughter and calling out to the eels that surrounded her, shimmying alongside her at her speed of accelerated travel.

The children agreed that their mother had asked her unseen guide about the body of water she had entered, but they couldn't quite correctly pronounce the name of the sea. Based upon their guesses of the name, I ventured that the name of the body of water they were searching for was the Sargasso Sea, especially since the eels were mentioned. The Sargasso Sea is known for being the only sea without a coastline but is also the spawning ground for the Virginia Eel. They remembered their mother laughing and whooping through this part of her journey, as though she were strapped into a thrill ride.

The excitement within the Sargasso Sea soon receded, however, as her underwater odyssey continued. Her children all remembered her then specifically asking, "So, I'm in the Bermuda Triangle right now?" before she succumbed to groans, cries and outright yells. Her children said she shook and twitched during this part of the passage before a calm finally came over her and she seemed to regain physical ease and stable consciousness.

With her eyes wide open, she struggled to shift her weight and keep her eyes open. Her children said she seemed to be looking right past them when she said, "I've always wanted to go to the Bahamas. I just didn't know I'd have to go all of the way to Atlantis to finally be baptized."

Gradually, she gave up trying to raise herself within her bed. Her voice softened as she closed her eyes. Her children related that they were standing beside her now, watching her eyelids flutter and her breathing slow. Her daughter said she "was making the sounds she made when she ate cherry cordial ice cream, like 'mmmm.'" Her older son added that she was murmuring "Wow" frequently.

They weren't sure how long this part of the journey lasted for their mother, but they do remember her really regaining consciousness after her body jolted and she started to retch, as though she had swallowed too much water and had just been resuscitated. Once she finally regained the semblance of herself with her children all beside her, she looked up to them and said, "So that was Atlantis."

After they related this last part to me, I redirected the conversation to the manifestation of their mother's voice at the well site. I emphasized to them that this most recent extraordinary occurrence should not be shared with anyone under any circumstances.

"That is probably even worse for me this time," the young woman realized aloud. "I mean I was the only one who actually heard Mom speak at the well."

"That's true," I agreed with her. "And I'm in the same boat because I was talking to an angel or a Siren, I mean, I really don't know what or who I was hearing, but the voice sure seemed beautifully divine and heaven-sent to me."

I tried to convince the three of them to make a pact with me that we would vow never to speak of what happened at the well site to anyone else, even the trio of men who were also at the well site. I held my hand out above the table and told them to place their hands atop mine.

"Now repeat after me," I began and they followed suit. "I do solemnly swear to know in my heart...that what happened today was a miracle between God and us...and that I won't tell anyone about the miracle that was meant just for all of us here today."

I felt like I at least gave them a fighting chance, especially the young woman. It was up to them to adapt to their circumstances the best they could with the help of each other. They already had plenty of practice doing just that. Their mother would have been exceptionally proud of all three of them.

I finished my cherry cheesecake then gulped down the last of my lukewarm coffee before I wished them all the happiness in the world. They returned my wishes with hugs and handshakes.

I asked them to send a copy of the audio recording of their mother singing my song while she was dying. The older brother said he did have even more recordings besides that one but thought they were stolen from his home.

"Stolen?" I remember asking him.

"That's all I can figure out," he had said. "One day they were there, then the next day they were all gone, except for this one because I had it put away in a different place than the others."

He added that he had not downloaded any of the recordings. I asked him to provide copies of these other recordings if they turned up. I provided my physical mailing address and an e-mail address but was hopeful deep down that I wouldn't have to communicate with them any further about their mother or anything else.

The entire reunion of sorts with her children made me realize that I still suffered from some nagging guilt over the way I had left their mother without my offer of friendship during her time of greatest need. I had considered her to be an extremely close and personal friend before I moved from Virginia. The relationship we shared together was ours, not anyone else's including our spouses, and for that I will always be eternally grateful to her for treating me like a true friend in return.

I had already started to think a great deal more about Brown Eggs after my first visit to Virginia when her children had first mentioned

her time in hospice care. In the three months that had elapsed from
that visit until my second visit to Virginia for my friend's funeral, I
had considered writing about their mother to help me better understand how I felt about her and the friendship we shared.

My newfound interest in my Kentucky friend Sirena had actually opened the floodgates for my memories of Brown Eggs when she
gave three cartons of brown eggs from her chickens to me just two
weeks prior to my visit to Virginia for my friend's funeral. The eggs
Sirena gave to me were the first brown eggs that I had even seen since
I moved from Virginia, where I would frequently buy brown eggs by
the dozen from Brown Eggs. Her seemingly non-stop availability of
brown eggs produced by her prolific hens was the source, after all, for
the nickname of 'Brown Eggs' that I conferred upon her.

Those memories of Brown Eggs took some sorting out for me, but
that catalyst of brown eggs from Sirena prompted me to start my
writing about Brown Eggs at the point when we were able to spend a
few hours alone together for the last time. I had met her at the local
community center before Christmas of 2009 so that our children
could participate in a morning homeschool education program
offered by the facility.

I wanted to spend time with her and have our children spend
time together as well before we moved from the region where we had
lived for the past decade. I knew Brown Eggs would have a hard time
with my departure from the region because she was having such a
difficult time with the effects of the Great Recession. Her looming
financial hardship was compounded by her own relative inexperience
in the workplace and her lack of technical skills or college education.

She was not a writer like my other friend whose funeral brought
her full circle back into my life nor did she have anywhere near the
worldly and perhaps otherworldly credentials as him. I hadn't known
her quite as long as I had known him either but still valued her
friendship all the same.

And in some ways, her friendship became an even more resolute
force for me than his because hers demanded a sincerity of heart that

I've not often found in other relationships. She also was truly pleasant to be around but capable of hardening when needed. She was quite capable of concealing it, but she had a vulnerability about her that sometimes surfaced in my presence and for some reason made me feel like I needed to protect her.

Of course, she is a collaborator in all of this in her own right and obviously implicated in the entire otherworldly intrigue that has saturated my life at this point. I write this now, knowing more than I ever wanted to know, or at least think I know, about the nature of reality and death.

I originally wrote the forthcoming story in Collaboration 2 of this book about Brown Eggs before I produced the preceding account about my friend and his death that constitutes Collaboration 1 of this book – "Brown Egg Resurrection."

I rendered this first part of the book in first person narration, but I have kept the original third person narration of her story – "Brown Eggs & Jam" – instead of changing the format for this second part of the book to match the narrative of the first part.

I decided to keep her account in its third-person form in order to preserve the authenticity of my depiction of her the way I knew her before I learned what I now know about her and her otherworldly, disembodied manifestation as an entity swimming her way through a portal that somehow might lead to the elusive Hall of Records.

I have to tell the full story of Brown Eggs in all of this because without her there would have never been this story to tell at all. There would be no discovery, no redemption, no revival and no resurrection.

And perhaps most importantly of all for me, without Brown Eggs there would be no Sirena.

Collaboration 2
Brown Eggs & Jam

———

December 21ˢᵗ, 2009
Kilmarnock, Virginia

———

"A RAT BIT ME," her voice shook, "when I reached for the egg. I think it was a rat or a mouse, I guess...or something. Maybe it was a spider. I didn't actually see anything because I reached down into a concrete block, but it sounded like something moving. It was big enough to make a noise when it moved. And it hurt like a bite, not like a sting."

He watched her finger trace the spidering raw blotch on the back of her hand that had further spread and reddened since he saw her yesterday. He did not notice her lift her eyes to him when she stopped outlining the lesion.

"Better get that looked at," he told her through his grimace. "That don't look right."

"I know," she sighed. "But I can't really afford to do that right now with my husband hurt and out of work probably for a long time now the way it sounds, but forget about it. Usually, stuff like this does just goes away on its own."

"I don't know," he said as he peered closer at her wound. "That looks downright nasty. I don't think I've ever seen anything quite like that. It looks like something might be wrong with your blood."

"Well, I've already claimed healing for it," she informed him. "Just like the woman who touched the garment of Jesus was healed of her abnormal bleeding and the cause of it, I believe my healing will come from my faith in Jesus. I'd still like to get a faith-healing preacher to lay hands on it, too.

"Besides, God's will is God's will. If it gets worse it's God's will. If it gets better, it's God's will."

"You've got three kids relying upon you," he remarked. "You taking care of your kids should be God's will. And to do that, you have to take care of yourself. You need to have that looked at by a doctor before it gets any worse. It wasn't anywhere near that bad yesterday."

Their eyes met. Hers welled up, but she did not look away. Her gaze surged plaintive but could not capture his attention. Instead, he first eyed the egg carton that she had placed between them on the round table in the middle of the community center computer room.

His gaze drifted to the garland Christmas swag draped all along the wall above the bank of computers. He then cast his glance toward the silver-tinseled Christmas tree positioned in one of the corners of the room.

"'Tis the season, I reckon," he said, returning his eyes to hers.

They were alone together in the computer room while their children participated in a homeschool educational program in another wing of the building. Her three children and his two had spent significant time together at the center over the past year taking advantage of all of the resources at the facility, such as the educational programs, the computer room, the sports courts, and the indoor swimming pool. Over the course of the year, she had frequently brought brown eggs for him laid by her chickens. He had literally bought dozens of these eggs at least a couple dozen times from her.

"Didn't know you'd need hazard pay for this batch," he tried to joke as he reached to the carton and opened it to look at the brown eggs inside.

As he reached to the back pocket of his jeans to pry loose his wallet, she touched his arm and gently pressed her fingertips against his forearm.

"Don't," she urged him. "You've given me way too much money for eggs already."

"I like them," he replied as he handled his wallet and removed a ten-dollar bill. "And if there's more between now and when I finally move, I'll pay for those too."

He noticed the tears swell from her eyes then drop to her cheeks before the corners of her mouth quivered. He watched more tear drops fall before she removed her fingers from his forearm.

"That's too much for a dozen eggs," she managed, pushing the ten-dollar bill toward him before she smeared her tears across her face.

"It's just ten dollars," he laughed. "Not a hundred, not even twenty. Give me the next dozen for free then if you think I'm giving you too much money. Besides I might as well be a rich man in this imploding world."

"I guess," she muttered past a sniffle before he slid the ten-dollar bill back to her. "Not like I can't use the money. Times are getting really, really tough now, and I'm not sure how or when they'll get better. I'm afraid we're going to have a hard time keeping our house with all the bills we're getting."

"Oh, no," he groaned. "How far behind are you on your mortgage?"

"We're not too far behind yet," she sighed, removing the money from the desk and folding it into the back pocket of her shorts. "But if we don't get enough for disability, I'm afraid it won't be long before we run into real trouble."

"You know there's been some legislative action in the works, state and federally, about mortgage assistance for homeowners who've suffered job loss and property value drop," he informed her. "It may be a while before all of that gets sorted out given how the financial markets are collapsing, but it would be definitely something to keep an eye on if it gets harder for you guys to pay your mortgage, especially if the house value goes significantly underwater in relation to your loan."

"Yeah, I've actually mentioned this already to the bank," she replied. "They're going to do what they can to help us find any resources available for us to use. I'm sure they don't want to get stuck with a house they can't do anything with if we did have to foreclose on it. It's not like we have waterfront property like you had."

"Just don't let them sweet talk you into a short sale," he warned her. "They may try to act like they're doing you a favor by eating some of the house's worth if it's underwater, but if the market is so bad overall that there's no way to close a good sale, all a short sale will do is put you out of your house with nowhere else to go unless you want to pay the ridiculously steep price of rent around these parts."

"Well, we would probably have somewhere to go because of the homeschool network here," she countered. "But I don't know for how long. So far no one at the bank has mentioned a short sale to us."

"Have you looked at all into finding work for yourself?" he asked her. "I know it's a hard time to try to find a job, but you might be able to get something."

"I've just put together a resume, but I'm afraid I don't have too much in the way of recent work skills since I haven't really worked at all in fifteen years," she managed to convey before she buried her face in her hands.

The outburst of her sobs caught him off guard. She tried to choke them back but lost control. She clenched her eyes shut and audibly cursed herself beneath her breath in between sobs. He knew she really wouldn't want for him to see her break down like this, but he understood her situation had taken such a dire turn that she couldn't stop the momentum of her surging despair.

He watched her back jerk up then quiver back down as she struggled to muffle her sobs. He placed the palm of his hand upon her lurching shoulder. He could only stay there with her while her anguish ran its course, realizing that she might be on the verge of total upheaval in her life.

"It's going to be all right," he tried to console her. "You'll see. Everything will work out."

But he didn't feel that he sounded too convincing or optimistic about a positive resolution to her predicament when he said all would be fine. He knew how bad the Great Recession of 2008 had already become, how long it would take for many people to recover from the economic fallout, and how much collateral damage there would be as the wholesale ruin of people's lives transpired.

It also struck him as he shifted his palm from her shoulder to her back between her shoulder blades that he and his family could have just as easily been in a similar financial predicament had he and his wife not sold their house in 2007.

Instead of being forced to use retirement funds to pay a mortgage in a virtually non-existent job market, he found himself in a financially stable position having cleared $250,000 from the sale of his own house. He and his wife had sold their house just before the housing bubble burst in a place where property values had skyrocketed to extreme proportions.

"The first thing you have to do," he began, "is cut every expense that isn't absolutely necessary. Make it a challenge to see how little you actually need and that might help make the situation more tolerable."

"I already had to cancel our health insurance," she finally managed to let out between her heaves. "The kids and us aren't covered at all right now. If anything should happen, I don't know how it would work out, but we do have about a thousand dollars in a health savings account."

She then buried her hands in her face again and sobbed in even louder bursts.

"Look, I know it's bad right now, but you have to believe things will improve," he said louder and more sternly than he intended then placed his hand across her forearm. "You know, my author friend likes to extol the virtues of the serenity prayer as a surefire way to lift himself up when he felt anxious about circumstances happening in his life that clouded his future. You know, God grant me the serenity to accept the things I can't change, the courage to change the things I can, and the wisdom to know the difference."

"I love that prayer," she managed to wheeze past a stifled sob. "It's such a comfort to say and hear. Thank you for that. You really are so very kind to me."

"I'm just here to help you," he told her, knowing that he wouldn't be of much help to her once he moved from the region. "And that serenity prayer will always be available to you for you to help yourself. Those words are as true as they come. Let them guide you through the challenges you face."

She resumed her sobbing but did so silently now. She shuddered nonetheless with each pang. He kept his hand on her arm and squeezed softly when he heard her grit her teeth and felt her tighten herself against the spasms gripping her body. At least now it occurred to him that there was something more tangible he could do to actually help her.

"I can actually help you right now," he snapped his fingers as he offered his assistance, perhaps too quickly and cheerfully.

"How?" she asked then sniffled, looking up to him with her suddenly swollen, red eyes.

"Come here," he directed her. "Sit beside me and we'll find what you need for insurance online right now."

He did help her. Together, they readily completed the registration and online forms needed to begin the process for enrolling her children in health care coverage. She qualified for her three children to receive health care coverage without cost and was advised through the registration system that she could expect confirmation of immediately retroactive coverage within two weeks.

She was relieved to know her children would receive coverage, but she wouldn't pursue any kind of subsidized or free healthcare for herself and her husband. She refused to let him continue with the forms on the website for that purpose. She also told him that her husband had been out of work but unable to collect unemployment insurance money because of restrictions applied against him as a self-employed subcontractor.

Now her husband was completely unable to do the physical work he had previously done for most of his adult life because of his chronic neck, back, and hip problems, but she waved him off when he asked her if her husband could perhaps change the type of work he does.

"There are now programs that can help him transition to a new career path if he can no longer perform the physical labor he used to do," he said. "At some point, he'll have to figure out something else to do anyway if he can't do what he was doing."

"I'd rather leave our health, our work, and our future in God's hands," she told him as she squeakily rubbed her eyes. "God has a plan for us. We just have to keep praying we'll be fine, and there will be enough work one way or another to meet our needs."

"Have you confided in anyone at your church?" he asked her. "I know a lot of the congregation there is involved with charity work for several non-profit organizations in the area. Those folks could be a great resource for ideas and support for you, too."

"I have talked a little bit with a couple of them," she divulged before retrieving a tissue from the box on the table and clearing her nose. "But nothing that's really helping me. I really don't want them to start passing around an offering plate just for me so I can pay my mortgage either. That would be too embarrassing for me."

"Embarrassment can't factor into your financial survival at this point," he chided her. "I'm not saying you have to go around begging for money or start trying to steal stuff, but if members of the congregation of your church want to help you, you let them help you in any way they can, even if it means giving you a dented can of green beans, do you hear me?"

"I'm really not looking for help," she declared. "I find it much more rewarding when I can dig my own way out of my messes. God's plan always seemed to get revealed one way or the other in the past when I just buckled down and gritted my teeth to make things happen. Sometimes it just takes longer to see what that plan is."

He respected her choice in regard to letting God's will play out, but it struck him as too simple overall. The choice didn't seem like a testament of faith or even pride in self-sufficiency at all to him. He felt like it smacked of the path of least resistance in the short term. Only when desperation takes hold does urgency reveal itself in full force, he thought to himself, and by then the relief needed might prove too far removed for her to access.

Still, he knew better than to minimize just how informed her decision might be by her faith. She had previously shared the details of her spiritual rebirth with him; how she had spiraled out of control in her twenties only to smash into the rock bottom conclusion of substance abuse and narcotics addiction.

She had willed her leap of faith by necessity and with the fervor that accompanies such a drastic measure. Her life-or-death reality perhaps made her faith a last resort, the final hope for some semblance of normalcy and purpose for prolonging her own life. Now that she had been a born-again Christian for several years, she had told him more than once that she knew in her heart she was the living testament of her faith, the veritable animation of Holy Spirit in human form by virtue of the gift of grace given to her.

She claimed that the saving grace of her descent into a reckless lifestyle was the salvation of both her body and soul that her path of self-destruction had precipitated. Without her suffering, she would have never known redemption. She found the support she needed through church-sponsored programs to help her shed her destructive habits and begin the path of recovery to rescue her true self from the vicious cycle of artificial consciousness and bottomless despair.

"I understand," he had conceded then waited for her to restart their conversation.

"We need to lighten the load here," she declared after extended silence passed between them and she had completely gathered herself. "Or else I'm going to drive us both crazy."

"Why don't you tell me about something you want to tell me?" he offered. "Try to make it something as far removed from the worrisome details of your day-to-day life as possible. That way you can escape a little bit here and take me with you for a while."

"All right," she said then paused while she rubbed her puffy eyes. "This will probably sound a little crazy, but the one thing that keeps popping into my mind more and more is this vision I have flying around on a pterodactyl during the times of the Garden of Eden and the Great Flood.

"When I wake up, it seems like I'm living this dream right up until the time my eyes open. It happened again last night."

"I remember you talking about this before," he replied. "But it seems like it's been quite some time ago since you mentioned it."

"The vision I have opens up the genesis of all creation to me," she began. "I'm riding on top of this giant pterodactyl and holding on for dear life to the rainbow-colored top of its head. Everything below me is in view: the lush beauty of an unspoiled world filled with all of God's creatures from dinosaurs to humans alive at the same time in a world without death in the Garden of Eden, just like the Young Earth Creationist belief says."

"Fascinating," he said. "People and dinosaurs living together, but I believe the prehistoric creature you're describing is the pterosaur Quetzacoatlus and not a pterodactyl, which were actually quite small.

"But carry on."

"In the vision I had, that's what I keep seeing," she glared at him before she resumed her story. "But then – WHACK! – One second I'm flying around through the Garden of Eden in all of its beautiful glory then the next second everything speeds up in the vision like a fast-forwarded time lapse. That's when the thing flies me smack dab into The Great Flood.

"The vision at that time is like I'm flying on the pterodactyl in a bubble and see all of the destruction happening below me, but I'm safe inside the bubble. All I see is water swelling up from the sides of the earth then crashing into itself with all of the dinosaurs, people and other creatures running for their lives before they are swallowed by the flood."

"I definitely remember the bubble part," he blurted.

"Right," she confirmed. "That's when my ride lowers us to the water and we float on the waves in the bubble once we do stop flying. We just lurch back and forth across high seas until I see Noah's Ark sloshing there in the water, too.

"Then the strangest thing happens over and over again without fail each time. While we're still inside of the bubble, the pterodactyl launches us into the air high above the Ark. It then pops the bubble with its beak. We drop like rocks until – BOOM – the bird jerks us level just above the Ark. Once it is right above the boat, it slams the brakes so hard and fast that it throws me from its head. I go crashing to the Ark, but a hatch opens and I land on a soft bale of something like wool."

"Wow, that sounds almost too real not to be real," he commented.

"But last night, the vision had a different ending," she resumed. "This time I meet this beautiful middle-aged lady who pops up from behind the bale and sings to me. Then she tells me that I am one of the same type of people as her, who were born of human women from the loins of angels."

"That's awesome!" his voice boomed. "You had a vision that you were the Nephilim offspring of an angel on earth and a mortal woman! Wow!"

"Nephilim sounds familiar from the Bible, right?" she asked.

"Indeed," he confirmed for her. "Nephilim is mentioned in the Book of Genesis. I've had to learn more about Nephilim than I ever wanted to know for a book project by my author friend. They were portrayed by some as the reason why God wrought the Great Flood upon the earth – to destroy the Nephilim born of fallen angels and humans so that the true human beings could be restored to their rightful province on earth."

"Yeah," she smiled at him. "I remember hearing about that, too, from the angel woman on the Ark. My God, she was gorgeous and glowing with such a soothing, uplifting voice."

"That's sounds amazing."

"But the vision last night got even more complicated because of the half-angel woman up and says she and I are going to be the only two of those types of angel half-breeds to survive the flood and that we were put on the ark by the actual angel who had told Noah the flood was coming. She said the name of the angel but I can't remember the name she said for the life of me. I just can't get it off the tip of my tongue."

"It was an archangel who told Noah the flood was coming," he replied. "I remember running across this archangel during research for a book project, but I can't remember if the angel name was Michael or Gabriel or Raphael or some other."

"The name she said wasn't any of those three," she informed him. "Must have been a different angel."

"For me, that kind of surrealistic odyssey you've described is much more vivid and visceral than this sort of Young Earth Creationist perspective that you've framed around your vision," he stated.

"Well, I believe in Young Earth Creationism," she told him. "I take the Book of Genesis literally in how God created man, everything else on earth, and the whole universe. I believe the earth is only about six-thousand years old based upon the lineage from Adam to Noah listed in the Bible."

"I know you do," he replied. "But what I mean is that this vision you're experiencing is just so imaginatively deep and textured. I mean, you're telling me a half-angel human hybrid woman told you that you are like her and you were both put on the Ark by the archangel who told Noah to prepare for the Flood! And all of that after the giant pterosaur you're flying around on pops an enormous protective bubble that contains both of you so that the creature can drop you out of the sky and down to the Ark? How on earth does someone evoke a vision that bizarre?

"That sounds to me like your belief in your vision is coming straight from within you without any filters to screen its content and not something you've memorized so that you can internalize it or explain that you believe it, like you had to do with your Young Earth Creationist Christian belief."

"Why can't I believe in both!" she glowered at him, flinging both of her hands into the air then slamming her palms down on the table. "And why can't the one be part of the other! I don't see why I can't believe my vision confirms my belief about Creation and the Flood and everything about Jesus, even if I don't really know or understand what the rest of all the angel-human talk was all about."

"Another one of the things I found most interesting about your vision," he interjected, "is that the creature involved sounds like Quetzalcoatlus, which ties into more research I've been doing for a book project."

"Why is that creature so interesting to you?" she asked with some semblance of calm restored to her voice once she noticed the door to the computer room open and their children file into the room with each of the five of them wearing a balled Santa Claus hat upon their heads.

"Because of the pterosaur's namesake – Quetzalcoatl," he answered. "You see, Quetzalcoatl is a principal deity by one name or another of ancient Central America from the Olmecs and Mayans to the Toltecs and Aztecs. Quetzalcoatlus couldn't have been better named since the deity namesake translates to 'feathered serpent.'"

"Feathered serpent sounds like a flying reptile-bird, all right." she muttered.

"Only in this case," he continued, "feathered serpent was more like a giant or biblical angel who embodied resurrection and not only advised humanity how to survive through the advance of civilization but also by some accounts actually shaped humans from the collected bones of extinct human life.

"Depending on how much affinity one has for biblical and nonbiblical accounts of angelic beings coming to earth, Quetzalcoatl might even be described as a fallen angel or archangel at that."

"Did youse guys have fun and get enough to eat for lunch?" she loudly asked the children, who all looked at each other briefly before unanimously agreeing aloud that they did.

"Good," he said before he smiled at them. "I hope you learned all you'll ever need to know today."

Her daughter and two sons laughed at his comment but his own son and daughter just shook their heads. The two girls paired together and went to a computer at the far end of the room, sitting with their backs to their parents as they shared the screen. The three boys went into the opposite corner of the room, where a mound of wood and plastic building blocks covered a large oval mat.

"Legend suggests that Quetzalcoatl was forced from his city of Cholula," he resumed his account. "But he escaped by floating to the Yucatan Peninsula on a raft of snakes. For the Mayans, his arrival might have fulfilled prophecy of the return of their divine deity, in some ways like a second coming of a messiah would fulfill in other religious belief, say through a happening like the Rapture."

"Now you're getting really far-fetched, Jam," she sneered at him. "And maybe even sacrilegious or blasphemous because when you start throwing around words like 'the Rapture,' you've got fire in your hands, especially when you compare the end times to whatever you're talking about with these Mayans or whoever.

"I don't know if you really understand what you mean when you say something like 'the Rapture' because what it means to me and other Christians who think like I do is that the true Christians who have been saved by Jesus rise from the earth to meet the Lord right before the Tribulation period of worldwide suffering. Those Christians who are dead rise first then those who are alive before the Tribulation starts also are brought up to meet the Lord. Then all return to earth with the second coming of Jesus to live under Christ's reign for one-thousand years after the Battle of Armageddon takes place."

"Well, the point I was trying to make," he resumed, "is what seems more far-fetched or whatever else you want to call it, the legend and creation myth of Quetzalcoatl or riding around on the misshapen, spectral forehead of a gigantic flying reptile in a world that was created six-thousand years ago?"

"Now I see what you're doing, you jerk," she nearly spewed at him. "I knew you'd throw all of this back in my face with the ridicule you just can't hide. You want so badly to call me and everybody that believes in the literal interpretation of the Bible and Young Earth Creationism an idiot."

"That's not what I'm doing at all!" he actually yelled back at her.

His rise in volume drew the attention of the children from their opposite ends of the room. When he noticed their wide-eyed looks of looming concern, he laughed before he spoke again.

"Sorry, folks," he smiled, waving one of his hands to the boys and the other to the girls. "Just getting a little excited over here about what I was talking about. I'll try to pipe down a little bit."

"Don't worry," she chimed in. "Jam here is probably just getting a little hungry. He's had to sit here and look at these brown eggs for a couple hours now."

The children all laughed at her words as he nodded his head in agreement.

"Yes, I just wonder if they're still good after they've sat here all morning." he added. "But I guess I'll find out when I crack half of them open, scramble them all up with a little milk, then fry the whole mess with a great big gob of shredded cheddar cheese piled on top of it."

"That sounds good," his son remarked from his side of the room before the children all returned their attention to each other and their activities.

"Look," he quietly said to her. "I'm not here to judge anyone, and for all I know you're as much right about what you think with regard to Young Earth Creationism as you would be if you suddenly announced to me that you were destined to be a courier for a mythical Hall of Records outpost of Atlantis somewhere in or near the Yucatan Peninsula that Edgar Cayce apparently detailed in a trance.

"I mean, there could be some kind of extraterrestrial Osiris Shaft right underneath the paw of some invisibly submerged North American Sphinx buried beneath the mouth of the Rappahannock River for all I know."

"I really don't think you have any idea at all just how badly it can make somebody feel when you say things like you're saying," she said through clenched teeth as she rubbed her brow. "You make it out like nothing in this world is possible to know because there's so much that might seem unexplained about it and that even the things that are explainable haven't been understood in the right way."

"I'd be the happiest man in the world just to know that you were flying around on a giant prehistoric creature," he countered, "for no other reason that you are actually a half-woman, half-angel courier from the Hall of Records. It'd be great if you were on some kind of mission in this world and the next to let people know that the Rapture is coming for believers and the earth is really only six-thousand years old based upon the Bible, regardless of what Edgar Cayce or anyone else says or thinks."

"Yeah, right, Jam" she half-heartedly laughed as she smacked down on the back of his hand, exposing the back of her own hand marked by the sickly scarlet sheen of the spidery blotch glazed beneath the fluorescent light. "I really couldn't care less about what Edgar Cayce thought or did, and what would I be doing wandering around something called the Hall of Records? I sure wouldn't be searching for answers like you're talking about anywhere else other than the Bible."

"I would say if you ever did find yourself in between worlds like that," he began. "If the Hall of Records does portend of such a thing, that you would have your very beliefs at your full command without any inconsistency between them and the experiences you would encounter because if the Hall of Records doesn't account for the reckoning of resurrection and eternal life, like the very Rapture itself, then its theoretical contents would be worthless as far as I'm concerned."

"Then to me," she surmised aloud. "I already have all that I could ever need from any Hall of Records because I already have the Bible. And based upon that I know the earth is around six-thousand years old. I don't need Edgar Cayce to tell me any differently."

"Good for you, you Young Earthian," he smiled. "And don't ever let anyone else tell you otherwise."

"How much longer are you going to talk?" his son asked him from the other side of the room. "I'm hungry."

"Hungry?" he shot back. "How can you be hungry? Didn't you just eat lunch?"

"Not much of it," he told his father. "I didn't like it."

"Well," Brown Eggs said, "we should probably get going, anyway. I think we'll come up here to swim tomorrow. Join if you want."

"Most definitely," he replied. "Now that I've got nothing but free time to burn, what better way to do it than poolside. Except for the excessive chlorine, maybe. Sometimes I come out of the pool and can't hardly breathe when I hit the outside air."

"I know what you mean," she concurred as she stood and smiled at him. "Don't forget your eggs, and thanks for all the help and conversation."

As she walked away from him with her three children in tow behind her, he couldn't help but admire the woman he had grown to know over the past few years. She was clearly determined to right her own life and did exceptionally well to that avail, but she was perhaps even more resolute when it came to the guidance of her children. She was determined to give them every chance to lead a less chaotic life than she knew. Their happiness and wellbeing became her purpose in life.

She had decided to formally homeschool her children on religious grounds, but deeper still beyond the desire to control the education and interaction of her children, she was a lot like him in that they both loved the pure spirits of their children above all else. In their children, they saw the purity they might once have had within themselves. That spirit was evident to him the first time he met her. The smile of her eyes was wider and brighter than the smile of her mouth. Her words were direct but resonated with the beauty of a survivor whose joy in sheer life was boundless.

Despite their respective choice to homeschool their children, both still wanted their children to actively interact with other children. Sports became an important outlet for this social interaction. In their case, that is exactly how they got to know each other – by watching their children play sports together.

He recalled how he would greet her by his original nickname for her after the two had gotten to know each other. For a while and much to her dismay at first, he often greeted her "Hey! Long Island" at their daughters' soccer games to jab at her about her Long Island background, only he altered it to sound like he was saying *Lawn Guy Land*. He could tell the name irked her, so he would keep up with his mock accent: *What youse guys doin'? Youse guys doin' awright?*

Eventually, she did blast him about the nickname. She told him in no uncertain terms that she didn't like his Long Island name for her even a little bit. She even asked him not to call her that anymore, so he had come up with 'Brown Eggs' on the spot, given the prolific brown egg output of her backyard flock of chickens.

She had immediately rolled her eyes at his new nickname for her but had conceded she was less bothered by it than the Long Island tag. She promised then that the time was coming when she was going to nickname him, as well. He wouldn't have to wait much longer after that before she kept her promise.

One day when her car was being serviced, he picked her up at the service garage so she could run some errands. As soon as she sank into the passenger seat, she gravitated to the music he had in the car.

"King Crimson. Pink Floyd," she had begun as she rifled through some of his compact discs between the front seats. "Now all you need is some Blue Oyster Cult and Black Sabbath or maybe Rainbow and Deep Purple."

"How cleverly prismatic of you, Brown Eggs," he had smirked at her. "You're just a veritable cornucopia of colorful commentary."

"That's it!" she had blared above the music from the car speakers. "From now on I'm going to call you *Jam*, since all you want to do is jam to that terrible rock-and-roll music sent straight from the mouth of Hell."

"Like you don't like it, too," he laughed at her. "You probably know every song ever played by every band you just named."

"Nope," she denied. "None of it anymore. It's all Christian music and church hymns for me now. Got to set a better example for my kids than the example set for me."

"I don't know about that," he countered. "Music is art and what I listen to inspires me. If choice in music helps someone feel better about themselves and motivates them, I don't see how it can be entirely bad regardless of how any religion tries to portray it."

"It's the Devil's music is what the preachers say, Jam," she turned to him with wide eyes and pursed lips. "I go to church with the kids every Wednesday and Sunday now, and that's what we're told among other things about what we should avoid in order to live a righteous life that will keep us from bad experiences and evil lifestyles."

"No question there's a whole debauched lifestyle associated with this kind of music," he replied. "But that doesn't change the cultural timeliness and relevance of the music itself. It doesn't change the energy the music can give you or the emotions it can evoke."

"I think you should throw away all of your satanic music and repent of your rock-and-roll ways, Jam." she said to him straight-faced. "You're just singing the sorry-assed song of a sinner."

"Not a chance I'm throwing any of it away," he smiled at her, knowing he could help her revitalize herself momentarily by listening to some of the music form her past that she had abandoned. "Want to hear some Led Zeppelin? I got *Houses of the Holy* in the glove box."

"Oh, are you trying to steer me down the wrong path, Jam?" she smiled back at him. "Trying to lure me back into your wretched fold?"

"Nope," he answered. "Just giving you the opportunity to hear something that might soothe your soul."

"All right then," she replied as she opened the glove box. "Go ahead, and let's see if I can resist the temptation to actually enjoy it."

"You know we are who we've become," he tried to sound serious. "And music has had a big part to play in how we've become who we are."

"You quiet down now, Jam," she demanded. "I want to hear the music right now, not you. This might be the last time I ever get to hear this for all I know."

"I'll quiet down then," he echoed her as he watched her remove the disc from the case. "Sounds good to me, especially if you go to track three."

Brown Eggs forwarded the disc to the third track. With the acoustic opening to the song, Brown Eggs propped the back of her head against the headrest of the passenger seat and closed her eyes. Jam watched her lips turn into a thin smile as the tranquil vocals at the beginning of the song harmoniously merged with the acoustic guitar.

But when the electric guitar ripped aloud and the vocals shot higher and stronger, she jerked her head from headrest and started to sing the lyrics. He grinned as he watched her sing and slap the beat against her thighs with the palms of her hands. He soon joined her in singing the rest of the song. He would glance at her during the drive as she bobbed back and forth, sung lyrics to some of the songs and otherwise enjoyed her brief but refreshing reemergence into music that meant a lot to her during her youth, for better and worse.

That memory of Brown Eggs bouncing around in his car while she sang the Led Zeppelin song at the top of her lungs was one that would always make him smile. That memory, however, wasn't on his mind when he and his wife visited Brown Eggs at her house to say their final goodbye just two days before relocating his family more than six-hundred miles away.

The three of them would walk the muted winter grounds

surrounding the old renovated farmhouse that Brown Eggs and her family called home. He already understood she, her family, and their happy home were all in limbo at that time, and her husband had suffered a permanent physical disability.

As he waved and smiled at her past the driver's window, he could feel the sadness in her face despite the smile she tried to forge. Now, when he recalls her waving to him with her children beside her and a few of her chickens pecking at the ground around her, he realized he didn't only leave her – he had in some way forsaken her.

Had he known what would happen to her a year-and-a-half after the last time he spoke with her, he would have tried to help her more. The sheer tragedy of her death lingered for him afterwards with an inescapable sense of dread and gloom. He learned later that she was spared from losing her house in the final months of her life because others donated enough to help pay her mortgage.

He felt like he could have done more to help her avoid or at least somewhat ease the fate that ambushed her and the suffering she endured. He also could have done something to help her children with their anguish. He genuinely had, after all, become friends with her. Had he been willing to maintain contact with more of the people he had known over the ten years he had lived at his previous home, he might have really been able to help her.

But he made the decision for a clean break from everyone in the area where he had lived when he moved with his family. His wife agreed with the decision to move on in every way to a new life with new people in new places. Despite all that was new and fresh in his and his family's new life, the horrible news about Brown Eggs ripped into him when he was told what happened. She died within two weeks after he found out she was admitted to hospice care.

The news had shocked both him and his wife, but the more it sank in for him that such a vibrant, happy person like Brown Eggs was wiped off the face off the earth, the angrier and sadder he felt whenever he thought of her.

Mercifully, the homeschool network available to her was tight-knit in the Chesapeake Bay peninsula where they lived. That support would be most needed. After the drug-overdose death of her husband just months after her own death, her children were left without any guardian and probably would have been subjected to state agency placement in homes unless there were some type of intervention. He was relieved to learn that her three children remained within the homeschool network after her death and the death of her husband. All three were taken in by the same sympathetic family whose grown homeschooled children were all successful professionals.

When her three children needed stability the most in the absence of any surviving family capable of providing that stability at that time, the people who had surrounded her in a shared vision of how to raise their children in a world wrought with deception and fear were there for her to glorify all that she held sacred, all that she believed and knew had saved her for the short time she would have on this earth. Her lifestyle choice that mattered most to him was her commitment to teach her children herself with the support of the homeschool network she sought.

All these years later, he still felt the warmth of her as she brightened the space she walked through. He saw her joyful exchange with her children and the decisions she made to raise them according to her faith and religious choice.

After not living in Virginia for several years, returning there for the events surrounding the dementia and death of his author friend had dredged up his past for him with a vengeance. His journey back into his past may have helped him better understand who he was and how he dealt with the circumstances in his life at the time, but he was finding that years after the death of Brown Eggs, she had reentered his life in ways he just hadn't expected through the agency of what could be perhaps characterized as paranormal. He wondered about just how he should process all of the events that had happened since he twice visited his author friend and then attended his funeral. There was nothing normal about any of it.

He recognized that this last trip to Virginia for the funeral of his friend had altered his perception of reality to no small degree. The interaction he shared with the children of Brown Eggs, especially her daughter, had jarred him deeply. He felt he was powerless to resist the pull of some unseen portal that might force him to shift back and forth between worlds: the world of the living and this other world where Brown Eggs and the disembodied voice of a beautifully mystical earth angel could yank him from his normal life to a landscape where everything that seemed real was not as real as the impossibility he experienced. He feared his mental faculties might be on the verge of betraying him. He was struggling mightily to find his way back to his full senses.

The upheaval in his life wouldn't transpire right away, however. The transfiguration that awaited him would first have to develop through his interaction with another married woman who had captivated him far beyond any level that Brown Eggs had.

For better and worse, the story that unraveled between him and Sirena would prove to be the consummation of everything he knew in this world and the whirlwind that swept him away into a world beyond any reality he previously knew.

The story between Sirena and him truly begins in the month preceding his departure for his friend's funeral in Virginia on June 20, 2016. The two of them had unknowingly embarked upon a course wrought with a thrilling terror that could liberate them both from the shackles of time, if only they were both willing to pursue the forbidden fruit – or brown egg – dangling in front of them.

Or their time together could damage him to the extent that he would have to view the whole story he was writing and living as either a prolonged and unrequited surrealist love letter at best or perhaps an epic suicide note at worst.

Collaboration 3
Brown Eggs Sirena

June 6ᵗʰ, 2016
Carrollton, Kentucky

SHE PLACED a stack of three egg cartons on the picnic table beneath the sprawling canopy of a gnarled white ash tree. He opened the top carton of eggs. The sky beyond the shade darkened from the shift in clouds as the pale brown of the eggs deepened with the dimming light.

"I haven't had brown eggs in a long time," he finally said. "This is the first time I think I've even seen brown eggs in years."

Shifting shapes conjured themselves from his scrambled past until he thought he glimpsed the silhouette of his departed friend Brown Eggs against the landscape. The shadow slid black and swift in its descent down the hill that fell away from the picnic table where he sat. He twitched when the shape suddenly reversed and instead surged toward him from a blast of wind that ripped across the stretch of ground below him. He shivered as the jolt of violent air buffeted him, but in its wake, he thought he saw the woman from his past standing fully formed before him. She smiled at him at first through the kaleidoscope of years before her eyes bulged, her face drained ghostly and her skewering image shattered into a splatter of flesh, blood, and shards of bone.

His vision blurred, forcing his eyes to cross before he managed to regain focus by virtue of some grain of crud stuck to one of the eggs in the open carton. He lifted his eyes to the woman standing before him now. She appeared vastly different than the woman he remembered who last gave brown eggs to him. Her green eyes gleamed with agate depth below her arching eyebrows. Her slender nose centered her unblemished face of lustrous skin hung tight from high cheekbones. Her sleek complexion sloped to dimpled cheeks, where her angular jaw framed her enticing mouth of an upper lip wisp tucked into a fleshy bottom lip that crowned the splendid curve of her chin.

He realized that the woman in front of him stood voluptuous from her face to her feet. Her supple arms flowed as the wavy volume of her silver-streaked, brunet hair cascaded through her long fingers. The turquoise, tangerine and slate hues of her paisley top swirled as her contoured chest heaved with her stretch and breath. Her hands then traced the taper of her hips thrust above trim legs wrapped tight in white capri pants.

The difference in face and form between this woman standing in front of him and the other woman from his past quelled his initial fear that he might address the wrong woman.

"These eggs won't last three days, Sirena," he managed to revive himself from his reverie. "Thank you."

She then sat across the picnic table from him and tossed the silky froth of hair that bounced along her narrow shoulders. Nothing in the way she comported herself reminded him of the other woman from his past. Elegance drifted from her as she arched her back then straightened herself and lowered her hands. She glowed with the light in the symmetry of chiaroscuro that overcame the darkness of the other woman in the aura of his perception.

"I had to give them to somebody," she replied, capturing him with the silvery resonance of her voice.

Her radiance coursed through him. He decides that sophistication sharpened her visage all the way to her alluring bottom lip that glistened moist as the returning sunlight brightened the shade beneath the tree. She teemed with an energy that transcribed the fluency of her understanding from her eyes and across her face.

Nothing was further from his mind than suffering and death as he sat across from her, mesmerized by her boundless beauty.

"Are you as excited by our rendezvous here as I am?" he asked once recovered from his jarred state of mind.

"Oh, yes, I feel electric all over right now," she chimed. "I'm not sure if I can really go through with this, though. It's been so long since I've really jumped in headfirst into anything, and this is unlike anything I've ever done since I've been married."

He closed the top egg carton before taking all three cartons of brown eggs and transferring them one-by-one to the top of the white cooler chest on the ground beside the table.

He tried to reassure her, but it's too late for him to know for sure what his words are because she triggered far more in him than just the memories evoked by brown eggs. He groped for a better understanding of his deepening connection with her as he shifted the egg cartons atop the cooler until the three were in a single stack again.

"What are you doing?" she throatily laughed, watching him handle the cartons.

"I'm just trying to get all of this straight in my mind," he replied. "I want to make sure I can do this with you. We're going to be deeply involved if we decide to take this plunge. The commitment is a very intimate one that can overtake us if we're not careful."

"Well," she recoiled with a slight defensive tilt to her voice, "if you'd rather not, I understand, I guess."

He brought his bare forearms to the rough table surface and etched his stare directly into her shimmering green eyes. But before he spoke, he averted his eyes from the confusion and hurt that lurked in her face. He remained silent instead.

"I thought you wanted this, too," her voice shook. "I am...or was... looking forward to everything we were going to do together."

"It's not that I don't want to do this with you," he leaned even farther forward to stare even harder into her eyes. "I'm all in. I just don't want to cause any real problems for you. This type of arrangement can change how we think and feel about ourselves, each other, and others who are important to us."

"I can handle it," she almost snapped at him. "Just because I haven't done this before doesn't mean I can't do it. In fact, I think this will be the best thing for me because I've never exposed myself like this before. I need to feel all of this force churning inside of me again. It will revive a part of me that I've missed."

The thread of a smile turned his upper lip. He recognized her engagement now. She really was ready to start something that might transform them both.

"It's actually good to feel a little vulnerable when you're in a position like this," he told her. "Let's see what you've got."

"All right," she said. "But I have to go to my car for just a sec then I shall return."

He watched her walk away, gripped by the fleshly switch across the back of her skintight pants. She opened the passenger door of her SUV and bent at the knees to reach to the floor. Her haunches flared as the fringe of her top climbed to reveal the hollow of her tapered back.

When she stood and turned around with a manila folder in hand, she smiled at him. He smiled back as he watched her place cautious steps over the soft ground in her return to the picnic table.

"I actually found one of the novels I never finished and lifted part of it for this," she informed him.

"Just as long as it fits the first assignment," he responded, grinning. "I'd hate to have to get our little literary affair here off on the left foot."

"Oh, it does fit the assignment just like a glass slipper," she beamed back at him. "It's about something someone really wanted but couldn't have, just like you said.

"Actually, it's about someone who really wanted someone but couldn't have that someone because the someone who was wanted didn't want the someone who wanted her."

The mischief he detected in her tone made him shudder. For a fleeting moment, he thought that perhaps her opening of the folder was like watching Pandora's box open for all the evils of the world to fly out and accost them both, leaving one or both of them helplessly lost in an inescapably ruinous state of mind. He hoped not because the last thing he would want in the world for her to experience was any undue stress, much less truly life-altering anguish. His mind again wandered back to the brown eggs and the tragedy that befell the other woman he had befriended those years ago. This is different, he told himself. This has to have a happier ending.

He righted himself by returning his attention to her delivery of his assignment for her. The assignment was simple enough: write a thousand words about something or someone that a character desperately wanted but couldn't have. The assignment marked their first meeting together with him informally as the teacher and her as his student in preparation for a new job she was taking as an administrative assistant with an online creative writing program.

She pulled a few pages of stapled notebook paper from the folder then set the folder down. She quietly cleared her throat then looked to him for her cue to start reading.

He felt he might have a preoccupation now that would disrupt his concentration while she read. He knew he had to revisit the shock that the brown eggs caused him as soon as he could. He had to try to understand why mere brown eggs triggered such a visceral and hallucinatory reaction within him.

But he pushed the conjured flurry of memory and emotion aside and signaled with his hand for her to read:

The first sentence she rendered was this:

The brown eggs are in your basket now.

She then proceeded to read the remainder of her assignment:

He handed the long-handled wicker basket to her. She took it and peered at the brown eggs nestled in the green plastic Easter grass.

"Thank you so much," she said, "You really are such a sweet guy."

"I have a cousin with a bunch of chickens," he explained.

She crouched to set the basket of brown eggs on the foyer floor.

"Besides," he added. "You make it really easy to be sweet to. I'd like nothing more than to be the sweetest guy you've ever known every day of the week."

"Thank you so much," she cringed. "But I don't want to lead you down a road where I can't go with you. You have to know that what we've done together is just fun for me. It's not anything serious for me at all. I'm sorry if I misled you, but it's probably for the best if we stop seeing each other the few times that we even do, at any rate."

He felt his face turn flush. She steadied her eyes on his, waiting for him to say something, but he just stood there with his mouth agape.

"You really are a very sweet guy and lots of fun to be around," she finally said. "You're going to make some lucky lady very happy one day."

"But I'd like to keep seeing you," he protested. "I love to be with you, and I love everything about you."

"Again," she stated, more sternly this time. "You are going to make some woman other than me happy. You're a well-built, good-looking guy who will make the right woman very satisfied to be with you.

"But that woman is not going to be me. I have way too much to do that doesn't involve settling down or anything like that at all. Besides, I'm hardly ever in town as it is now. It's just not going to work out for you with me. Just move on from me and find someone who can give you the time and attention you deserve to make you happy."

"I don't want to be happy," his voice cracked. "I want to be with you. You are the right woman for me."

She sighed as she stepped forward across the threshold of her front door. She glared at him to his face. His gaze turned from hopeful to embarrassed. He realized he was losing the battle to keep her in his life and was afraid what she might say next.

"Don't make me get nasty," she warned him. "Because I can get there really fast if you can't get it through your thick skull that you and I just don't go together. You are not my type, and I'm definitely not your type."

"What does any of that even mean?" he nearly cried. "I thought we were getting along great together."

"You're dense," she snapped at him. "Don't you know I just wanted to have some fun with you without any real commitment?

That's it. That's all it was for me – fun. I used you to feel good and
have some fun, okay? You really don't mean anything to me at all more
than that. And I don't even want that anymore, do you understand
me?"

She stepped back into her condo and tried to slam the door shut,
but he wedged his hand against the jamb just as the solid wood door
reached full force.

"Christ!" he shrieked before the door bounded back open and hit
her on the side of her head, knocking her off balance but not toppling
her.

"Get out of here and don't ever come back or I'll call the cops!" she
screamed at him then slammed the door even harder.

His hurt pride was more painful to him than his throbbing hand,
but the hand hurt bad enough that he thought it might be broken. The
sudden swelling made it hard for him to grip the steering wheel of his
van as he headed back to his house, defeated and forlorn.

He just couldn't understand how something so good could turn so
ugly so fast. They hadn't been together for two weeks prior to her
change of heart, but they had shared their most mutually passionate
exchange of their brief relationship during that last night they were
together.

There was no doubt in his mind that he loved her and that this was
the woman he wanted to spend the rest of his life with. The tears
silently flowed from him as he negotiated his way through darkness in
his return home.

When he did reach his home, he felt even more distressed by the
turn of events. He wanted to call her but instead buried his head in his
hands and sobbed for several minutes, thinking about how unlucky he
had been in life and love and wondering if anything different with
more promise awaited him in his future.

Since he met her just three months ago, she became the light in his
life. His heart raced at the first sight of her when she opened the door to
let him inside to work on an electrical issue at her condo unit. He had
checked with her the following week to see if the problem was resolved

but stammered as he let his eyes wander along the curves of her body. She smiled and laughed then rescued him from his awkwardness by informing him that she was satisfied with his work.

It wasn't until a couple of weeks later that he saw her again. This time it wasn't work related. He was out with friends at a restaurant and bar where she had also shown up with a couple of her girlfriends. Both trios were in line together waiting for a table when she suggested that the group eat together because there was a table for six available. After a rather lively dinner, they all decided to go to a neighboring nightclub to dance and drink. She eventually asked him if he would take her home to her condo. Much to his delight and surprise, she let him inside and they spent the night together.

He met her three more times after that, but her out-of-town work schedule prevented him from seeing her as much as he would've liked. She always seemed so glad to see him when they were able to meet. She was also always passionate with him when they met, and he ended up spending the night with her at her condo after each one of their dates.

He just couldn't understand what would make her act the way that she did this last time he saw her. She had turned completely vicious. It made him want to just give up on the idea of finding the one right woman for him in this world. He knew he shouldn't feel that way, but he already felt so deeply in love with her that he just didn't want to be without her in his life.

When he reached his house, he immediately went to his bedroom and opened his gun safe in his closet. He removed his .45-caliber pistol from its mount and drew back the slide to force a bullet into the chamber.

He left the closet with the gun in his hand and went to the bathroom. Light flooded the room when he flipped the switch. He stood in front of the large oval mirror above the sink and held the muzzle of the gun to his temple.

She stopped reading and looked to him.

"Well?" she probed. "I feel like I'm really exposing myself writing about stuff that relates relationship intimacy like this does, but I wrote this twenty years ago before I became a Christian, at least a real reborn one anyway.

"The only reason I'm compelled to share it with you now is that it's really all the written material that I have that's developed fiction. I thought it would be good for me to shake some dust off, you know? This could help me with my new job."

He sat stunned, embracing her swath of beauty from across the picnic table. Now, she seemed even more appealing to him for her delivery of her thoughts through language that organically blossomed before his eyes into this lush texture of meaning that resonated within him.

But he knew he had to keep himself grounded in the moment. The sole purpose for their meeting was to discuss her writing so that she could prepare for her new job, which would require her to handle student matters and possibly even their compositions.

"Well?" she asked again, this time more sharply and slightly louder.

Her eyes widened a little as she tilted toward him. He recognized that she was very much waiting for him to respond to her reading. He studied her face, realizing that the woman before him was perhaps more talented and soulful than he imagined.

"Not even the most hauntingly seductive of Sirens off the island of Capri could present a more enchanting and enticing thousand-word creative writing assignment," he smiled, but her wrinkled brow seemed to express confusion to him. "You've produced a compelling piece that definitely captures the truly transformative yearning for an object of desire that ultimately proves to be unfulfilled because of unrequited affection."

"That almost sounds facetious to me," she nearly sneered at him. "I really want you to be straight with me. Don't heap praise on me just because you don't want to hurt my feelings."

"I'm not being facetious!" he fired back. "I thought your writing was outstanding. Your story and characters are quite compelling to the point that any prospective reader will be intrigued enough to want to read more."

"Really?" she queried further. "You don't have to go overboard just because you might like it a little bit."

"Rest assured, I'm still in the boat," he said through a laugh. "You have a very compelling part of a larger work there, but is this the style of writing or type of content that you normally read?"

"Sometimes," she confirmed. "But I mostly read historical novels and Christian fiction. I'm a voracious reader regardless, and I think that's a big reason why I'm being hired for this new job. I've read so much that I guess my new employer thinks something valuable to them has stuck with me over the hundreds of thousands of pages I've read."

"You are going to do so well at this," he remarked. "I just know you are because your depth is acute and authentic."

"I really appreciate the vote of confidence," she smiled at him. "But I'm just so anxious about this job and this whole direction in my life. I'd really like to pick your brain as much as I can before I get started with this fresh start.

"I'm most nervous about what kind of material I'll have to read from students. There's no telling where they'll be coming from. It could range from sappy to sordid, so I want to be mentally ready for anything really."

"By all means then, pick away," he smiled back at her as he held his hands apart. "My brain is at your fingertips."

"Okay, great," she gathered herself. "I have some misgivings about the propriety of the physical relationship scope of some of the text, but what I really want to know is what you thought about the unresolved ending of possible suicide. Did you think it was too much to have the spurned character ready to kill himself in the end?"

"I would say it is less believable and desirable only if he does in fact kill himself," he began his reply. "The main reason I find the measure of suicide an unfitting vehicle for story development is that it makes the character too easily disposable. The more you write, the more affection or empathy writers should feel for their characters."

"Well, the only real reason I had him on the verge of killing himself at the end was because I had to wrap the story up to stop at a couple hundred words over the thousand," she explained. "That part is not in the original novel. I just added it to see how it reads."

"Then tell me more about your original novel itself," he prodded her. "When did you start it and why did you feel compelled to write it?"

"I wrote it while I was pregnant with my first born," she informed him. "I was twenty-five years old at the time and basically on maternity leave. I finally had time to write, so I figured it was now or never."

"Besides having the time to do it," he began his next question for her, "why did you feel compelled to write your novel then?"

"Well, my motivation was actually a source of divine inspiration," she revealed somewhat hesitatingly as she adjusted herself on the picnic table bench. "I had a vision that I was visited by an angel who told me to write down the story that would come to me.

"I know it sounds crazy, but this angel came to my bed one day early in my pregnancy and instructed me to write what would be revealed to me. He even introduced himself to me, but I can't remember his name for the life of me. Still, he seems so familiar to me even after all of these years like the proverbial guardian angel."

"Really?" he managed to ask straight-faced despite his disbelief and urge to laugh. "You dreamt a guardian angel told you to write a book?"

"No," she countered. "I didn't dream it. I was wide awake at the time. I was probably half-hallucinating from prescription drugs related to complications during my pregnancy and total lack of sleep from stress, but it wasn't a dream."

"Exactly what did this angel say to you?" he asked her.

"Something like that there was an alpha and omega to life in this world," she began. "And that my own transfiguration was coming, but I can't remember exactly how he said what he did."

"Oh, my God." he murmured, stunned by the coincidence of Sirena's account with the message of the woman from the Dali performance. "That has to be some kind of miracle."

"That's exactly what I thought at the time," she resumed. "I have never felt such serenity overcome me in my life after the angel told me that. Then he said he loved me and that he would come again for me one day when the time arrived."

"Was this angel by any chance named Uriel?" he asked her as he felt himself start to tremble.

"I don't know," she replied. "Isn't that the angel name you said when you had come back from Virginia after watching your friend's weird Salvador Dali show or whatever it was?

"That name did seem to ring a bell for me when you said your friend started screaming that you were the angel *Uriel*, but I really don't remember what the name of the angel was who visited me because I was pretty loopy at the time."

"What else do you remember me sharing with you about the Dali reenactment in Virginia?" he asked her as he felt himself starting to wobble on the bench.

"Just that your writer friend with dementia had arranged some kind of Salvador Dali thing in a coffin," she replied, knotting her brow. "And that he thought you were an angel. Also, that there was something about half-angel, half-human creatures. Nephilim, I believe. Why?"

"Oh, it's nothing," he said with a wave of his hand as the sky darkened from a shifting cloud. "It's just peculiar that the biblical part you just said about *Alpha and Omega* and *transfiguration* also factored into the Dali reenactment by my friend.

"But let's get back to your novel for now. You say the visitation by the angel prompted you to write your novel, which includes what you just read, right?"

"Yes, it does," she confirmed. "And the revelation that came to me was to write a story about the spiritual rebirth of a young woman who was led astray by her lust for the physical world. It even occurred to me to have the angel visit the character during a key scene in the book when her life really spirals out of control because of her wayward lifestyle. After that she's the one who actually ends up on the verge of suicide."

"Sounds like a lot of conflict and turmoil," he said, struggling to remain focused because of her admission about the visitation by the angel. "But is the woman who undergoes such a spiritual transformation the one you just read about?"

"Right," she said. "The first part that I read is before her life starts to crumble."

"So, it's the same woman who is deliberating suicide in the second part," he surmised aloud, still unable to quell the implications of her proclaimed angelic visitation. "And not her jilted lover from the first part."

"Correct."

"So, now, what I would like for you to do is provide another one thousand words to the opposite effect of what you just read," he instructed her over his growing anxiety about the angel in her life. "Write about something or someone that a character wanted so badly and then actually did get what he or she wanted."

She smirked at him a little.

"That's exactly what my novel is all about," she revealed to him. "That's how it actually progresses."

He then suddenly suspected that the confrontation and rejection depicted in her reading probably were drawn directly from her experience in relation to her own husband. This evoked another emerging suspicion for him that the angelic visitation she said was also in her book really reflected her own personal turmoil in circumstances that were hers alone and not those produced through the figment of fiction.

"You know," he began with a sigh, relieved that he might have explained the function of her angel better to himself than its manifestation as the archangel Uriel. "Writing obviously can be very cathartic. We can find ourselves answering questions most pressing within ourselves through the actions and interactions of our characters."

"That's partly why I do really want to pick this thread back up," she declared, perking up on the bench. "I see now after all this time that I had started something powerful and now that I have lived my life as a mother taking care of my kids at home for all these years, I feel like I have a very compelling story that I can craft from the standpoint of a writer rather than someone who is tweaking life events that people experience or just making stuff up."

"That is a very astute insight about part of the writing process," he observed aloud. "When we can come to that realization, we have matured as writers to the point where we can actually offer something genuine to share with readers who will be better positioned to appreciate the integrity of the work through both the story rendered and the intent of the writer."

"I like that," she smiled at him. "That's exactly why I'm interested in picking up where I left off with the novel I had started all those years ago.

"Well, that, plus the fact that it's my basis for how I understand character and story from a standpoint of reading a manuscript rather than a published book by an actual author, and I think that fact will help me with my perspective for this new job."

"Well then maybe we should change the assignment to something more specifically related to your long-delayed, work-in-progress?" he offered.

"Actually, no need," she replied. "This new assignment falls directly in line with my two characters anyway. The next sequence of events changes things around quite a bit."

"Can you first tell me a little more about the novel?" he requested, settling into his teacher role now that the initial jarring effect of her angel upon him had passed. "Such as length, chapter structure and the most important events that take place in it?"

"It's all handwritten in two parts and something like a total of forty-thousand words," she answered. "What I read here was the end of the first part, which dealt with how the pair of them met and the details of their respective lives leading up to their developing relationship."

"So, the second part reverses the ending of the first part," he concluded. "The unrequited protagonist doesn't really consider killing himself but instead springs into action in the second part, which results in his fulfillment with the object of his desire."

"Pretty much," she confirmed. "So much of the storyline is driven by the woman's predicament. Her situation changes dramatically from the end of the first chapter. She goes from this hopeful horizon in her life that she might be able to get the man she really wants by becoming pregnant to an absolutely nightmarish scenario where she loses her dignity, her hope, and basically everything else."

"This other man not mentioned in your reading is the one to whom she has devoted herself, but he decides to dump her in the second chapter?" he supposed aloud.

"Exactly," came her reply.

His attention fixed on her eyes as their agate green brightened with the increase of sunlight emerging from the clearing of a cloud. He was all but certain now that she was telling him about the events in her life through this fiction. He realized he might have to tread lightly through this written landscape of her past if he wanted her to continue to meet with him. Any remarks too pointed or criticism bereft of empathy in this regard might cause her to withdraw from him.

"The woman in the novel thinks this other man ultimately loves her more than his wife," she elaborated. "The two of them had known each other for almost seven years by this point, starting at college when he was a senior and she was a freshman and going on for four years after that when she worked for him as a traveling secretary and his personal mistress more or less.

"She thinks that he will leave his wife for her in the first part, then she basically is stripped of any and all hope of that in the second part when she loses both him and her job."

He could see her eyes moisten as she said this. He wanted her to continue without feeling like she was disclosing something she would otherwise feel too uncomfortable to divulge, so he referred her statement back to their discussion of character development.

"Our female protagonist has a confrontation with this other man, much like the first man had with our female protagonist?" he speculated aloud.

"At one point in the book, the other man's wife even gets on the phone and screams at her to stay away from her husband or she'll kill her," she disclosed through her quavering voice.

"You know," he quickly began matter-of-factly, "the most compelling characters can be those whose identity for us as readers is formed through anguish and conflict. We identify with these characters based upon how real they seem to us in terms of the situations they face and how they react to both the opportunities they have as well as the predicaments they find themselves within beyond their own ability to control."

"That is so true," she gathered herself in reply. "Most of the romance-oriented novels I read have this same kind of tension about choices that determine the course of the story and circumstances. The characters are put in positions of either victim or vanquisher based upon how they react."

"Tell me more about the events that materialize in the second part of your work," he urged her.

"Well, my heroine tries to take her ongoing affair with her boss to a whole other level besides her being just his travel companion," she began. "She decided to stop her birth control to see if she can become pregnant by him, suffering from the delusion that if she is pregnant with his child, he'll leave his wife."

"Wow," he said. "That sounds like one ill-conceived plan."

"Indeed," she agreed. "It blows up in her face in Las Vegas. After she's with him, he tells her that this is the last time they'll be together because he wants to be only with his wife from now on.

"For good measure, he adds that her position with the company has been eliminated, but at least she'll be able to take some time off and draw unemployment for a while."

"So, she loses the man of her dreams and her career position in one fell swoop," he voiced. "She should complain or sue."

"She is too distraught to think straight," she replied. "She doesn't even tell him that she went off her birth control just two weeks prior. Instead, she just lets him take her to the airport and put her on a plane to get her out of his life for good."

"She sounds better off without him," he remarked. "Does she end up pregnant with his child?"

"She doesn't know at first," she answered.

"What does that mean?" he asked.

"Let me explain how the rest of the story unfolds then you'll understand better," she began. "She is so beside herself on the drive home from the airport that she finds herself veering toward an over-pass piling on the interstate at about one-hundred miles an hour.

"But then she hears a voice that tells her to slow down. She does slow down then straightens out the car and calms down."

"Divine intervention, I'm guessing," he said.

"Not necessarily," she countered, peering at him. "But would that be a problem?"

"Could be," came his answer. "I told you about how I frown upon suicide for character resolution. I regard divine intervention as even less viable because it's just way too easy and not something that can be very believable anyway."

"I feel the same," she concurred. "But I do see a place for it. In what I wrote, the divine intervention comes after the character returns home. When she gets there, she's still a nervous wreck, but she finds 'guess who' waiting for her at her front door."

"No way," he feigned disbelief. "There was her knight in shining armor or maybe her future husband in electrician uniform."

"I don't know that I'd make him a cliché or demean him," she glared at him. "I mean, the text conveys the struggle he had to go through when she jilted him in the first part of the book. Plus, the decision to go to her house was a gamble because he knew he could be risking a restraining order at the very least and maybe even the loss of his job with the property management group."

"Very true," he admitted. "He would have faced quite a bit of risk by going to her condo after he was told in no uncertain terms to leave and not come back."

"Yes," her voice scratched. "He risked a lot to be there and waited there for her for quite some time. He told her he was just about ready to get up and leave for good when she pulled up.

"Then he saw the distress in her face and placed his hands on her shoulders, asking her if she was all right before she buried her face in his chest and just absolutely bawled."

"Wow," he grinned. "That's almost miraculous."

"She embraces him there for quite some time before they walked arm-in-arm to her door," she continued. "She realized she wanted him then and there without explaining anything about what had happened to her.

"There was something pure about how they interacted with each other, or maybe uncomplicated is the better way to describe it. Even though he kept asking her why she was crying, she pursued him physically without answering until he finally consented to her desire. She wanted him to have the chance to be the father of her baby, if, in fact, she was going to get pregnant by the end of this awful episode in her life. She wanted him to at least have the chance to be the one who straightened her mess of a life out for good. And if the child wasn't his, she still felt in her heart that it wouldn't matter to him because of how much he seemed to love her."

"I'm guessing that the chords of true love were struck that night," he ventured.

"Pretty much," she smiled.

"Is it ever revealed in the novel exactly who the father is?" he asked.

"I try to convey that the child was like a miraculous conception," she answered somewhat sharply. "*Miraculous*, mind you, not hardly immaculate by any stretch. The whole idea is that her own misguided quest for pregnancy with a man who didn't love her actually led her to the person who God wanted her to be with and have a child together that would bind their lives from that day forward."

"Does it turn out that the father of the child is the electrician after a paternity test?" he asked her.

"Yes," came her delayed response. "I mean there's no mention of any paternity test taken, but it's assumed."

"And they lived happily ever after," he surmised aloud.

"Eventually," she affirmed. "But not until she is rescued from her turmoil and depression through divine intervention. You see, as much as she wants to find peace and happiness in her new life, she can't quite shed her attachment to her old one. Her longing for the lifestyle, career, and man she lost beckons her louder than the rather humdrum, domestic life she sees in her future. The action, travel, and excitement of her previous life all were truly in her blood, and a big part of her self-identity. She believes she has sold herself short by not pursuing someone and something more fitting her personality and ambition. She isn't too sure she wants to stick out what this new future holds for her."

"Not uncommon," he commented. "But do you mean she feels like killing herself? I mean, there are other much more compelling reasons why a young woman might want to end her life. This doesn't seem like there's enough motivation for such drastic action."

"It's not so much intentional suicide as just this acquiescence into an overmedicated merger with oblivion," she related to him. "That's how the vision that leads to the angel starts. She's in her bed, naked, overdosed, and drifting away but descending like a leaf falling through space until her body more or less splats in a wet mud that forces her to open her eyes.

"That's when her terror starts. Screams erupt all around her as flames singe her dream flesh. She tries to pry herself from the muck that holds her but can't budge. She can only turn her head to discover the horror of all of the bodies and parts of bodies strewn around her, and that's when she sees that the mud is not made from water but blood instead."

"What is it that you hope this vision relates?" he asked. "Hell? Armageddon?"

"Neither," she replied. "It is the battlefield of angels, those who have fallen from their heavenly height and those angels who would kill to restore God's own image in man.

"That is where the angel descends to her and peels her soul from her body."

"The angel *peels* her soul from her body?" he probed, suddenly realizing her described landscape referred to the supposed slaughter of the fallen angels and the half-angelic race of Nephilim.

"Yes," she answered. "I describe it like the angel removes her skin from her body then the skin inflates with her soul inside as the angel rises with her in his arms. The angel holds her in his arms at first just to comfort her above the scene of mutilation and destruction. He lets her know that her despair will subside and she will be resurrected with restored life on earth.

"But then, after he soothingly explains this to her, his embrace inexplicably firms. He tells her that he is not there only to comfort her. He says she is part-angel and that he loves her angelic nature in the same way she understands physical human love."

"You mean part-angel, as in Nephilim?" he asked her. "Like half-human, half-angel?"

"I believe that's what I envisioned at the time I wrote it," she confirmed. "And this scene is supposed to portray the slaughter of the race of those born of fallen angels and human mothers by the angels who seek to restore the order of God and human creation.

"The angel tells her that he is going to spare her from this fate because she is his true soulmate, even though she is like those being killed: born of an angel and a human mother."

"And she's one of them," he laughs. "She's one of the ones who got away. And it's got to be Uriel who saves her.

"You know I told you about Nephilim and Uriel after I came back from Virginia in the spring from my friend's bizarre Salvador Dali reenactment. You sure you didn't write that part of your novel since then?"

"All of this that I've written is from twenty years ago," she reiterated. "And the angel is unnamed in my story. But he is definitely a hero for my heroine.

"When the scene below the two of them erupts into a wind of fire, a rain of blood, and the horror of even more hellish screams, the angel kisses her mouth like a man would kiss his lover or wife, deep with passion coursing through his entire being into hers."

"That seems incongruous," he managed to say. "And that would be a euphemism."

"I know," she admitted. "But the angel tells her that the kiss and embrace are his signature and that's how she'll know him when they meet again so they eventually can be together for eternity. Until that time of their reunion, she must have the same passionate affection he conveys to her for the man who will become her earth husband.

"He promises her that the day will come when he returns for her and they will be together for eternity when Alpha and Omega proclaims the transfiguration she awaits."

When she waved her hand in the direction of some circling bug, he thought he glimpsed the woman in his friend's film of Salvador Dali who held the brown egg and said: *Alpha and Omega. Your transfiguration awaits you, my love.* But with a blink and shudder the fleeting image vanished.

"That is quite a bizarre exchange," he managed to comment, feeling faint from the convergence of the jarring flash of the woman with the brown egg, the utterance of the cryptic Alpha and Omega phrase, and the stunning swerve of her novelized character into the realm of Nephilim.

"It most definitely is," she agreed with him. "But anyway, after the angel kisses her and she kisses him back, he flies with her away from that awful place. She holds on and feels her body moving through space like she is flowing through some kind of current. Her soothing travel finally ends when she revives on her bed with a splitting migraine and drug hangover. She thinks she is dead and in the quiet of heaven at first, but then she slowly realizes what has happened to her."

"I would imagine that an experience like that could give someone quite a start," he remarked, still grappling with the Nephilim revelation by her angel, who he dreaded was really Uriel after all.

"I should think so, too," she said once she looked up into the twisting tree branches above her. "I try to vividly describe her flight with the angel so that it seems too real not to be real, you know?"

"I know exactly what you mean by too real not to be real," he nervously grinned at her, trying to swallow the otherworldly implications that her vision had for him.

She paused from relating the details of her story while she kept her eyes on his, returning his grin. He broke his stare to reach over to the eggs on top of the cooler. He picked the eggs up and moved them to the picnic table before he retrieved a bottle of water from the interior of the cooler. He untwisted the cap from the water bottle and extended it across the table for her to take.

"Thank you," she said as he transferred the egg cartons back into the cooler. "You know this is really sweet of you to do all of this for me."

"I'm just happy to help you," he managed to chirp through his looming doubt about his sanity. "I admit I had reservations about meeting with you at first, but only because I was afraid that if I started talking with you like this I wouldn't want to stop talking with you. You make for just the most delightful company, especially when you're telling such a riveting story."

Her face flashed blush before she turned her eyes from him and drank gulps of water. He tried to watch her slender neck undulate as she swallowed but had to avert his eyes from her. Her assignment had proven interesting enough, but this twist of Nephilim and Uriel had waylaid him. He realized he needed to restore his full attention to her and drop her tale of divine intervention from his mind for the meantime.

"It sounds like your next thousand-word assignment will relate how the woman and the man who truly loves her both get what they want," he said.

"It will," was her reply. "That's exactly what happens. He gets her, and she gets her earth man – tall, handsome, muscular, striking and just a great big hunk overall."

She glanced at him somewhat off-angled, and he again grinned at her. She then stared at him with knotted brow until a smile spread across her face as she blushed again. She brought the opening of the water bottle to her lips and swallowed another gulp of water.

"Now to get back to the story," she continued, smiling wider at first before she regained her composed storytelling countenance. "Our heroine embraces her fate with faith in a destiny fulfilled, one that has purpose in God's plan."

"You sure that's all that happens?" he remarked in the hope of restoring his ease across from her. "Or is there some other bizarre or lascivious twist of fate that awaits disclosure somewhere else in your enthralling work? The return of the angel for a divine tryst, perhaps, and the pitter-patter of little Nephilim feet?"

"No more of the angel!" her voice merged with her laughter. "Nothing but a happily-ever-after human ending!"

Her grace and radiance mesmerized him instantly when she laughed and her eyes sparkled in sunlight. She was such a beautiful woman, not just physically but also by virtue of her captivating demeanor. The literary expression that she shared galvanized his esteem for her, now that she had presented such an apt exclamation to the depth of beauty that beamed from her. He let himself momentarily bask in his appreciation of her, surprised that this pull he felt exerted from her wasn't manifested long before now because he definitely had gravitated into her orbit.

Even though her physical beauty struck him the very first time he saw her over four years ago, he had never talked with her much until the spring of this year. During past years, they had only conversed briefly during sports events that involved their children.

This year was different because he brought his children to the park to meet twice a week with the homeschooled teenagers of other families, including her and her youngest daughter. He and Sirena almost always stayed together to supervise the homeschoolers while the other parents went to run errands. That was how their ongoing conversation began.

During these gatherings, the two found that they shared mutual interests besides the fate of their respective children. For him, this came as a surprise because he had not really thought about her in a context different than the mother of homeschooled children acquainted with his own children. Their conversations grew in length, detail and depth. He felt drawn closer to her each time they talked. It seemed to him that she also drew closer to him. When she looked into his eyes and conveyed her meaning to him, he felt a sensation like levitation start to overtake him. Her guarded enthusiasm and measured passion beckoned him. He had started to value her for who she was, what she said, and how she said it.

When she mentioned one time that she had started a novel but never finished it, he was aroused. He knew she read fiction profusely but never suspected she had aspirations of writing novels. The idea that she wanted to be a writer had flooded him with possibilities about their potential interaction. It was partly why he had offered to help her develop her writing style. He was hardly a writer with credentials to make her swoon from his literary prowess, but he had proven his salt as a writer enough for her to recognize his value as someone who might be able to help her.

There was also the other reason why he offered his assistance. At the outset of spring, she had informed him that she would be looking for full-time employment now that the last of her children was finished with homeschooling. All three of her children would be in college in the fall.

"I feel like my main job is done," he remembered her saying. "I haven't worked in twenty years. Now it's time for me to get on with the next stage of my life."

A few weeks later she was asked to interview for the administrative position to help coordinate an online creative writing program that was headquartered about an hour from her home. After a second interview, she was offered the job.

It was at that time that he shared his idea with her about helping her develop her own writing style. That would allow her to hone her own writing skills and also review written work critically with him to help her prepare for her new job.

He explained he would share what he had learned about writing not just creatively in terms of fiction – novels, short stories, and poetry – but also non-fiction related to his countless newspaper and magazine articles and several book projects over the course of his sporadic writing career. He would also share what he knew about the business side of writing as a literary agent, credited collaborator, and ghostwriter.

"I can bring some of the articles I've written and material from books both published and unpublished," he had said to her then. "That way you have a direct source to ask specific questions about everything from character development in fiction to source confirmation in journalism."

"The more diverse, the better," was her reply. "I have absolutely no idea about the range or type of material I'll have to sit down to try to evaluate, if that part of this job does develop along those lines."

"What might be best is your own work," he had added. "Anything you have written or something you want to write may be the most direct way for you to learn about all the components of writing because it will be most immediate for you and you'll know more about the content than anyone else."

"Don't know about that part, but all right," she finally did agree. "Let's give it a shot. How do you want to set this up?"

Once she accepted his initial proposition, he had to devise a plan and schedule for them to follow. They would try to meet three times a week for two hours each afternoon over the two months before she began her job. The next time they would meet would be alone together in the park. He hoped this arrangement would open up another dimension that would inspire him as much as it hopefully helped her.

Their initial meeting with the thousand-word assignment had hardly been a disappointment.

The return of Nephilim and the smack of Uriel had shocked him at first when she related the angelic intervention in her story, but he had relegated them to freakish coincidence, even though he had virtually hallucinated Sirena in the guise of the haunting woman holding the brown egg in his friend's film of the Salvador Dali performance.

The brown eggs Sirena had unexpectedly given to him had ambushed him with even more force than the angelic visitation. The memory of his dear, deceased friend Brown Eggs had evoked a much more drastic reaction within him that he felt compelled to pursue further. By the time he and Sirena parted from their meeting at the park, he had already formulated how he would address the impact her gift of brown eggs was having upon him. That could only mean one thing for him – he would have to write about it.

And write about it he did.

Once he had transcribed about three thousand words of his literary flurry from his on-screen document to notebook paper in cursive, he realized that the inspiration Sirena had unwittingly instilled in him had the prerequisite substance for a book-length project. That alone intrigued him, but he found another aspect about the potential project even more stimulating: she could collaborate with him to produce the book. She clearly had the ability to write narrative, and he couldn't think of anyone with whom he'd rather spend more time right now than her.

He knew from experience that a proposition of literary collaboration could get tricky. He was basically sticking his neck out with the offer, which may prove to be much more than Sirena wanted to consider. He knew through a previous collaboration with a married woman that outside tensions could surface into the process from both sides due to the proximity of interaction and the amount of time the collaborators spend together.

Still, he wrote about his friend Brown Eggs with this gesture of collaboration in mind. He had to stage the writer's showroom for Sirena to properly gauge the depth and course that the project could have. If she could grasp that scope and felt excited enough to embrace it, they would be off and running, and where they would end up was an unknown that thrilled him with possibility.

After he stapled the fourteen notebook pages of the composition together along the side, he circled the last sentence that he had handwritten:

The brown eggs were in her basket now.

The composition began the same as it would appear in the fully drafted book form of the project, "*A rat bit me,*" her voice shook, "*when I reached for the egg. I think it was a rat or a mouse, I guess...or something.*"

He then titled the composition at the top as *Eggsquisite Corpse* so she would understand that the rest of the composition might proceed in three ways:

1. The composition could be an exchange of paragraphs or chapters in the collaborative sense if she decided she did want to try to create a new novel with him.
2. The composition would be based upon her comments about what he wrote or, as it were, didn't write. In this case, he would include the dialogue between them as it developed from her perusal of the composition.

3. She would decline any further participation and perhaps never mention the composition again or otherwise delay any commitment regarding it if he asked her about her opinion of the composition.

Part of the reason for his deliberation about the third possibility listed was the way he described her in the material he would provide her. The last three pages of his writing were about Sirena, not Brown Eggs. These three notebook pages could clearly be interpreted as a written admission of his attraction to her. He knew there was a chance she might recoil from what she perceived to be a cloaked attempt at seduction.

In truth, he knew that the last three pages of the material he prepared did not limit the possibilities of a significantly expanded relationship between them. He had intentionally crafted his description of her to further the appeal of developing a more intimate relationship.

He tried to convince himself that whether or not any relationship between them would intensify at some point was secondary to the larger purpose he thought he recognized with her. At its most basic level and value, the content of his written material clearly centered upon how the two of them would proceed together under the premise of a collaborative literary project. That seemed to justify the highly energized content of those three pages for him in which much of the language seemed laced with suggestive undertones. Nonetheless, the expressed purpose proposed in the writing truly did remain just a literary collaboration and nothing else.

He had checked his impulse to really write how he might ultimately feel about her because the potential description would most likely portray her as one of the most – if not the most – desirable woman he had ever encountered. He had already understood that he was not only drawn to engage with her at every level but also perhaps even consider starting his life anew just for the opportunity to be with her on a daily basis. He found himself enticed by the notion of waking up beside her every morning, enjoying life with her during the day every day, and knowing she was next to him every night before he drifted into his dreamscape.

He knew how disruptive these thoughts were for him in the hypothetical realm, as well as how destructive they could be if he decided to act upon them, but she had made him feel more alive than he had in a long time. He had never felt this strongly about another woman since he fell in love with his wife. Now, after nearly a quarter of a century of marriage, he never felt closer or more physically intimate with his wife. Moreover, he had never felt more certain that their marriage – and marriage in general – was a true sacrament between a man and a woman that should be honored in all ways as such.

And yet here he was struggling with this newfound whirlwind of passion he felt for another woman who engorged him at the mere thought of her. Sirena had overtaken him body, mind, and soul despite the fact that he hardly knew her and had never even touched her.

He was painfully aware that he was allowing this feeling to fester to a potentially unhealthy mental level, but it was a risk he was willing to take even if it so saturated his subconscious that it became increasingly more difficult for him to function normally. If she did not feel the same intensity that he did, he understood his feelings would be unequivocally unrequited at every level. He was prepared for that and felt that he could accept that stoically enough. He knew that would almost certainly be the case: she would not return his affection and he would have to figure out how he would at least be able to occasionally see her or hear her voice now that his infatuation with her was already coloring his every thought.

He convinced himself that he could manage without her utmost affection in return, but if he had disclosed too much about his true regard for her, his literary pursuit of her could betray him. If she felt that his intentions were directed toward an unseemly design, she could very well deem him as an impostor merely using his literary leverage to try to command her attention for his own manipulation.

That would almost certainly be the end of the relationship kindled between them.

For now, he had to operate under the supposition that she had no attraction to him beyond his insight as a potential teacher who could help her with her own endeavors. If that's all that came to pass between them, he knew he could be happy with that and only that.

He also knew he could explain his lavish and sensual description of her in the last three pages of his written material as literary chiaroscuro. He fully intended to delineate the contrast between the stark, morbid reality of Brown Eggs with the promise and potential of Sirena. It was a matter of life and death, light and darkness.

Then there was the matter of his reference to surrealism.

He had previously talked at length with her about the bizarre Salvador Dali reenactment he had witnessed his friend with dementia perform in Virginia. He had just returned that week from Virginia and described in detail how his friend replicated the rise of Salvador Dali from a coffin-like repose with an egg on his face punctured to allow the escape of ants.

He shared with her that his friend reenacted the Dali performance by rising from a sarcophagus modeled after the one in the Pyramid of Unas at Saqqara. He had informed her that the faux coffin was made by an institute with which his friend had been associated at one point as a writer of paranormal alternate history books and a devotee of Edgar Cayce.

"That's messed up," he remembered her saying, as she leaned closer toward him to hear every word of his lowered voice. "But it's fascinating, even if it is demonic."

He had also related his friend's peculiar identification of him with the archangel named Uriel, whose name had resurfaced during their first literary meeting. He had mentioned his friend's espousal of the Nephilim hybrid human race born from the union of fallen angels and human mothers. He had told her of her friend's account of how some women born of these unions became the Sirens like those depicted in a variety of ancient mythologies.

"My mother named me Sirena after the Sirens," he remembered she had announced at that time. "She was going to name me Elizabeth, but then she heard my newborn cry and said that I had the haunting wail of an angel trapped in a human body, like a Siren stranded on a rocky island somewhere, luring explorers to their deaths."

He had paused in his recollection of how she had been enthralled by his description of the account in Virginia. He then underlined *Eggsquisite Corpse* at the top of the first page of his fourteen-page handwritten text and wrote *Exquisite Corpse* beneath it. He wanted her to be able to further research the surrealist concept of *Exquisite Corpse* in case she was unfamiliar with the surrealist collaborative technique. If she weren't familiar with *Exquisite Corpse*, he would explain to her that it basically involved taking turns writing in their case, ideally with freedom from inhibitions that would also encourage surrealist automatic or stream-of-consciousness writing.

However, he anticipated that if she wasn't familiar with *Exquisite Corpse* that the phrase itself might not exactly comfort her or entice her with some promise of flourishing creativity. The connection of this surrealist technique with the more familiar surrealist artist Salvador Dali might coax her to collaborate with him, even if she agreed only for the fun of it to see where it took her own writing.

But he still had misgivings about how ultimately receptive she would be to the idea of literary collaboration with him regardless of how it was phrased. Even if she weren't averse to the idea itself, his own material and the commitment of such a proposition might so alter the course of what she was now expecting from their meetings together that she might start to look for ways to avoid meeting with him.

"But this all is becoming more urgent than I ever imagined," he had told himself. "She might be gone for good soon with her new job on the horizon. This may be now or later. We owe it to ourselves to at least find out how we are together."

Sirena's seductive presence had opened the floodgates of inspiration for him. He swooned with uncertainty about all of it, but because she had agreed to meet with him regularly over at least the next month, he knew he stood somewhere with her.

Still, he didn't want a collaboration to seem like the end-all of the process between them in case she balked at the *Eggsquisite Corpse* concept. He had already mentioned some of their interaction would involve published material that he had written, so he located a few of his articles from copies of magazines and included them in the manila folder in which he also placed the fourteen-page *Eggsquisite Corpse* composition.

The other contents were as follows:

1. "Dog Days of Summer" article that comprised his "Reelin' in the Big Ones" fishing column for the Summer 2016 issue of *River Times* newsprint magazine. He wanted her to have this because it was his most recent published writing at that time. The fishing column about the benefit of wading during the hot month of August ended with this: "It provides an appreciation of the timeless quotation from the pre-Socratic Greek philosopher Hercalitus, who said: 'You can't step into the same river twice.'" The other purpose behind inclusion of this was to express the urgency of time in relation to their emerging relationship.

2. "Venus Envy" article in the "Channel 9" news section of the April 2005 issue of *Chesapeake Magazine*. He wanted her to read about the collaboration by a husband and wife team of Bulgarian painters who rendered Botticelli's *The Birth of Venus* on a jib sail for a 50-foot yawl. He wanted her to appreciate the close working

relationship between two artists who were also lovers and
spouses.

3. "The Underground Railroad Revisited" article from the
    February 2000 issue of *UPSCALE* magazine. This article
    details a guided tour of Underground Railroad sites that
    originated in Maysville, Kentucky, and ended in Ripley,
    Ohio, at the John Rankin House. This article had a
    specific regional reference for a topic of national
    relevance. It was also interesting because the article itself
    was printed on a black background with white text,
    which gave him some inroads into his planned lesson
    about literary *chiaroscuro*.

4. His "Rosie" article about a benefit concert by singer
    Rosemary Clooney to raise funds for the Russell Theater
    in her hometown of Maysville, Kentucky. The theater
    premiered Clooney's movie, *The Stars are Singing*, in
    1953. The article appeared in the February 2000 issue of
    Preservation Magazine. He wanted the success of the
    singer and actress to make her feel empowered as a
    woman artist in her own right..

Another part of his rationale for providing the additional material
was to set the expectation that the end result of any prospective
collaboration between them actually could lead to publication and
ultimately some form of payment.

The packet also served notice to her that she was dealing with a
competent, experienced writer, one who would have a difficult time
pulling back from his vision for the project once it started to materialize beyond the concept stage. That might not mean as much to her
without having gone through the process to market her own work
herself, but it could be a node for him to hang his expertise upon
whenever awkward moments or confusion surfaced.

He recognized that she was most likely the raison d'être for the book now formulating in his mind. She had become his heroine both on and off the page.

Part of his characterization of her would have to address her faith. He did understand and truly appreciate that Sirena was a professed Christian, who was discretely devout and aligned with the stalwart born-again ilk from what he knew about her religious belief. As much as he did appreciate her faith and wanted to respect her religious belief, he had come too far to turn back now from a purpose that he could not abandon because of any religious protocol or directives from the Ten Commandments.

Regardless, he could neither defer nor otherwise scrap the project because he recognized its potential impact transcended both of them together and either of them individually.

It wasn't lost upon him that the only connection between Brown Eggs, Sirena, and him were their provision of brown eggs to him. Just a few dozen brown eggs and yet here were all of these words gushing forth as though dictated by some unseen medium to conjure his past with Brown Eggs and the fervor that steamed from his thoughts of Sirena.

The realization staggered him. The idea that Sirena and Brown Eggs could somehow be connected through the medium of brown eggs was absurd. Yet he had found himself so bombarded with such subconscious force by this connection between the two women and the brown eggs that he felt submerged in some ceaseless stream-of-consciousness coursing through him.

It was like he was living in an underwater dream himself now, and the delirium of interpretation from every action he took and every thought he formed effervesced with clusters of irrational knowledge that spewed like a barrage of bubbles from some submerged source in a different world. The impetus for this unexpectedly heightened awareness was triggered by external factors that had altered his perception to the point that he felt the very palpable gravity of some otherworldly realm where phantom objects animate themselves from the void of shadow and death.

And at the center of it all, he was starting to absorb the yolk of his predicament: the fact that the brown egg held by the alluring woman in the Salvador Dali film now really loomed like a veritable phantom object plucked from a surreal dimension for him to consider in all of its numinous profundity.

As for the elusive woman in the film, her haunt had deepened for him when he convinced himself that he glimpsed her subsume the form of Sirena herself. Fleeting though that hallucination was, its impact shook him in the recognition that he had perceived one reality emerge from another as visual phenomenon and not just inter-pretation.

"This is starting to polarize like paranoiac critical activity," he blurted to himself in his office. "I'm inducing a hallucinatory state of mind that will transport me to a surrealist landscape where phantom objects lurk and reflection is reality."

His surprise surrealist baptism was a brown egg resurrection.

He was also very aware that he felt another presence with him now. He rationalized this sensation as part of the paranoiac critical activity he believed he really was experiencing. This presence seemed stronger and more immediate to him now, like it shifted closer to him and was more directly responsible for arranging his circumstances, controlling the outcomes of his interactions and even manipulating him to act on behalf of some purpose besides his own.

He liked to think this force now at least partly in control of his thoughts and actions was a kindred spirit that could guide him through the induced paranoiac critical landscape for artistic discov-ery, like he was following a path already traversed by Salvador Dali. He hoped for visions and signs that would delight him first in his imagination then become even more powerful once rendered in language.

The trigger for him to induce his jaunts into this other world remained the brown eggs and the two women. The perceived relation between women and brown eggs couldn't possibly be linked in any rational way beyond the shared generalized qualities of women and eggs. He knew that.

But he no longer believed that there was nothing more to it than that. The future awaited him now like an odyssey into the heart of the unknown and the unmanageable. He understood that this could mean his identity itself was in the process of starting to disintegrate. He also knew too well that there was the very real risk of not coming back to normalcy at some point. This permanent departure into mental imbalance was the one ominous aspect of this experience that he knew he would have to safeguard against.

The computer showed 3:48. He needed to stop the momentum in his mind and go to bed. He had to meet Sirena at noon.

June 8th, 2016
Carrollton, Kentucky

WHEN HE MET Sirena in the park again, he desperately wanted to give the packet of his writing to her as soon as he set eyes on her, but he restrained himself. Instead of showing his hand right away, he let her show her hand to him. Once again, he found himself transfixed by her reading of the second thousand-word assignment, which began with this sentence:

Sometimes you have to crack some eggs to bake a cake.

The mention of eggs from the outset once again instantly focused his attention on her every word. She paused to don her reading glasses this time before she resumed reading her assignment:

That's what she told herself.

Poor decisions and the sinful way in which she had lived were the eggs in her case. Those eggs had cost her everything she had. She had lost her job, was trying to sell her condo for no profit if she was lucky, probably would lose her car, and any shred of her dignity was gone.

She doubted she could find another job that paid as well as the one she lost and couldn't even make it through an interview for a job that paid far less without breaking down into tears. To add insult to injury, she wasn't able to draw unemployment insurance. She was told in Las Vegas that her position had been eliminated, but the company had decided to block her access to unemployment because they had found her at fault in her termination instead. She had lost her initial appeal without revealing she was the mistress of her former boss. Now, she would probably have to file a civil claim to try to access those funds, and all of those details about her extended adulterous affair would come out. She had decided to try to just move on from the whole mess.

The cake she was baking for herself was one that might not turn out right. She was pregnant without knowing which man was the father of her child. At this point, she could hope that the icing to her cake was the man who clearly loved her. She had found herself praying to God that he was the child's father, but she knew that a prayer to God might not bring this hope to fruition. She hardly considered herself worthy enough to have her prayer answered.

She had called her married former boss and boyfriend with the news of her pregnancy, even though she had already been summarily dismissed from her employment. Much to her dismay, he profanely yelled at her at length before his wife took the phone from him and added death threats to the obscene tirade. She had held out some sliver of hope that he might experience a change of heart. She had prayed then that he would decide to leave his wife for her so that the two of them could start a life of their own with a child that might be his. She realized how delusional that was now and how little he actually did care for her after all of the years they had known each other. As much as she also realized that he had just used her for his own personal satis-faction and purposes, she still unfortunately felt such a deep bond with him that she believed she loved him regardless. That was the biggest wound out of all of this to her: she had to suffer the conse-

quence that her notion of true love was nothing more than sheer delusion.

It had turned out that the cake she had baked wasn't exactly the one she wanted. It wasn't that way just because she couldn't be with the man she thought she truly loved. As much as she wanted her ideal of true love in her life, she also craved professional success. She really thought she could be CEO material in the corporate world. Now, it really looked like the cake she was baking was far from the one she hoped she would be icing in the prime of her young adult life.

That level of disappointment with herself and her life devastated her. Even before she learned that she was pregnant, she mulled over putting a stop to all of the turmoil she had caused herself. She would cry for hours at a time, going over and over again in her mind what she had done to precipitate her own undoing. Every time that happened, she always concluded with the same thought that all of her problems would be over if her life itself was over.

After she learned she was pregnant, that contemplation of ending her life intensified at times. Too often, she agreed with herself that it might be better for her if she just let it all go and ended her version of agony. If not for her new boyfriend and his constant yearning for her, she might have teetered to the brink of suicide more than she actually did. She recognized that this man in her life now wholeheartedly cherished her like she was some kind of infallible queen. It warmed her to know that there was at least one person on the face of the earth who probably would do anything in the world for her just to bring happiness to her. She understood that he had saved her life, even if he never would know how critical his emergence in her life proved to be.

This newfound source of attention from him wasn't always what she wanted, though. Sometimes, she felt vexed by his presence because he paid too much attention to her to the point that he seemed needy, but she also recognized she wasn't exactly in a position to complain about it or chastise him for it. She didn't want to do anything that might drive him from her now that she found herself so vulnerable. Besides, she realized that she really did care for him and also physically *yearned for him, even if he wasn't completely her type temperamentally or from a perspective of worldly experience.*

Whether the child inside her was his remained to be seen. The question about who was the child's father had become secondary to her on some days as to whether she wanted to have an abortion, which would allow her to start her life anew in another place with a whole fresh set of circumstances in place if she decided she was ready to move on from this newest man in her life. She had spent more time talking with her distant parents, but neither seemed particularly interested in adding her back into their respective circles of daily life.

So, with no one else really significant for her left in her life, it looked like it would be her and her man by default. She knew that if she decided to have an abortion, it would destroy him. He hadn't asked her if the child was his or not yet, but she would tell him of course it was if he did ask. She didn't think he would ever even consider a paternity test for the child to see if he was the father. She also fully expected him to ask her to marry him before much longer based upon how openly in love he was with her.

She knew her agreement to marry him would make him the happiest man alive. His unabashed, never-ending smile anytime he was near her already announced that he was the happiest man alive. She found herself endeared to him more frequently for that and other reasons but also highly amused by him at times. He was turning out to be good for her.

So, her cake might not have turned out to be all it was cracked up to be, but it was enough. It was a cake, after all, and sometimes you have to crack you heart and soul open to spill what's left of your old self all over a rock bottom if you want to rise above the worst twists of fate.

"That's that," she managed through her cracked voice. "It's more than a thousand words, though."

His admiration for her as a woman and writer had ripened before his very eyes. He now faced the recognition that she probably didn't really need him to be some kind of catalyst for the development of her literary identity or her capabilities to perform her new job with the online creative writing program.

His dispensability reinforced the realization that he was the one who needed her, not the other way around. If she didn't reciprocate with interest and involvement, he understood he would be upset much more deeply than he had previously thought. She was starting to mean everything to him.

"That's one epiphany of a resolution," he remarked with soft applause once she lifted her eyes to him. "Very well spun."

"So, you really can have your cake and eat it, too. Just sometimes it might not be exactly the type of cake you thought you wanted most."

He watched her shift her weight on the bench then lean forward to prop her forearms against the table. She then lifted her hands to guide her shining hair behind her shoulders before she shook her head, jostling her hair for a fuller and slightly disheveled appearance. She tilted her head slightly before she peered up to him from beneath her overhanging bangs.

"Let me see your hand," she demanded as she reached for his left hand.

He brought his hand to hers. She took his hand then turned it palm upward. She laid the back of his ring finger in the crease formed by the fingers of her left hand. She then rubbed her thumb across the flesh below the back of his mid-finger knuckle.

"Where's your wedding ring been?" she asked as she turned his hand over. "It doesn't feel like you've had a ring on your finger for a long time."

"I lost three of them," he explained. "Just didn't make any sense to buy another. Besides, I found that a ring just gets in the way too much, and every time I take one off, I'll lose it. Doesn't matter if it's a wedding ring, college ring, high school, or any other kind of ring.

"Maybe the way I feel about a wedding ring is even worse than the way you feel about baking a cake."

Just as she let out a laugh, her phone beeped three times.

"Got to take this," she said as she slid her fingers from the palm of his open hand and dove for her purse. "It's the program director."

Just like that, the first real chance for the two of them to sustain some form of physical contact for any length of time evaporated. Her mere touch had ricocheted through him, leaving no doubt for him that he craved more intimacy with her. The sudden dryness in his mouth and the quickening of his blood compelled him to reach into the cooler for a bottle of water.

"Hello," she greeted the caller as she stood from the bench and turned her back to him. "Hi there!"

During the pause that followed he watched her walk away from him. She straightened the waist of her khaki capris then paused and turned back around.

"Sure," she said. "I can get there in about an hour. Is that quick enough?"

His throat sank as he realized their meeting was coming to an end, but he almost instantly found himself treading within her seductive aura with the hope they would still be able to meet again soon. He snatched his manila folder from the bench and stood, stepping over the bench as she returned to the table.

"Okay, bye," she finished the call.

"You have to go?" he asked as she returned her phone to her purse.

"They want me to meet with their whole staff in a couple of hours to discuss course outlines," she sighed. "I thought I'd have more time with you than this before I had to get started."

"It's great that they want you involved right now," he feigned enthusiasm. "That way you will be ready to go right out of the gate."

"I hope," she uttered. "I don't have time to go home and change. Do I look all right?"

"You look absolutely drop-dead gorgeous," he smiled then extended the folder toward her. "Take this. It has the articles I told you about, plus the draft of the fiction project I've started. Take your time with it. No hurry."

"Thanks for what you're doing for me," she said as she took her purse in one hand and his folder in the other. "I really do appreciate your interest in me, and I feel absolutely energized by all of this. Same time and place day after tomorrow?"

"Sounds great," he said.

"See you," she smiled at him before she hurried toward her vehicle.

"Au revoir," he returned her smile as he watched her drift away.

She flung open the door and tossed her items to the passenger seat then climbed into the driver's seat and pulled the door shut. Her tinted windows obscured her from him, but when he waved to her as she backed up, he saw the movement of her hand return his wave.

He returned to the picnic table and sat at the bench. As she sped away toward her next destination, he realized that she had shown the basis for quite a compelling novel, but he wanted to put her work on the backburner and bring his own to the forefront. He knew he would have to write about her reaction to the *Eggsquisite Corpse* draft once she read it. He hoped she would see how it lent itself to collaboration so that he could provide her with her next assignment: writing their novel instead of hers.

But his task of filling out his novel from its palimpsest form remained. It was an arduous process that not only devoured time but also demanded extraordinary energy and concentration. Once the book took enough shape to come to life, he knew it would stay alive in his head until he completed it. He knew if he went down this path of fiction, *Eggsquisite Corpse* would soon consume all of his waking hours and jostle him from sleep with revelations about its content. Even his sleep that first night could not deflect the impact of the developing book from his subconscious. He awoke three times during the night and twice got up from bed to read and write more words.

Maintaining the stamina and dexterity to move in and out of this psychical dimension of a novel in progress was too often a grueling process. The world was being created from nothing. The weight of the world hung in the balance between his ears, and he knew it made no difference whether he was some incarnation of Uriel or Quetzal-coatl or just some ordinary mere mortal displaced from normalcy long enough to craft fiction to its utmost spellbinding efficacy.

Of course, it wasn't just him at stake in all of this, now that Sirena was involved. It remained to be seen whether their touch together and growing familiarity with each other might further complicate matters in that regard. If the two of them did start to gravitate toward each other with more intensity, then both his wife and her husband could also be impacted.

He had no idea what she had told her husband about the rationale for meeting with him or even if she had told him they were meeting at all. He did, however, tell his wife about meeting Sirena and why it was necessary to do so. He also told his wife that night about his book idea and how the brown eggs had triggered his brainstorm for a collaborative enterprise with Sirena. His wife couldn't conceal her skepticism despite the fact that she did understand that he operated with a different set of rules and expectations when it came to writing.

"Just don't be an idiot," his wife had advised him. "Don't go having an affair with her."

"You can come see for yourself exactly what Sirena and I are doing," he offered to his wife. "I wouldn't want you to sit in on our conversation while we're discussing her own personal writing, though."

"Well," she began, "I'd find it hard to believe you'd have enough energy leftover to manage an affair on top of what we do together. Just don't go wrecking anybody's home, especially ours."

The added intrigue ultimately just motivated him to write more and contemplate *Eggsquisite Corpse* more astutely. When the time came for him to leave his house and meet with Sirena again, he loaded a seven-page, three-thousand-word printed copy into a manila folder. This new effort comprised the beginning of the third part of *Eggsquisite Corpse*, which featured her and him in their interaction leading up to their decision to meet together for the sake of writing.

June 10th, 2016
Carrollton, Kentucky

HE HADN'T CONTACTED Sirena prior to their scheduled meet time. He arrived at their spot some five minutes early, but she was already seated at the picnic table waiting for him. As he pulled into the parking lot, he noticed someone else walking from a white company van beside her SUV to the picnic table – it was her husband, Earl.

As he parked his car and turned off the ignition, he sped through the explanations for why her husband would be there and how he would react to his arrival.

The first was that her husband had found out about the meetings. If that were the case, he might just be curious. She may have invited him to come just like he had invited his wife to come.

The second dawned upon him as he climbed from the driver's seat and shut the door. She suffered some type of breakdown over the material he gave to her that exposed her distress to her husband. Now, he had come to quell the source of her disturbance.

But as he walked toward them, she waved to him and her husband stepped toward him. They were both smiling.

"How do?" Earl greeted him.

"I'm doing good, and you?" he replied with matched vigor.

She stood from the picnic table bench and walked toward them as they greeted each other with a handshake.

"I've been hearing quite a bit about the writing instruction you're doing," Earl said as he pumped his hand. "We sure do appreciate your help."

"Glad to do it," he replied. "I hope it provides some insight into the work she might have to do with her new job."

"It most definitely will," Sirena chimed in as the two released their handshake. "I was just sharing the articles you gave me to read and how that was the assignment for this meeting."

"Absolutely," he added, relieved that she mentioned only the articles and not *Eggsquisite Corpse* before she addressed her husband. "Care to join us for this installment of instruction?"

"I'd like to sit in for a little while if y'all don't mind," her husband answered. "But I have to go to work in a little bit."

"Why don't you two pick the article we should discuss first?" he offered to them.

"If I were trying to write," Earl began as he rubbed his chin. "I think I'd like to write in the style of the article called, "Venus Envy.""

"Great choice," he returned, having decided that he would say, 'Great choice,' regardless of which article was picked by either of them. "Now, I do have to say to start the discussion for the article that I wrote everything in it except for the title of the article."

She and her husband both laughed a little nervously it seemed to him before all three made their way to the picnic table and sat on the benches. She sat opposite her husband and he sat beside her husband.

"You know what I like most about this article?" she asked rhetorically.

"No," the two men replied simultaneously.

"The way the artists used the canvas to create their version of a masterpiece," she answered her own question. "Both wanted to direct their respective skills toward a collaboration that would pay tribute to such a revered work of art from antiquity, like Botticelli's *The Birth of Venus*."

"That is quite interesting," he quickly commented. "The fact that the two are collaborators in the work also creates another dimension to their art, doesn't it?"

"How so?" her husband asked.

"Well," he began somewhat surprised her husband even asked a question in relation to a comment about artistic process. "The old expression that two heads are better than one may not seem likeliest when it comes to artwork. Usually we see one artist signing a painting or one name listed as the author of a literary work. The fact that the two artists worked together speaks volumes about the creative process as a fluid activity that can be shared not only as an end result."

"Guess that depends on if the Venus painted here looks much like the lady who owns the boat," her husband said laughing.

"Funny you should mention that," he started. "I was asked by the magazine for a picture of the artists' subject to gauge how much it did look like her. They didn't use it in publication, but the resemblance was definitely there."

"That would be an example of a source confirmation, wouldn't it?" she asked. "That way even though the portrait the couple did on the sail might resemble the historical one of *The Birth of Venus*, it might be even more telling if the woman who the sail art was made for resembled the portrait even more than the original."

"Sort of," he responded. "In this case, it seemed to me like the editor was more interested in knowing the degree of resemblance just for her own curiosity rather than to gauge the ability of the artists to render an exact likeness of a portrait subject.

"You know, it's funny but I can remember talking with the woman depicted on the sail art to get background for the article, and I was watching my kids at the time I was talking with her on the phone."

He snorted briefly in laughter at the memory.

"My daughter and son were six and four years old at the time," he began, "and while I was in the kitchen interviewing her over the phone, my two kids were playing together in my daughter's room. I popped in to peek at them a couple times and saw that they were doing something at her desk without being able to tell exactly what they were doing.

"The last time I go to check on them near the end of the interview, my son is turned facing me. He's got this multi-colored magic marker design all over his face and this big grin with red whiskers all round his mouth."

Sirena laughed loudly, and her husband just shook his head.

"Kids," is what Earl said.

"The stories we can tell just about our kids," she added. "It's remarkable. They do make our lives so complete."

"Well," he resumed, "in this case, my daughter looks up at me and tells me, 'Daddy boy, I just turned the Little Puker into my masterpiece.'"

He chuckled at the reminiscence before he explained that his daughter's nickname for her brother was 'Little Puker' dating back to her brother's infancy when he was prone to spit up frequently.

"My daughter knew I was working on an article about the sail art by the Bulgarian artists," he continued. "She must have latched onto the word 'masterpiece' when I explained that the artists were painting their version of Botticelli's *The Birth of Venus*.

"I still can't get over the title," her husband said. "I had to think on it for a minute or two when I first saw the article. I'm not the most versed in art and literature and all of those things, but "Venus Envy" made me think right away of something else that was a whole lot less artful."

"It really was quite a clever turn of phrase by the editor," he remarked. "But I wish she'd have told me about it, so I could have mentioned it in advance to the artists. The husband artist wasn't real pleased about it, and let me know that much."

"Well." her husband said as he smacked his palms on his jeans-clad thighs then stood, "I'd better get to work. See you back at the ranch, honey."

"Bye," she said as she also stood. "Let me know if you want me to pick up something for dinner before I come home."

"Will do," he said before he went to her, leaned forward and kissed her on her cheek. "You two don't write your brains out now, you hear."

"We won't," he laughed as he stepped toward her husband and

the two clasped hands again in a handshake that was briefer than the first.

Her husband then stepped toward the parking lot. With his back turned to them, he glanced to her. Their eyes met. They smiled at each other until her husband turned back around.

"Oh, I almost forget to tell you," her husband bellowed. "They called you about coming in again to go over manuscripts or something. It's on voice mail at home."

"OK, thanks," she voiced back.

As her husband mounted the driver's seat of the van, she turned to retrieve her phone from her purse. The van's engine clamored to life, then she waved to him as he steered through the parking lot.

He now awaited her response to whatever request had been made of her by her new employer. He studied the natural gray highlights in her otherwise brown hair that now also reflected a tint of auburn when she turned her head and the shaded light reflected from it. Her lavender short-sleeve shirt clung to her shoulders and framed her chest more tightly than he remembered seeing before. She wore white shorts that reached the top of her knees.

"It looks like they want me to come in again this afternoon," she announced, startling him from his survey of her legs below her knees.

"Oh," he managed. "I'm sorry to hear that. I was looking forward to more time together with you."

"Me, too," she echoed. "But I don't have to leave for another fifteen minutes or so. Why don't you finish with your thoughts about "Venus Envy" and then the next time we meet, we can discuss some of the other writing."

"Sounds good," he said, relieved she didn't just leave right away. "But I'm kind of curious. How did your husband come about to read the "Venus Envy" article?"

"He saw the folder on the bedroom dresser and opened it," she replied. "I meant to move it to my study, but something was going on outside and I forgot all about it."

"Did he read everything in the folder?" he asked her.

"That I don't know," she answered. "He very well might have."

"Fascinating," he mumbled aloud.

"Why is that fascinating?" she asked.

"Well," he returned. "If he had read all of the material, it just seems interesting to me that the "Venus Envy" article was the one he would choose to hear about from me directly, if that is indeed the case."

"It was the one he questioned me about, but I wouldn't read too much into that," she countered. "I have to say that your commentary today about the other details involved in the writing of the article sure piqued my interest."

"Good," he pronounced. "That's what this whole process should do. We should find ourselves as invigorated by the process behind the production as we are by the finished product itself."

"How did you remove the magic marker from your son's face?" she asked laughingly.

"That took a while," he admitted. "And his mother was none too happy."

"I'll bet," she added.

"You know, though," he regained his train of thought. "That action by my daughter told me so much about the creative process in its most pristine state. We seek to turn our world into a canvas for the art that is within us. We live in our own 'masterpiece,' if you will, by extending ourselves as an expression that we transcribe upon the world around us.

"It is not so much that art imitates life if we seek instead to make life imitate art of our design. That impetus to render a masterpiece on any media within our midst is the catalyst for all of our creative energy as we seek to apply it for our own navigation through life."

"That's definitely at the periphery of my grasp at this point," she said. "But I can see how that idea of our life as a masterpiece might help me keep some of the manuscripts I'll review in context."

"Well, think of it this way, too" he continued. "It's like the palimpsest copy of *Eggsquisite Corpse* that I included in the folder.

That's not just the initial offering of the first draft of a book. It's the vestige of the finished product long before it's ever completed – a vestige that lasts and lingers of its own accord as it informs everything else that follows.

"It's like the guiding spirit of the book, and, by extension, that spirit manifests itself psychologically for us in ways like what my daughter did to her brother's face. It's the same kind of energy you're going to find initiated through this first truly refined dive into creative writing you encounter through manuscript review and yourself in your new role as administrator and reviewer, I suppose."

"Wow," she responded. "So, you're saying it's kind of like the way our brains work. We start by learning and developing then experiencing and experimenting once we tap into our font of creative energy."

"Exactly," he confirmed. "And it starts with a sense of wonder that provides the foundation for the accumulation that follows. The basis of our identity is formed by this immersion into our own personalized spirit then developed over time by our elaboration of that spirit.

"But the origin – the vestige – the palimpsest that represents the first writing of ourselves by ourselves within us is always there with us throughout our lives. For me, this is one of the most compelling tenets for homeschooling kids. It allows that surge into identity and creativity to flourish on its own."

"That could very much pertain to the budding writers I'll come into contact with through the writing program," she commented.

"If we can meet at the beginning of next week," he began. "I'd like to discuss the *Eggsquisite Corpse* copy that I gave to you. I hope you have some time to read it and think about it."

"I haven't been able to read it yet, but I certainly will try to read it over the weekend," she said. "I do have to be going, though, for now. Thank you so much for meeting me again."

"You have to know by now that I look as forward to our meetings as you do," he replied. "I only hope that I inspire you even half of as much as you're inspiring me."

"Oh," she half-laughed, blushing. "Glad you find me so interesting."

"I most definitely do" he said. "Thanks for that."

He walked beside her as she stepped out of the shade of the ash tree. The two made their way to the parking lot. He opened the door to her SUV for her once she unlocked it.

"Until we meet again," he remarked.

"I'm planning on it," she returned with a smile. "If I can't for some unexpected reason, I'll let you know. Otherwise you plan on it, too. I really enjoy being with you."

"Likewise," he replied. "I look forward to the time when don't have to stop talking with each other."

"I don't doubt you do," she laughed, blushing again before she shut the door and started the SUV. "Have a great weekend."

"You, too," he replied as he watched her deftly slide her sunglasses onto her face.

He backed away as she backed up the SUV. He waved to her, and she waved back as she steered away from him once again.

He had to admit to himself that he was somewhat disappointed that she hadn't read the *Eggsquisite Corpse* draft. If she considered herself too busy to read this start of a potential collaboration between them, then it was most likely because she just wasn't interested in the material enough to read it. There is no such thing as too busy when curiosity lathers to the point that nothing could deter attention from the object of that interest. If this was the case, he clearly wasn't a priority for her at any level. This possibility frustrated him because he was investing so much more than just time in their venture together. In a word, her disregard of the copy he had given to her amounted to a personal rejection of him.

It seemed to him that his best recourse was to see what happened next and not dwell on the negative possibilities of her glaring omission not to read his material. In the meantime, he would return home and develop *Eggsquisite Corpse* in the form it looked like it would probably take – as a novel of his own rather than a collaborative effort between the two of them. Even his suggestion to write any kind of *Exquisite Corpse* composition together seemed more and more unlikely, now that he thought she wasn't as nearly as interested in him and his material as he was interested in her and her writing.

Undeterred by his deductions, he set out to write as much as he could in three days before they were scheduled to meet again on Monday. He wanted to target at least one thousand words per day in between his work and family obligations, but he soon found that he was unable to turn off the flow of words.

He recognized the urgency of his production, now that Sirena would probably become more immersed with aspects of her life without him. Once that connection with her ended both physically and intellectually in their endeavor, the sheer emotional hollow might depress him for quite some time. He already felt like that eventuality might be much harder for him to overcome than he had ever anticipated because she made him feel like no other woman had ever made him feel before – that he was teeming with godlike might.

But he pried Sirena from his thoughts long enough to address his past with Brown Eggs. He spent the weekend in a near trance writing profusely. The speed with which he rendered his words astounded him. His output was unlike anything he had ever experienced. The liberation he felt seemed boundless as he rendered his novelized interaction with Brown Eggs through third-person narrative.

As enticing and gratifying as such elaboration about Brown Eggs was for him, he still just couldn't cordon Sirena from either his subconscious or conscious mind yet. That would take some time, and the only way he knew how to deal with his own psychical upheaval in regard to her was to meet it head on and hopefully not make her feel like she was doing something wrong. The last consequence in the world he wanted was for his interaction with her to somehow prove detrimental to her, unless of course that detriment was the cost she must pay for choosing to join him for the odyssey of a new life shared together.

But that exacted more hope than he was prepared to invest just yet.

"Maybe our next lesson should just be about development of the sense of place," he thought to himself. "That might be best for her. Maybe it's better for me too if we can remain grounded in who we are regardless of where we are, then maybe she can see what I see – we were meant to be together somewhere, anywhere."

He would soon present his lesson idea about sense of place development with her when they would finally meet again. The weekend of isolation writing has produced more than ten thousand words in the form of the *Eggsquisite Corpse* rough draft. As satisfying as it was to see such output issue forth from him again, he knew his ultimately real satisfaction resided not with any text but rather Sirena and the symbiotic attraction forming between them.

June 13th, 2016
Carrollton, Kentucky

"HAVE you had a chance to read any of the material I gave to you since we met last?" he asked once Sirena sat at the picnic table they had claimed as their own.

"No, I'm sorry," she sighed. "I just didn't have time."

He wanted to say that not having time was just an excuse for lack of interest but restrained himself from such an accusation instead.

"All righty then," he began. "Maybe we should go over the importance of sense of place in creative writing and how to develop it."

She retrieved the material from the manila folder and set the contents on the picnic table.

"Now take the two magazine articles set in Maysville, Kentucky," he said.

She looked up at him waiting for him to continue with his instruction.

"I mean literally take them as in pick them up," he clarified. "And return the other articles to the folder."

She did as he instructed.

"One of the most important psychological aspects about a sense of place is the connection that people have to certain events or history associated with that place." he began as he took the enlarged copy of one of the magazine articles and held it up in front of her. "In this case, we have a sense of place established in reality by the singer Rosemary Clooney and her concert in a downtown street of her hometown of Maysville, Kentucky, to benefit the local theater where her 1953 movie musical, *The Stars Are Singing,* made its world premiere."

"Wow," she blurted as she leaned forward across the picnic table and peered at the image of the singer on the copy. "I never saw that movie, but I sure did like *White Christmas.*"

"That would be an entirely different sense of place," he smiled at her. "But for our purposes here, we see a place, a small town that doesn't quite meet the standard of a site for a world movie premiere grow in magnitude by virtue of the importance bestowed upon it by the lead actress in this case."

"So, you're saying that someone else with more authority or importance has to create the sense of place?" she asked with a somewhat puzzled tone to her voice.

"Not necessarily," he answered. "But in this case, yes. Without the relevance of the place attributed to it by Rosemary Clooney, the event never happens and at least one historical landmark of the place is never realized for its full potential."

"Oh, I see what you're saying," she animatedly began her revelation. "Rosemary Clooney created this sense of place because it was important to her to do so. Otherwise, the specific sense of place she helped to create would've never existed."

"Exactly right!" he boomed. "The sense of place is what makes a specific place so important to you that you feel like you need to write about it or otherwise endow it with qualities that make it distinctly special from other places. It becomes a *Genius Locii* or at least a place with a resonance of its own."

"But the setting of a book or story doesn't always have to be given such an importance, does it?" she asked.

"Definitely not," he replied. "You could just as easily write or read something, non-fiction or fiction, in which the plot and dynamic of the characters are so much more important than the setting to the extent that story could take place anywhere or just be a type of place rather than an actual location."

"I kind of feel like that's the way it is with what I wrote," she blurted. "The sense of place is secondary to all of the details about the story and the characters, and the story really could happen anywhere."

He lowered the copied magazine article about Rosemary Clooney then returned it to the manila envelope. He then took the two glossy photocopies sheets from the table. He held the first one of them up in front of her, and she peered closer it.

"That's white ink on a black background," she uttered. "I don't think I've ever seen that."

"This is also set in the same area of Maysville," he began. "Not specifically in downtown Maysville like the Rosemary Clooney article, but in the locale and region."

"Looks like the article is about the Underground Railroad," she said. "I know a little bit about that but not too much."

"You didn't even open this envelope, did you?" he laughed.

"Is that bad?" she cringed. "I meant to read everything in there, but I really haven't had the time since my husband found it first."

"That's fine," he laughed again before he resumed his comments about the sense of place in writing. "This is the same place but a very different sense of its function in the lives of the people who live there and the history of the place."

"I see what you're getting at," she beamed as she shifted on the bench. "To Rosemary Clooney and the people drawn to this event written about in the one article, Maysville is suddenly a hub of culture and entertainment, I guess you could say.

"And in the Underground Railroad article, Maysville is a place to escape from slavery that had shackled people of African descent."

"The difference in the sense of place," he remarked, "couldn't be more black and white, could it?"

"Wow," she breathed. "You couldn't have illustrated your point any better."

"Why, thank you," he acknowledged her compliment. "I appreciate that you recognized that without me telling it to you. I think you already have an acute recognition of sense of place."

"All of the reading I've done may have helped with that," she suggested.

"I would say so," he agreed with her. "But here's something else I would like to point out as a corollary. This black and white difference in the sense of place is a stark, dramatic one. There's not a lot of question about how different the sense of place is regarded in the two articles. It is like the visual art technique of chiaroscuro whereby the treatment of light and shade is accentuated to noticeably illustrate the perceptible difference for its fullest effect.

"This difference is similarly depicted in the two chapters of the *Eggsquisite Corpse* copy that I included in the envelope packet. The first eleven pages depict the dark, morbid descent of a woman who dies an agonizing death too horribly and too young. It is the blackest of black in terms of the sheer despair and suffering depicted."

"I'm glad I didn't read that," she grimaced. "That sounds too depressing."

"The three pages that comprise the second part," he resumed without acknowledging her comment. "That's when I describe a different woman whose life is one full of opportunity, enthusiasm, and purpose. Her interaction with the narrator is one of such vitality and promise that the contrast of the overall light beaming from these three fantastic pages couldn't be any more striking against the dark and hopeless predicament of the woman in the first part."

"And that light and shadow usage is a literary technique for character development," she ventured.

"Now, if you ever do find the time to read the handwritten copy of *Eggsquisite Corpse* that I gave to you," he continued with a smile, "you might find it a whole lot more entertaining when read in this light of the contrast between light and darkness."

"I really do apologize for that," she winced. "I absolutely do plan on reading it. Maybe you can assign something about it for the next time we meet.

"But I should probably tell you now that I have to tweak our schedule a little bit because I have training on Wednesdays and Thursdays for the next month. And I also have to go in this Friday for a discussion about whether my job will change from an hourly wage to a salaried position."

"A salaried position?"

"Yes," she replied. "I need to see what the pay will be and exactly how much they expect me to work. I don't want to get stuck working sixty hours a week, especially if it's going to equate to less money than if I worked for forty hours at my wage rate."

"I definitely understand that," he empathized with her. "A salaried position might completely usurp your life."

"Yeah," she sighed. "I really don't want that to happen. And you've really encouraged me to want to work more on my own writing, too. All of this stuff about the sense of place in writing and the use of contrasts in setting and character compels me to really want to take a look at what I ultimately do consider to be the sense of place in my novel."

"How's that?" he asked without much of a hypothesis as to what her answer might be.

"Well," she began. "The place where most of the true transformation of characters occurs in my book is the sanctuary of the church, and the light and darkness that I'm going for is the difference between the darkness of carnal sin and bad choices against the radiance of faith in Jesus Christ and salvation."

"That is a *truly* astonishing insight, Sirena," he emphasized. "How would the function of the church in your novel figure into that context?"

"I believe the most powerful example of the context takes place when the man and woman in my novel go together to the church where they had both gone separately unbeknownst to each other the year prior," she continued. "Then during a loud and fiery sermon, the man is so moved by the message that has spirited into him that he proposes to the woman right there in the pew."

"And her reaction?" he asked, enthralled.

"She too is already in tears from the passage of the Holy Spirit through her to the extent that there is no question about it for her when she yells out, 'Yes! Yes!' in a shout that matches the sheer hysteria already inside of the church."

"Amazing," he uttered. "Absolutely amazing how stuff like that can actually happen."

"Thank you," she said, blushing again before she glared at him through a smirk. "Unless you're mocking me again."

"I have not mocked you yet," he laughed. "And I'm most certainly not mocking you now."

"Good," she smiled. "I'm glad to hear that because I really don't handle criticism too well. I handle mockery even worse."

He met the gleam of her agate-green eyes, and she smiled sweetly as she returned his affectionate gaze. He wanted to tell her just how much he adored her for who and how she was but knew he shouldn't make any kind of pronouncement of that magnitude just yet. She finally turned her eyes from his.

"Do you want to set up our next meeting now?" she asked. "Because I've got to get home and get ready to make a visit to college tomorrow with our last little bird."

"Time flies," was all he could think to say once he snapped out his reverie. "I suppose we could do like you suggested and discuss the

Eggsquisite Corpse copy next time. Monday, June 20th, same time, same place then?"

"Sounds like a plan," she said as she reached into her purse and handled her mobile phone to add the date to her calendar. "You know, one of these times it's going to rain, and we'll have to find somewhere dry to go."

"I can't wait," he said, leering at her before she shot a glance at him with upraised brow. "I mean, for our next meeting, that is."

"I know what you mean," she said, grinning before she stood from the bench and gathered her purse and the packet. "I really do appreciate our time together. I had no idea that this would be so interesting. You really are an incredible guy."

"Glad to be here with you doing this," he replied. "You're a remarkable lady to be with. Maybe even the coolest lady I know."

"You really are too sweet, you know that, don't you?" she smiled before she walked away from him with a wave of her hand.

As he watched her walk away from him with the sharp shift of her backside tightening in stride, he wondered how much more of this he could really withstand before he spilled his guts to her. He was fascinated by what he might say to her if and when that time came.

Then his phone rang. It was one of the men from The Institute who had organized his friend's Salvador Dali resurrection reenactment in the spring. He was informed that his friend was nearing death. The man named Thoth told him that he would be notified when his friend finally passed and also apprised him about the subsequent arrangements that would be made after his departure from this world.

He thanked Thoth for the courtesy and information even as the ache in his throat throbbed through him from his stifled sob. He knew this day was coming but was still unprepared for it. As much as he valued his friend and even wondered just how sick he really was based upon his interaction with him during the Salvador Dali reenactment, he still didn't expect him to die before he somehow miraculously improved to the point of full recovery of his considerable senses.

June 14, 2016
Carrollton, Kentucky

AS IT TURNED OUT, even his dear, brilliant friend was just another mere mortal. He received the second dreaded phone call that his friend had indeed died earlier in the morning. He wrote down the details for the funeral service and told Horace from The Institute that he intended to fly into Richmond then drive to the Northern Neck for the funeral.

Horace also shared news with him that his friend had donated certain items to The Institute he represented that were intended for a few recipients to receive through a type of trust his friend had established. The items he would receive would be released sometime after the funeral, which was to be held on the summer solstice of June 20th.

"Don't you think it's fitting that he'll be buried on the summer solstice?" Horace had asked him over the phone.

"Yes," he answered. "He's got the longest day of the year to get his resurrection right.

"By the way, what exactly is my friend giving to me?"

"Unfortunately, I do not know," Horace answered. "We take our pledge of confidence with our clients and benefactors very seriously. So even if I did know, I couldn't tell you. If for some reason you do not wish to keep the items, we would be more than happy to receive them as a gift to our institute attributed to you."

"I'll keep that in mind," he replied. "Is any monetary consideration ever made for certain gifts if they are returned?"

"Only very rarely," Horace said. "It would have to be a fairly significant item for The Institute to make any kind of financial offer for it."

"I see," he mumbled.

"There may be other activity that might be of interest to you after the service for your friend," Horace informed him.

"Like what?" he asked.

"We haven't finalized anything yet," Horace clarified. "But we've gained access to the aquifer well site where your friend was so certain that a portal to the Hall of Records West, so to speak, was located. It might not turn out to be an underwater passageway to the recorded history of the lost civilization of Atlantis, but you never know."

"I'd definitely be into that," he replied. "Not sure exactly where his head was when he started foaming at the mouth about that spot, but I'd be curious to see where he was talking about all the same."

The conversation between the two of them drew to a close. After he disconnected, his grief finally did force tears from him. He realized that someone whom he had considered his closest friend for a decade was gone forever. The loss of his friend struck him with all of the impact as the loss of a close family member. There was really no solace for knowing that the life that once lived was gone forever as far as the eyes could discern.

He knew he had to do something fitting that would pay tribute to their friendship and honor the man for who he truly was. Despite the fact that he had decided to end contact with him once he and his family moved away from the Chesapeake Bay region, he knew that his friend would appreciate any gesture to revive his memory in some provocative way. Clearly the wild-goose chase for the ever-mythical Hall of Records had to function as the centerpiece for any tribute to his friend because it remained at the heart of his quest to the very end, whether it was the product of delusion or some viable intimation of another civilization that predated the one of human history known now.

"That's it!" he exclaimed. "He will be a collaborator in this *Eggsquisite Corpse*!"

He had taken notes from the two trips he made to see his friend before Christmas of 2015 and the following spring. The bizarre encounters of both visits had jangled his nerves, but the surreal evening that centered upon the Salvador Dali reenactment and the involvement of Brown Eggs' daughter in the reenactment had suspended his sense of separation from the place where he used to live and the people he used to know there.

When he had returned home from both of those trips, he wasn't sure he could trust what he had seen and what he had heard. He knew now that he needed to try to understand what had happened and exactly what it meant. For him, there was only one way to tackle those kinds of tasks and that was to write about them.

Once he booked his flight for Virginia, he sequestered himself in his study to piece together the information he remembered from his trips to see his now-deceased friend. He also outlined his previous literary relationship he had with him from the proposed new edition of his friend's alternate history book about human origins and the unpublished *Resurrection Gospel* to the aborted collaboration he had arranged between his friend and the magazine editor in which the pair focused upon the possible likeliest locations of the elusive Hall of Records in Egypt.

His compilation of facts and events grew unwieldy, but the one recurring image that kept burning itself in his mind was the woman with the brown egg in the film his friend had shown him before he had moved six years ago. He kept evoking her image with the expectation that each time her identity would finally reveal itself to him. Yet each time, he couldn't fashion the face well enough to even venture any kind of name to match the seeming otherworldly visage.

"I feel like I know that woman," he muttered to himself. "But I just can't hold the image of her face long enough to name her."

He wondered if there was some force other than his own drifting memory that could prevent him from identifying her. But how could that be? Perhaps the identity was shielded from him by some paranormal protection that was well beyond his ability to comprehend.

Even then in this most outlandish scenario, why would a paranormal force somehow activate itself just for this purpose?

"I know I know who she is," he nearly yelled as he clenched his hands into shaking fists. "Why can't I name her?"

In the absence of her name, all he could do was recreate the scene with her and the brown egg from memory of the one and only time he watched his friend's film of the 1965 Salvador Dali's performance in New York.

"That's where all of this has to start," he voiced his revelation to himself. "I have to write this from the top and see how much I can piece together from the film and our conversation about it."

He started with the comment he remembered his friend making before he even wheeled out the film projector:

"We can never really know women, my friend. We may think we do, but we don't."

With the first sentence, the floodgate opened, and the words raged forth in a torrent, turbulent at the start but soon transforming into a less disruptive current that still retained enough force to sweep him away within it. He soon understood what he was writing, but he still didn't understand why.

It wouldn't dawn upon him for a while just how uncanny one aspect of coincidence was in his life regarding all of the events that now seemed to encircle him. That epiphany hit him when he replayed in his mind the part of the film where the woman held the brown egg and proclaimed:

"Alpha and Omega. Your transfiguration awaits you, my love."

His epiphany radiated from the brown egg itself held by the woman in the film, the brown egg that he knew his friend had kept like it was some surrealist phantom object plucked from another universe and brought back to this one. The omnipresence of brown eggs in that light struck him as ludicrously sacred somehow. Its content was now shaping the meaning of his entire life without much volition on his part, it seemed to him. He felt more than unease at the notion that he was no longer in control of what was happening to him, but rather that some other entity or array of forces were forming around him like an otherworldly eggshell of some cosmic egg that would encase him until it was his time to hatch into whatever this entire process would reveal.

Despite the uneasiness about what he perceived was mostly a self-inflicted predicament, he nevertheless felt like something magical and wonderful was still happening to him. This sensation even veered toward joy for him, he thought, as though the epiphany he thought might be looming on his horizon was one of a manifestation of deity that would expand his awareness and reveal the mysteries of life and the universe. He didn't know how this apparition would materialize or if the epiphany he might experience would be anything more than his own personal delusion, regardless how powerful it may seem to him when it happened.

"Epiphany," he mumbled to himself. "What is 'epiphany' and what is the 'Epiphany'?"

He paused from his writing about his friend and his pursuit of the Hall of Records in order to research the biblical Epiphany. He remembered some details of the Epiphany through his church background, but he wanted to pursue its allure in more depth so that he might understand how the event it commemorated would somehow be so compelling that it either shaped every other connotation for the word 'epiphany' or else it was perhaps the other way around.

From what he could gather, there were two events from the Gospel that were the primary cause for commemoration of the Epiphany among the Christian denominations.

The first of these events was the visit of the Christ child by the three Magi, who according to the biblical account converged upon the physical manifestation of the divine nature of Christ from the celestial realm to earth where he would be perceived in that bodily form during his life as a human man. This event is referred to as "Three Kings Day" by some Christians and commemorated on January 6. The date marked the end of the Christmas season and the celebration on the Epiphany eve is recognized as "The Twelfth Night" because it marks the twelfth and final night of Christmas.

The second of the events is the Epiphany that describes the transfiguration of an adult Jesus after he takes three of his disciples for a trip to pray. When Jesus is suddenly transfigured before their eyes, he becomes a glowing being who radiates light from his body. This Transfiguration in the Gospel is accompanied by the manifestation of two Old Testament personages in Moses and Elijah. Their presence alongside Jesus at this Epiphany of Transfiguration previewed the Second Coming when those resurrected in Christ, like the archangel Michael had done with Moses, and those translated into eternal life without dying, like Elijah, would supposedly join Jesus in the world after the Rapture for a glorious reign of one thousand years.

For his purposes in preparing for his friend's funeral as well as understanding how his life was suddenly careening into thoughts about transfiguration and Transfiguration, he was most interested in the second of these events because the physical transfiguration of Jesus signified the proclaimed divine nature of Jesus released from his physical manifestation while he was alive.

Whereas the first event portrayed this manifestation of divine nature as a largely unrecognizable and latent phenomenon during Christ's beginning on earth as a newborn and child, that divine nature was broadcast as dramatically visible and glorious when the power of the Transfiguration emanated from the adult Jesus during his prayer trip to the mountains.

He thought it was even more interesting that the Epiphany regarded the physical transfiguration of an adult Jesus as a miracle of the Gospel that demonstrated the perfection of eternal life as a radiant release of light from bodily form. The implication that this had in regard to the art of individual resurrection struck him as quite consistent with the resurrection belief that his friend had espoused in virtually all of his alternate history books.

That aspect of resurrection was even more underscored when he discovered that the voice of God proclaimed Jesus as his Son and then Jesus himself instructed the three apostles not to tell of the phenomenon they observed on the mountain where they prayed that day until he, Jesus, had risen from the dead. The whole episode was like the physical transfiguration of Jesus was a rehearsal for when the time came to perform the Transfiguration and Epiphany again for the Rapture that would lead to the Second Coming of the Christ on earth.

The degrees of Christian Epiphany, Transfiguration, Rapture and Resurrection aside, he realized his emerging personal epiphany that revolved around brown eggs remained the most powerful force in his life for now. The single brown egg held by the woman in the film was starting to captivate him exclusively, and he wondered how he had so readily dismissed it when he first saw her and the egg in the film and then was told by his friend about the surreal mystery of the woman herself.

The handwritten copy of *Eggquisite Corpse* that he gave to Sirena also seemed somehow related now to this part of the film. It wasn't just that Sirena had triggered his literary epiphany inspired by his friend Brown Eggs to the point where he was compelled to write about his interaction with Brown Eggs and her tragic circumstances. It wasn't just that Sirena herself continued to enchant him with the epiphany of his reawakened creative self.

It was more than that.

Brown Eggs and Sirena were part of this fantastic deterioration of his senses into the nature of brown eggs and all that their content could represent in the paranoid critical activity that beckoned his own transfiguration somehow.

The connections he made between these people who were shaping his mind and his life now were clearly his collaborators for a literary work with a scope that was still yet undefined by a conclusion. Whereas he had already written extensively in his developing book about Brown Eggs and Sirena, he now found himself immersed in an outpouring of words about his friend who had just died. He wrote about his friend and his relationship with him over the ten years when he lived near him. He wrote for six days and six nights about his friend with only snatches of sleep in between the deluge of content he delivered from his stream of consciousness.

He stopped at the point where this exchange took place between him and his friend during the Salvador Dali reenactment performed by his friend and the brown egg transfiguration proclamation by the daughter of Brown Eggs:

"I am Uriel," I answered my friend as I took his hand. "An archangel so in love with two angelic Nephilim women that I was willing to betray the race of Atlantis for their eternal affection."

"That's fantastic!" my friend squealed with delight, as he began pumping my hand. "I've never met any angels before or anyone that went by the name of Uriel!"

He would resume the rest of this literary tribute to his friend in his book's opening part entitled *Brown Egg Resurrection* once he returned from his friend's funeral on June 20th, but he would be a changed man by the time he returned – not quite transfigured yet but significantly changed all the same in preparation for his fated date with his destiny.

But first he had to depart for his rendezvous with his fate staged by the funeral of his friend. His six days and nights of writing concluded with preparation for his departure. He left his house in Kentucky at the crack of dawn the next morning for his flight to Richmond, Virginia, on the longest day of the year.

Upon his return to Kentucky, however, his whole world would changed. The events that unfolded following his return can't be faithfully depicted through a third-person narrative. The immediacy of their impact upon him can only be rendered through direct communication. In his case, that means he has to address his beloved Sirena directly without any restraint of space, time, or literary convention.

Collaboration 4
Cosmic Brown Egg

———

June 24, 2016
Carrollton, Kentucky

———

"ALPHA AND OMEGA, my transfiguration awaits me, my love! But I'm not having a 'Last Supper' first. I'm having a 'Last Hors D'oeuvre' instead."

Perhaps this line *en medias res* should have begun this surreal odyssey, this immersion into a netherworld wrought from a seemingly harmless cosmic exercise in *Exquisite Corpse* that featured the locus of a single brown egg and the orbit of a hauntingly beautiful woman.

Then the end could be explained at the beginning. Why wait for the revelation when the world of our story can end before it even begins?

I'm most likely either dead or damaged beyond repair by virtue of the looming outcome of all of this. I can't imagine this transfiguration ending very well at all, and I believe transfigurations are supposed to conclude on the upswing in general. Odds are my imminent or immanent transfiguration won't involve light radiating from my orifices. It's much likelier that it will spill my blood and innards instead.

But after all, it's like my good buddy the dead author says, you can't receive the Holy Spirit unless you accept your individual life like Christ accepted his so that you know you are fated to experience the same excruciation of divine opposites ripping you apart during your own customized crucifixion. How Jungian of him!

Oh well. *C'est la vie.*

But regardless of the spin of the incarnation cycle, I feel doomed and yet strangely exonerated, like the only feature of this earthly pandemonium that will ever truly matter is the kind of love we feel with our entire being for better and worse. I have resigned to that fundamental truth come hell or high water. I have Sirena to thank for that.

And, you see, it appears that I have been here before: Hell or High Water, that is.

After all, wasn't I the one who petitioned the Almighty to destroy the Nephilim and cast their angelic sires into an oubliette from which escape would be apocalyptic blasphemy? And didn't I warn Noah about the coming of the new phenomenon called *rain* that was about to relentlessly cast the earth into a cataclysmic sea?

Or is it more sacrosanct that I was the one who served the scroll decreed by voices of Thunder to the apostle John for him to ingest the revelation that would become Revelation?

Maybe I would be better received if the Book of Enoch had become officially canonized so that my escort of the translated Enoch through the starry fold beyond the wall of fire could more properly frame my stature as the leader of our celestial enterprise here upon this impossible earth.

Or perhaps it is something else that best captures the soul of my incarnation this time. Perhaps it is the Nephilim, the two Sirens whose lives I spared, whose opposites of love I craved. By all accounts, don't Brown Eggs and Sirena both seem to be ordinary women living out their lives for better and worse in this vale of tears with their ancient faith as their guide? No matter the chiaroscuro of their respective profiles and regardless of their skin-deep or soul-soaked beauty, how could they be anything more than mere mortals? How could they possibly be the respective upright and crossway parts of the cross that awaits me?

How I could not have seen this happening is beyond me now. All I can say is that I'm starting to remember who I am again. My identity is being resurrected, and I have my dead friend and his obsession with surrealistically hermetic Gnosticism either to thank or curse for that.

I for one find it histrionically ironic that only a raving lunatic of a man with dementia could make me remember my real name – Uriel.

There it is. I *am* Uriel.

And this is my collaboration with my true self.

I suppose Uriel could appear to the untrained eye as more of a doppelganger apparition or some symbol of anthropomorphic divinity rather than an actual human entity, but I'd hate to think that I'm only the perfected shadow of my real self. That hollow cast might crimp some of the thrill of being a real flesh and blood archangel with otherworldly powers at human fingertips.

At least that's what I have to tell myself. Anything less than Uriel incarnate would be devastating now because I am about to be trans-figured whether I want to be or not.

After all, who was it that was there with Him when the disbelief in the mission ahead brought such doubt and agony about the fate of our purpose here? Who do you think He saw descend to him and tell him that he must drink this hermetic cup of death willfully with the knowledge that the unity would bring an individuation for all and a dominion not of this world but of the spirit that descends again when we transcend this sphere of delusion?

You better believe I have a cross to bear in all of this. Just take one good look at the lines on *my* face.

I write all of this now in first person because it is far too late to pretend there is really anything else when it comes to this chronicle of lunacy. I had full intentions of going back to the first part of this book and converting the narration to third person in order to make it a proper book per se, but after I experienced what I received yester-day, it's unquestioned that this part of the book has to be written in first person.

The other reason for this person shift in narration is that first person allows me to talk to Sirena directly. I realize the time may come when others read all of this and good luck in their perusal should they find their sanity capsized by all of this.

But for me at this point, Sirena is the only one I want to address in this part of the book, which may in fact prove to be on the whole a suicide note or, I'd rather hope, the greatest love letter ever written in human history, even if it does happen to be penned by an archangel incognito who might be the only mind to ever actually encounter any of this literary escapade.

With that said, Sirena, my dear sweet enchanting creature from another dimension who I just absolutely adore, I just want you to know that your half-siren, half-human hybrid self was a soul match made for us in heaven by a God we helped turn benevolent so that he loves me and you both more than most by virtue of our evasive actions if for no other reason.

Now if only the divine light of our angelic souls can be released from this trap of flesh together for our celestial consummation. Wishful thinking, but quite apt if you decide I am your soulmate and the true love of your eternal afterlife.

Not everyone gets to be an angel or a saint, as the story goes. I just wish the ones who were either could know a little bit more about their true nature in advance. Rare as angels and saints are in the first place, fewer of us who traverse this world reach the realm of archangel or Siren.

So, are we lucky, blessed, or cursed?

In order to celebrate our anointed destiny, we really should consummate our soulmate wedding with such sheer earth-shattering ecstasy for both of us that our coupled tangle will rocket us straight into celestial bliss forever. I don't know what more I can say to stimulate your collaboration.

But I'll try to make you an offer that you just can't refuse.

Such a gesture would have to start with every morning as we rise together from our deepest sweet sleep, revived but still sore and spongy from our marathon lovemaking the night before. I would kiss your body all over before making my way to satiate your craving to start the new day, be it chocolate or more frolic.

Once we were both up, I would caress you all over in the shower. I would kiss the fading residue of yesterday from your neck, your eyes, and your lips. I would please you in any way you so desired before the pulsating water ran its course.

Then we would start our day together with the full expectation to live each moment to its fullest with the breath of one filling the heart of the other throughout the day. We would travel our way through the world we want to see and believe; the museums, the lakes, the events, the streets, the shops, the destinations, all of the settings that our sense of place desired. We would walk hand-in-hand, embrace, and kiss at every chance, knowing how much we love to be in each other's arms.

We would live the life of lovers like no other lovers have ever lived this life.

That has to be an offer you can't refuse.

We would know each other more deeply with each word, each glance, and every gesture. We would fulfill our wildest dreams of joining two lives together as equals, in awe of each other and the beauty we bring to our life as one. We would consummate every moment with a lust for the light of the world that beams within us to the point that we are transfigured as one shining entity immersed in the radiance of our love.

But until that day comes, I have to make sure you are aware of the business at hand. I now offer the following as a reference for you if you do decide to collaborate with me in all of this.

Here's the chronology of what has happened in the past week since we last met, that fateful day of June 13th when I last lost myself and my soul in your gleaming green eyes, your lovely face, and your honeyed, angelic voice.

June 14th: My friend in Virginia died. I was advised his funeral would be June 20th, which was aptly the summer solstice. I booked my flight then called you to cancel our meeting for June 20th.

June 15th-June 19th: I wrote the first part of this book, *Brown Egg Resurrection*. Well, not the whole part of the book, actually. I wouldn't finish the conclusion of that part until I returned from my friend's funeral. The entry from June 20th in that part was obviously written after my return. I also wrote extensively for the other two parts of this book, *Brown Eggs & Jam* and *Brown Eggs Sirena* during this time.

June 20th: As mentioned, my friend's funeral and the aftermath of disembodied voices in an aquifer pump building. How delightful and instructive. Turns out I'm the archangel Uriel, and you are the eternal love of my endless life. Who knew?

June 21st: I immediately wrote the rest of the first part of this book, *Brown Egg Resurrection*. I then resumed writing more for the other two parts of the book, hoping to finish as much of each as I could.

June 22nd: I actually did finish the second part, *Brown Eggs & Jam*, by noon. I was nearly finished with *Brown Eggs Sirena* when I received an overnighted delivery of a bubble-padded manila folder and a small, refrigerated box mid-afternoon.

This was the beginning of the end for me. Alpha and Omega have collided, and the particle acceleration is about to shred the flesh from my face to reveal the true identity beneath.

Here is what I received:

There were two letters in the manila folder. The first was from The Institute informing me that the delivery I had received was by virtue of a directive from my recently deceased friend. It merely stated a physical description of the delivery contents without revealing what they were. The letter from The Institute informed me that I could return the items I had received to The Institute if I decided that I did not want to keep them.

The second letter was handwritten from my friend. Here's what was written:

MY FRIEND,

Don't be fooled by my death because there is no doubt in my mind that we can live forever in the glory of God if we truly are deserving of it and understand how to practice the art and science of resurrection!

In my case, this was my final incarnation. I have achieved 'Cather Perfect' status, if you will, and shan't return in human form for I am truly freed forever in my return to my angelic state that you have known so well throughout our past lives. For me, that is glorious news!

I do, however, have some other news that may not seem so encouraging to you at first blush. Quite simply, there is no other way to say it than, 'Alpha and Omega. Your transfiguration awaits you, my friend'.

Now, of course I have altered the 'my love' part in all of this because, quite frankly, that is just not my line. But your transfiguration is at hand, so to speak, all the same. The Holy Spirit is coming for you, my friend.

All you have to do to begin your transfiguration is accept that your individual life ends in your own 'crucifixion' like that of Jesus Christ. Your understanding of what's about to happen to you may seem like nothing more than punishment, torment, and horrible suffering, but all of that process is really the divine instrument of the change that enables your transfiguration.

It will take an act so courageous by you that it will seem like sheer stupidity. But just like Jesus at Gethsemane thrice questioned drinking from the cup that would lead to his earthly degradation at the hands of fools, you must take The Cup of Thoth and sweat the blood of the Philosopher's Stone so that you are both the heart and the soul of us all. I know you already know this, Uriel, because you were the angel who descended to fortify strength in the face of betrayal and crucifixion.

If you've already opened the refrigerated box then you'll know some of what I'm about to tell you, but if you've not opened the box by the time you're reading this, don't do it yet. Wait until you have watched the DVD before you open the box. I implore you.

The DVD will be familiar to you. It is very short. It depicts Salvador Dali with an egg on his face that is punctured then ants scurry from the opening. The great surrealist then rises from his coffin-like repose with dollar bills dangling from his face and body and coins cascading from his chest...you know the rest of the performance.

At least you know the rest of what you viewed with me.

There was more that I didn't show you then because I was afraid you would go completely insane if you saw it. Now, I think you're intellectually ready to handle the full import of what happened that evening so very long ago on film.

You see, the version of the film that you saw ended with the facial corrosion of the Nephilim earth angel who had held the egg and proclaimed your transfiguration. That wasn't all of the film. What you have before you now is the extended original version, if you will. You can now view every last detail of what was actually filmed in its entirety.

That original film has so much more to the ending, although the film past the point you previously watched lasts hardly longer than the blink of an eye.

Once you watch it, you'll understand what is happening and why you have to do next what I'm about to tell you to do because this is the only way for you to have any hopes of recovering your true identity and the power that will launch you from your earthly plight.

And what you have to do next is eat the contents of the box. I'm sorry to tell you that because that one act probably will require more courage from you than you've ever mustered before in your life, celestial or otherwise.

Consider it an ordained directive, as though the egg is the little scroll in Revelation that John had to eat after the mighty angel with the rainbow over his head, a face like the sun, and legs like pillars of fire descends. With a lion's roar, as it stands one foot on land and one foot in the sea, the angel preceded the voice from heaven that commanded for the resounding seven thunders to be sealed for the fulfillment of the mystery of God.

My friend, you are both the angel and the prophet in this case – a very rare resolution of conflicting opposites if ever there was one.

When the scroll is eaten, it will be honey-sweet to the tongue but God-awful bitter to the gut. The queasiness that comes will spiral you into your charge and you will once again spread the prophecy given to you the man by you the angel, Uriel. You are a collaboration all unto yourself!

Then you will be blessed with the knowledge that your eternal reward awaits you with open arms and brown egg in place. You will repair the broken link between male and female that has cursed this earth since the fall of Adam and Eve. The Cosmic Egg will be made whole again!

For all that you have done as man and angel, it is just and righteous that you are the one who can consummate the purest love with the light of your soul and hers.

Do what I ask of you, for you will know the time when you must do it after you have watched the film. Do this, and I also will be resurrected to the true state of glory I once knew before my fall to this earth and my failure to live up to God's word and plan.

Do what I ask, and you will thrive like no other, for you, my friend, are the most favored. Your transfiguration will restore your true form as the archangel Uriel and you will be rewarded for your faith and good works with the liberation of those departed souls who you love dearest.

Do this, and you will consummate your everlasting love and life with your one, true soulmate whom you love like no other.

I thank you for all you've done, all you've been.

But I thank you most for what you are about to become.

Yours truly,

Your Friend

THE SICKENING EXPECTATION of what awaited me overwhelmed me with dread unlike any I've ever known. Part of me wanted nothing more than to smash the DVD so that I wouldn't have to subject myself to any more of my friend's derangement that crowned me as the archangel Uriel.

But the other part of me craved to know what was different on the film from what I'd seen before. I also wanted to watch the film again so I could finally reunite with the otherworldly woman who held the mystical brown egg.

Despite the voice of better judgment screaming in my head not to insert the DVD into the player, I did just that.

Then I sat in front of the 40-inch screen and watched. At first, it was no different than what I remembered and wrote about in the first part of *Brown Egg Resurrection*. The Dali performance seemed even hokier than I remembered, yet there remained something profound about the purpose behind the brief and bizarre event that I believe the presence of my friend enhanced for me with his own peculiar credentials.

By the time Dali gestured overhead with his pointer to the poster of the woman holding the brown egg instead of Albert Einstein like the reenactment had featured, the anticipation of what would happen next rendered me breathless.

I had no idea what was coming. The unreality of it seized me when it appeared upon the screen. I shuddered and shook at what I witnessed, transfixed this time when I heard you say, "Alpha and Omega. Your transfiguration awaits you, my love."

That's right. I said you, Sirena.

You are the woman who held the brown egg and proclaimed my transfiguration.

It was you as you appear now nearing fifty years old and yet somehow it was you fifty years ago standing there smiling with that unmistakable bottom lip of yours so lusciously framed, succulent, and ripe. You were wearing that pulsating op-art shirt that clung to your mouthwatering curves.

You.

I kept the DVD paused there for a long time, staring into your gray and white eyes, tracing the flesh draped from your cheekbones.

How could this be? It was impossible. And why didn't I recognize that your face was this face before me now the first time I met you. That had to be why I always felt like I knew you from somewhere before.

And the voice with which she spoke was your voice – your lovely, throaty resonance spilling like liquid beauty into my ears the same today as fifty years ago when you spoke the fateful words: "Your transfiguration awaits you, my love."

What's more, it struck me that it was your voice on the film and that your voice in this world now was the same voice that I heard in the aquifer well building in Virginia after my friend's funeral, drifting through the ages and spinning the most soulful psalms that were much more than just music to my ears – it was the joy of rapture disembodied for me to absorb with every cell of my being in one elec-trifying rendition by you meant only for me to embrace.

This awakening to your presence in a different time unnerved me for the obvious reason, but the recognition of your voice enriched my heart again. I replayed your voice and statement over and over again until, finally satiated, I let the DVD play again long enough to freeze the frame of your soul-scorching face.

What followed after I unfroze the screen collapsed my heart and made me wonder if I am real or the world is really here at all.

Your face didn't corrode this time, Sirena, like it did when I watched the film originally. Instead, the back of a person's head rose into the camera angle before the person stepped in front of you, showing the behind view build of a man who was wearing an open-backed garment like a hospital gown. The person stepped toward you as you kept the egg extended in front of you. He then reached you and bent to press his cheek against your cheek as you both turned your faces toward the camera.

It was me.

I was the man.

I was the man there in this film with you fifty years ago. There we were in a different place and different time together.

Together. Somehow.

Although neither one of us was smiling, the expression upon both of our faces gave no indication that our presence there together was a surprise to us.

I then turned to face you and enveloped you in my arms as you continued to hold out the egg. You leaned to the side with the egg still held in front of both of us between the index finger and the thumb of your right hand while you brought your other arm around my back.

I hovered over you as I cradled the back of your head in my hands. We kissed each other so slow and deep at first but then I grabbed you behind your shoulders and thrust my mouth more forcefully against yours. You brought the egg and your hand to my back as you met the intensity of my kiss and embrace.

Then with a mere flip of the wrist, you spun the egg from your fingertip and thumb before you seized my back with both hands.

The brown egg hung spinning in the air for a moment until the hand of my friend – the cameraman – popped into view and the camera jostled out of focus. By the time the camera lens found us again, we are wildly kissing with our lips apart and your tongue finding mine within our merged mouths as we tore at each other with our arms and hands. We coupled ourselves together like this until I abruptly pulled my mouth from yours and we both turned to face the camera while still in each other's arms.

We both smiled at my friend before I lifted you up by your thighs and you straddled me tight. With you in my clutch, I launched in one upward thrust, and we vanished from sight in a swirl of sparkling vapor trails as the rest of the group of people in the film continued their gathering like we had never even been there at all.

I know this will seem as impossible to you as it did to me. But it happened, and it's filmed. You will see it because I'm giving all of this to you. Ultimately, it's yours to do with what you will because all of this is nothing if not a surreal romance between otherworldly soulmates, angelic by nature but trapped in a world that seems intent upon keeping us hopelessly apart for earthly reasons.

So once again, do with all of this what you will, but I've also contacted someone who has been the most vital part of my literary life to this point and can help you decide what you would like to do with the book aspect of this brown egg *Eqqsquisite Corpse*.

I call this person "Anima" because of her expertise in Jungian psychology and her role in my own understanding of the anima archetype that is the innate filter through which I interact with women. I've known her for over thirty-five years, and she has worked with me on virtually all of my extended literary projects. She knows me perhaps even better than I know myself, except for this new angelic side I now seem to own.

I have already contacted her for this reason: if I should become incapacitated or die from the results of what I'm on the verge of doing, I would like for you two to work together if you agree to see that this literary odyssey I've started should continue without me. That may mean that you will have to become not only the spokesperson for this work but its copyrighted author, and she will be the editor of the project for all intents and purposes of establishing author identity behind the work as well as guide it through all of its stages through other media production, if that should happen.

I know this may all seem nuts, but trust me about this part of it. You might have an opportunity awaiting you that will never present itself again. Once this flight goes, it's gone for good, and you're either on it or you're watching from the ground as it climbs through the sky and hurtles beyond this world.

The last part of our surreal romance here is about the contents of the refrigerated box, which you have probably guessed by now contains the very same egg from fifty years ago that you held in the film. At least, my friend states that it is the same egg in the note that he included inside of the box.

So just know this: I'm consumed by my love for you and I don't really know why. It seems like there really is something larger than us at work between us that has brought us together, but I have no real idea what all of this means or if we'll ever be together in any way.

Clearly, we have other obligations to other people and other purposes, but those can't be enough to contain us from what presents itself now as the everlasting romance of our very souls.

So just know that I loved you to the utmost of my comprehension of the word, if I do not survive my cosmic egg outcome.

But you will have to decide what to do with our love if I do survive this.

And if I do survive, I really do pray that you will want to see me half as much as I want to see you and that you will want to spend time together with me to start our conscious journey together through this eternity made just for us. If I had my way, that time together and our love for each other would be so strong and real that it would transfigure both of us together into eternity itself. We would both radiate all light all of the time.

The last part of this book is now being written at our bench. I have the egg in front of me now. I have taken a photo of it with my phone, which I will also leave for you here. I am checking periodically to make sure you haven't called to cancel our meeting because that would dash all of this, but once I crack the encasing around the egg, I may not be able to check my phone again.

The entirety of this manuscript ends here in the next few paragraphs for now. I have advised Anima that there is one more part that should be written if you decide to collaborate with her. One of her Jungian specialties is the study of death and dying issues. She has interacted with hundreds of people in the various stages of the dying process. I hope to find her somewhere in the nebula of her own particular brand of otherworld interaction if my fate does indeed entail my death.

Should I not return, I have advised her – pending your agreement – quite simply to collaborate with you for this final part of the book, which should detail a conversation between her and me about this book and what has happened to me as a result of this egg I am about to eat.

The fifth part should also depict exchanges between me and the other deceased people presented in the book, namely my friends the author and Brown Eggs. These exchanges should be guided by the presence and intervention of Anima because of her overall familiarity with a Jungian perspective, but I would like for you to author all of these exchanges based upon your gleaning from this manuscript and your discussions with Anima.

Lastly, the fifth part should conclude with you and me talking to each other. At that point, the future that awaits us both will be known, and the true ending of the book can reveal itself for us to write together or for you and Anima to pair up without me.

Just so there's a record of how all of this was presented to you, I'll list what you already know for future reference whether it's just for you, just for me, or for both of us.

1. The nine cursive-written pages paper clipped to the printed copy of the manuscript comprise my final entry for the book before I consumed the egg. I have written across the top of the first page in underlined red marker that these pages must be read first by you even though it is the end of the book as far as I know. These nine pages address you directly and are the only time in the book that you are addressed in this way.

2. At the bottom of the last of these handwritten pages is Anima's name and phone number. She will be there for you to answer any questions you may have and help you through all of this.

3. The letter written by my friend and the DVD that shows you and me together fifty years ago during the Salvador Dali performance are both in the padded envelope that I placed beneath the manuscript.

4. The box in which the egg was shipped now contains only the clods of material that had formed the encasing for the half-century old brown egg.

5. All of this is given in the spirit of my truest of true love

for you. The last thing I would wish for on this earth is to cause you any undue anything. Please forgive me if I do cause you any grief or hurt because I would rather be dead than to see you suffer any turmoil. I consider you to be my soulmate, regardless if you never do believe it and our union together never does happen.

It is now an hour before we are scheduled to meet. The egg is open, revealing nothing but black inky, rank ooze. I am about to dip my fingers into this primordial rot and lick it from my fingertips. I'm almost positive that it won't be sweet as honey like the little scroll of Revelation, but I'm guessing the ache I get afterwards is going to be a whole lot worse.

Collaboration 5
Brown Egg Revival

———

July 4th, 2016
Florence, Kentucky

———

"YOU COULDN'T WAIT, COULD YOU?" the woman leaned over him and asked once she saw his eyelids flutter open.

"Where am I?" he asked, oblivious to her question.

"Anywhere you go, there you are," the woman replied. "So, what difference does it really make where you are?"

"I'd like to know all the same," he said as he looked at her then to the surface above him. "What is that?"

"That's a table, Sunshine," she answered. "You're lying on a floor underneath a table in a bar of your own imagination."

"Where am I?" he yelled.

"Well, let's see," she said then paused. "I'd say you're somewhere in your own deluded version of heaven."

He struggled to lean to his side and shifted his weight beneath him before he attempted to crawl from underneath the table. Once he had cleared himself from beneath it, he remained lying on the floor but tilted his head up to look at the woman, who he had grown to call "Anima" over the course of the thirty-five years the two had known each other.

"Looks like you're going to have to save my hide once again, Anima," he muttered. "At least you got me to some kind of version of Heaven."

"I hope you like what you've selected," she said. "As your perception of your designated other, better half, I really am only here to try to help you restore yourself so that you are ultimately whole and no longer in need of any external source for your own peace of mind."

"It's good to know you're in my corner," he sighed.

"Allies are good," she nodded in agreement. "But you do have to understand the depth of your particular predicament this time because it is far more precarious than we've encountered before.

"You think you're in Heaven with a capital 'H', but the truth is that you're closer to turning your version of Self into Hell with a capital 'H'!"

"Dear Jesus!" he trembled aloud. "What have I done?"

"You really might be better off praying to Jesus," she told him, "because I'm not sure a theoretical partner like myself can unequivocally rescue your wretched, shadow self this time. You've really mucked things up. Jesus sure would be a whole lot easier for you now.

"But there is some hope. You do understand that the actual encounter with your anima is the masterpiece of individual development. You just have to reemerge intact and in some ways wiser for the debacle you've caused."

"That's all good and well," he managed. "But I can't change who I am now. And I can't part from Sirena. She's part angel and out of your jurisdiction because of it."

"That's what I mean when I said you've really mucked things up," was her retort.

He sat beside the table now, feeling the throb of blood ebb and flow within his head and chest. He panted as he tried to focus on her face. Shortness of breath gripped him while he waited for his light-headedness to pass.

"I ate the egg and died?" he finally asked.

"That remains to be seen," she told him. "But you still didn't answer my initial question: Why didn't you wait for Sirena to arrive at the park so she could be there with you when you ate the egg?"

"I don't know," he wheezed. "Why should I have waited?"

"You have no idea the sheer horror you've put that poor woman through," she explained. "She had absolutely no idea what was going on when she arrived and saw you lying in a pool of your own vomit and the blood gushing out of your split scalp from the fall after you collapsed.

"She called 911 immediately before she did anything else, but for her to have to put up with your ridiculously selfish act is something I think she will have a very hard time ever forgiving you for."

"Is she okay?" he nearly cried.

"She told me she's fine physically when she called me," Anima answered. "But she was terrified by what she saw, and she's probably going to be livid once she truly understands what a crucial part of your design she has unwittingly been."

"What about what I wrote to her?" he asked. "Dear God, tell me she read what I wrote to her!"

"She read it all right," she informed him. "But not until she tried to resuscitate you. Can you imagine her doing that for you while you're lying there unconscious from your own self-inflicted delusion to make Sirena all yours? She can't like you very much at all right now. Do you understand what I'm telling you?"

"I don't know what I was really thinking," he admitted to her as he pressed his palms against his temples. "All I know is I love her with such thoroughly consuming force that I have no doubt that she is my one true soulmate."

"Love and soulmate?" she asked. "This soulmate love you profess for Sirena sounds more like physical attraction to me than anything else. You mistake your feelings for her as love. I get that you are ultimately trying to recapture the intensity of lovers' love through her, but it's like catching lightning in a bottle."

"Great," he muttered.

"You can't force the reality of love like that," she resumed. "That's not how it works. You've gotten hooked on phenylethylamine, norepinephrine, and dopamine, is all. Perfectly natural, and a delightful ride until the horse ends up riding you instead of you riding the horse.

"Eating that egg smacks of the desperation that you felt you had to exercise in order to guarantee a relationship that you were too scared wouldn't happen otherwise."

"I love Sirena," he claimed.

"All of your interactions with women should be spirited through me by now," she continued, "so that you can avoid such a regression like this. You must understand your perception of women through me is what makes you complete, not an external attraction to a woman like Sirena. You have ruptured through all levels of understanding the anima – physical, intellectual, spiritual, and cosmic – with a most unfortunate result."

"Maybe so," he replied, after exhaling a deep breath. "But like I said, she's only half human. Your control over my mind isn't strong enough this time to overpower the bond I have with her."

"Perhaps all you really see is the reflection of a familiar mirror," she countered. "Only instead of seeing a Narcissistic view in the reflection, you've decided to project the persona of a rather dubious archangel named Uriel upon your perception of her."

"I'm afraid there's much more than reflection or projection involved this time," he resumed as he gripped the top of his throbbing head with both hands. "Sirena and I together contain the perfect unity of two souls yearning for bliss aligned forever."

"What in that egg-poisoned brain of yours would make you believe that this poor woman loves you or could ever love you?" she asked him. "Especially after this harebrained stunt you just pulled?

"And why on earth would you think that somehow your version of God would condone your union with such cosmic approval of your delusion? I think that all you're really interested in doing is planning to commit adultery with a woman who you decided was going to mesmerize you without any intent on her part."

"Maybe your right," he conceded as he removed his hands from his head. "But the film, the meetings, her voice, the way she is with me when we're together, everything makes me believe we're destined for an eternity together or at least the remainder of this lifetime."

"Your belief in destiny is also a delusion," she countered. "This is all the delusion of your own doing. You have so successfully induced an altered state of mind that you've quite clearly deteriorated into a condition of clinical insanity. This paranoid critical method that you've borrowed from Salvador Dali has just led you to your own mental disintegration and perhaps your physical demise."

"You mean I'm crazy and almost dead?" he asked her.

"Crazier than a loon," she laughed. "And clinging to life by a thread.

"At this point, I consider you a mental patient for my purposes here, not a friend or your anima in the flesh, as it were. You've created such powerful archetypical material in your recent undertakings with such deep hermetical and Gnostic parallels that you have divorced yourself from any remote recognition of everyday life or functional setting."

"Thank God I'm just crazy then," he blurted. "For a while, I thought I was right about all of this, and that I really am the archangel Uriel and she is a half-human, half-angel hybrid Siren."

"Well," she began. "I never exactly said you were wrong about anything in particular. I just said you are crazy.

"The funny thing about delusions is that sometimes our beliefs prove to be the actual truth for us even if the facts and all rational argument completely point to the fallacy of a belief or perception of reality. We can actually become what we believe."

"What are you talking about?" he barked at her. "Either I'm crazy and wrong about everything or I'm sane and right about what is essentially the nature of this reality we exist within and my purpose in it with Sirena! How can it be any other way? How can I believe both at the same time?"

"That all remains to be seen," she sighed. "The only real issue for you now is whether you're going to physically live. She did what she could for you at the scene of your egg soufflé mishap. I do believe that she helped you survive long enough to at least make it to the hospital.

"Now I will tell you that she did read what you wrote her, the handwritten pages that addressed her directly, as well as most of the book at this point, I believe."

"Good," he groaned. "I did all of that for her."

"Well, like I said, she's not at all happy about the way you used her without her knowledge and certainly without her permission or expressed cooperation," she informed him. "She's actually quite pissed off and hurt that you wrote about her the way you did and that you included her writing in your text. She was aghast to learn how truly lasciviously you conveyed your feelings for her, even if you did so largely through innuendo and through the guise of some larger purpose and connection with her."

"But I had to make sure she knows how I truly feel about her!" he interjected. "And the purpose is higher! The DVD and the letter clearly show that the ordained union between us far exceeds any physical craving I might have for her!"

"That ordained part is also delusional," Anima countered. "Don't be too traumatized if it turns out that there was a trickster involved in all of this. Said Trickster, with a capital 'T', would be one with a hellacious sense of humor at your earthly expense.

"But she hasn't had the chance to decide for herself either way because the last time I talked with her she told me that she was afraid to watch the DVD. She gave it to me, and I watched it. Then I gave it back to her. She has it now but said she hasn't watched it yet."

"But she has to see what I mean!" he pleaded aloud. "If she doesn't watch it, she'll never fully understand or appreciate that we are destined for each other for eternity! There's just no earthly way possible that all of this isn't real and true. No way! We were meant for each other for eternity!"

"Please pipe down already about all of the eternity stuff!" she implored in return. "Neither you nor I can know about eternity until it comes to pass.

"In my anima expert opinion, it still looks more like you just want to get in her pants more than anything else. I know how powerful the film is and what mind-boggling implications it has, but I also know how you are. You really are nothing more than just another man who lusts women. That libido of yours is truly astounding! Maybe you do genuinely like women as people and appreciate them a little more than most men do, but the bottom line is that your first and strongest level of perception when it comes to an attractive woman is your immediate physical gravitation toward her and your invariable lust for her."

"That would trivialize the rest of this," he begged to differ. "That might be partly true, but there has to be more to it than just me wanting to make physical love to her, too.

"No. All of this now has a life of its very own. I'm just the medium at this point."

"I can grant you that much about the medium part for sure," she agreed. "You do understand that at the very least she's your muse. All of your prolific literary output resulted directly from her infusion into your life. Without her, you're not here right now, and you definitely don't have the manuscript you've cobbled together through this whole surrealist *Eqqsquisite Corpse* endeavor of yours."

"I just can't reduce her to a mere muse," he said. "She means much more to me than that."

"You mean like a half-human, half-angelic Siren?" she teased him in return. "And one that has descended from some Atlantis Hall of Records race that can't possibly be proven and even if it could be proven would sound even more ludicrous to most people than saying the earth is only six-thousand years old?"

"I really don't care at all how old the earth is, for starters," he snapped back at her. "The only reason I would even think about the age of the earth is because the case is made for that age in the Bible and some people believe it."

"The Bible or the BlahBlah," she said while making a talking gesture with her hand. "You're really an old enough of a soul by now to know better. At its most metaphysical, the Bible is an allegory of the interaction between the ego and the Self. Don't get me wrong; the Bible is a powerful piece of work, but the pseudoscience required to authenticate it is truly delusional. You know that."

"I'm not sure what I know," he began to counter her bias toward the Bible. "Say what you will, but all I know is that a literal interpretation of the Bible can literally save someone's life and their soul, especially the New Testament and the teachings of Jesus."

"Body and soul safe!" she boomed as she gestured like an umpire signaling a sliding base runner safe at a base in a baseball game. "What do you really know about a soul? I've seen the life leave hundreds of people and have yet to have any one of those lives visibly or otherwise indicate that there is anything that lingers after death that could be considered a soul with a consciousness that continues past the individual expiration date of their earthbound bodies.

"The collective unconscious endures just the same, but the personal psyche seems to pretty much crap itself out of existence. It's just a simple matter of biology. Sorry."

"Perhaps you are right, Anima" he replied, rubbing his eyes. "But I would like to hear that from someone other than you. Can you summons someone for me who might have a different opinion?"

"Let me just snap my otherworldly fingers and with a magic crack," she giggled with a snap, "let's see who arrives."

"Really?" he glared at her. "Shouldn't be a problem for such a Jungian Buddhist as yourself, should it?"

"Just close your eyes, now," she smiled as she wagged her finger at him. "And close your holy-moly mouth. How about we go to an island with a beach full of guilt? You can make your Hermetic castles for the surf of your own delusion to wash away, if you wish."

"That sounds like a boatload of joy," came his sardonic reply once he clenched his eyes shut.

"Keep your mouth shut, but you can open your eyes now," she advised him after she snapped her fingers again.

When he did reopen his eyes, he saw nothing but blue sky above him. He then lifted his head from a pillow of sand to find himself on

Mosquito Point Beach in the community where his author friend had lived.

He grappled to lift himself to his feet then noticed a large bird – either an eagle or an osprey – hover high above the middle of the river. Suddenly, the raptor dropped like an earthbound missile, revealing itself as an osprey. When its speed of fall peaked, it ripped head first into the river. He waited for the bird to surface for what seemed to be far too long of a time, but it didn't reappear.

Instead he was treated to the sight of the hoary head of his recently deceased author friend surface first before he fully emerged. He wore a wet white t-shirt clinging to his thin frame and jean shorts as he waded through the shallows to reach the beach.

"I can speak to you again like I know who on earth you are," his friend bellowed as he stepped across the sand to reach him. "Other than when I spoke to you at the Hall of Records aquifer site, it seems like the last couple of times I saw you I had no idea who I was or who you were."

"I'm not so convinced that you didn't know who I was or what was going on around you at all times," he said to his friend. "Seems to me that you were actually orchestrating quite a symphony of moving parts with the reenactment of Salvador Dali's resurrection performance."

"Perhaps," his friend conceded before the two of them shook hands. "But I can assure you my wits were wasted overall at the time."

"I really never knew what to completely make out of you when you were alive," he admitted. "And I know even less about what to think about you now that you're dead."

"Dead relatively speaking," his friend corrected. "It's all about the frame of reference. I've come to understand that our resurrection is the sole means for our soul to traverse by astral flight the dimensions that await us after our physical deaths."

"Well, there's a lot of that going around," he replied. "So much of it that I have to wonder how much does any of that really even matter anymore. I mean, your whole point in the letter you wrote was that you needed me to eat the egg in order for you to become an angel. I'm getting to the point where I'd probably be as content to die and have that just be the end of it all.

"But then there's the woman in the film there to keep me wanting more life. Her name is Sirena, and I've fallen madly in love with her, I fear."

"It is quite a fascinating dynamic," his friend returned. "When I realized that you were the man in the film I shot fifty years ago, I was astounded by the possibilities that such an impossible event entailed, and that intrigue is compounded for me now by the fact that you've discovered the woman with you all those years ago and now are together."

"I'm pretty much fascinated by it all, too," he added. "I'm so fascinated by all of this mess in fact that apparently I've killed myself in some kind of half-assed suicide attempt."

"I wouldn't say that you've killed yourself just yet," his friend countered. "You still might recover from your condition, and if you do, then what?"

"Well," he began. "Like I just said, I'm so utterly in love with the woman Sirena who you filmed holding the egg that I can't even think straight any more, brown egg or no brown egg.

"I've known her for a few years now and have been meeting with her during the past couple weeks for in-depth discussions about writing. I was really on the verge of losing my mind before I ate the egg, but now, all the rest of this existence just seems like an unnecessary formality if I can't be with her."

"Really?" came his friend's voice. "That's sounds like it has all the makings of a psychological thriller and surreal romance, especially if she really is Nephilim."

"I'm really not sure what to think about her divine nature or our interaction," came his reply. "On the whole, none of this gives me a very good feeling. I'm chronically lovesick about her, and she has no idea how hopelessly in love I am with her. I consider her to be my soulmate, but I have my doubts that she even remotely considers me in any like vein. Even if she did feel the same way, we would be destroying the lives of other people for whom we care a great deal."

"I'm very sorry to hear that part about your perception of unrequited love," his friend tried to console him. "But I do know this: you are destined to be together with her for all eternity at some point. Any earthly fallout from that is merely incidental. All others will eventually forgive you both.

"You are the living incarnation of the archangel Uriel, even though you can't understand that or apply your powers at this stage leading up to your transfiguration. She is a Siren, an enchanting hybrid of divine and human mix who is truly one of the loveliest creatures on the face of the earth."

"It sounds like you're going to confirm all of this insanity about her and me?" he probed. "How can you say for sure that her nature and mine are truly what you say they are?"

"This is where your transfiguration answers all of your questions for you," he explained. "You have absolutely no inkling how powerful you will become once you transcend the limits of your own current understanding of yourself and your situation.

"The self you saw on the film from fifty years ago wasn't just your doppelganger or spirit double if you will. It was one of the most powerful entities ever known in the universe."

"Great," he muttered with a wince. "Right now, I'm losing sleep, losing weight, losing my mind and now maybe even losing my life because of all of this disruption over everything from Sirena and Salvador Dali performances to subterranean passages that lead to some kind of delusion about a time-immemorial Hall of Records."

"Well, the Hall of Records is very real," my friend remarked. "But probably not as what may be perceived as a structure containing documents or other artifacts that describe and relate the secrets of a lost civilization that no one can find any trace of."

"What do you mean?" he asked with a puzzled look.

"Well," his friend began to explain. "The Hall of Records is most likely a physical portal to an intra-dimensional process or rite of passage through which individual consciousness traverses by virtue of the power of awakening to the true nature of the inner self and our eternal identity that exceeds our bodily form. The end result of real-ization is more like immersion into the celestial Akashic Record that Cayce expounded upon through trance."

"And that all undoubtedly has to get back to the angels, the saints, the sirens, and the hybrids," he said through a prolonged sigh. "This is exactly what Sirena said to me at the well site where you also heard her. She said I would eat the scroll and become the messenger in flesh of the revelation from the Hall of Records."

"You are what you eat, in that case," my friend confirmed. "This is how you will know who you are because you will remember who you were. Once that happens, as I have said, your individual power will be so awesome on the angelic scale that you will instantly regain the eminent domain you commanded before you chose to wear human form."

"So, again," he sighed loudly this time as he grabbed the top of his head. "I'm not really a human at all, Sirena is my soulmate, and together we will actualize ancient prophecy that will restore some kind of pre-Biblical order befitting a mighty archangel like me and quite possibly also usher in the Tribulation and the Rapture."

"Think of it like this," my friend offered. "You and she are ordained to be together, and once you fulfill this destiny, then the very universe itself will resonate with a harmonic convergence that can actualize the redemption of the lost civilization that preceded this one. Then the angels and the humans will be unified again with a much more harmonious outcome and that readies the path for the Rapture.

"You two won't be the cause or end fulfillment of the Rapture because that will only come with the second coming of the Messiah, but it will be a cleansing of souls whose divine natures will soar to meet the omnipotence of all creation and existence."

"And all I have to do is lay my hands on this woman, or half-woman and half-angel, rather?" he asked.

"Yes," he confirmed. "And you will bear a child together, but not an earthly or an angelic child. Rather, the consummation of your union will be a radiant energy so pure and complete that the two of you will glow in the glory of your transfiguration together even as you travel this world and beyond in your resurrected state of your celestial incarnation."

"That sounds just lovely," he replied. "But will we still be bound to an earthly body?"

"Yes and no," he seemingly contradicted himself. "You will be a human in physical form who will be subjected to all of the physical features of bodily existence, but your spiritual being will be so empowered that you will no longer gauge your life in full by the navigation of your physical form through this world. You will be able to shift in and out of your materialized self in an ongoing cycle of psychogenesis that will allow you to live like a doppelganger without the constraints of time and space."

"So that's how I end up in a film from fifty years ago?" he asked.

"Exactly," his friend replied. "Remember, you are a celestial being – an archangel. So, start acting like one."

"Well," he said as he clapped his hands together once. "That sounds like a wrap to me. I certainly like this delusion you've helped me to create."

"Be that as it may," his friend said. "You still have to stay alive for now or else none of that can happen."

"I'm going to do my utmost to survive the effects of the fifty-year-old egg or whatever it was that you advised me to eat," he promised.

"And I will be eternally grateful if you do," his friend chimed with a grin. "Your consumption of the fifty-year-old brown egg fulfills the first part of the reenactment described in the Book of Revelation when the apostle John eats the little scroll given to him by the mighty angel with one foot on land and one foot on sea."

"And if I survive that revelation reenactment," he ventured, "I get the girl of my dreams. I honestly am more interested in having her with me forever than I am interested in anything else."

"Maybe so, but there's much more to it than just you having her," he replied. "By virtue of your survival and consummation with her, you become the angel who provided the scroll to John. You become Uriel once again.

"That consumption so internalizes the resurrection message and prophecy of the Rapture that is forthcoming afterwards that the course of world events is altered by the reality you will be bound to project of its own accord, and for me personally, if you succeed in your surreal romance with your soulmate, I shall complete my own resurrection and gain my own wings, so to speak."

"Glad to help," he chimed in return with a wider grin than his friend's. "And I do want to tell you, whether you or I are real or not now, that you were the single-most fascinating person that I ever got to know and for that I too am eternally grateful."

"You are most certainly welcome," his friend replied. "It's always a blessing to have a friend who is equally as intelligent and capable of comprehending complicated subject matter."

"There's one other thing I want to say to you now that you are like I remember you before your mind turned to mush," he informed his friend. "I'm sorry I couldn't have done more to help you. I feel like I have forsaken you by not keeping in contact with you before it became too late."

"No need for an apology," his friend reassured him. "What we have to remember most about the interaction we humans have with one another, especially those with whom we grow closest and share a genuine affinity that has depth and substance, is that every minute we can enjoy together is a blessing that glorifies the true nature of ourselves and God. In Jesus' name, I pray."

"Adieu, my friend," he bid before he extended his hand for his friend to shake.

The two released their handshake before they flashed one final smile at each other. His friend then turned upon the shimmering sand to return to the water. He watched his friend wade through the shallows before his hoary head vanished beneath the surface.

He wept as he kept his eyes focused on the spot in the river where his friend had submerged, but his sorrow halted when the osprey exploded through the surface and launched skyward. He watched the osprey flap its massive wings faster as the raptor faded faster and farther into the spotless azure above until finally the bird reached its vanishing point and surpassed his vision.

"Goodbye, my friend," he said with a wave of his hand toward the point where the osprey vanished.

"And hello again," came the voice of Anima. "You certainly created a much lovelier setting for an afterlife interaction to take place this time around. I couldn't have picked a more splendid place myself. How much do those houses down the beach here go for?"

"Glad you approve, Anima," he said. "If this place on the Rappa-hannock River and Northern Neck Peninsula was good enough for Captain John Smith to say that heaven and earth never agreed better for man's habitation, then it's good enough for me to choose as a setting for heaven, or at least a stopover, I guess."

"I do have some good news for you," she said. "You see, these afterlife interactions of yours take quite a bit more time than the normal human time frame, so it allows me to get some work done behind the scenes while you fall all over yourself about your angelic aspirations and sexual conquests.

"In the meantime, I've managed to make sure that the soulmate you so yearn for has agreed to watch the DVD of her brown egg proclamation."

"That's great!" he cried. "Now maybe this party of ours can get started because I just absolutely can't wait to get my hands on her for keeps."

"Well, hold on to your halo party hat there, angel boy," she cautioned. "Just because she's going to watch herself in action fifty years ago with you swooping in by her side to whisk her away to your own little rendezvous love nest doesn't mean she's going to be willing to go just yet."

"Why not?" he nearly shrieked at her. "She'll see for sure that we are meant to be together, won't she?"

"I doubt it," she answered. "This whole sordid mess is probably just going to scare her shitless, especially when she sees just how far you were going in your unabashed attempt to seduce her."

"Please give me some credit!" he protested. "This is a surreal romance! She's got to appreciate that all of this is just for her because she's the only one I really want to read it anyway. Surely she'll see that all of this is really only written directly for her to read like one long novelized love letter."

"Or one pathetically porous suicide note," she countered. "If you do survive your little Revelation quest with the egg and this doesn't end the way you hope, you are going to be so devastated that I'm afraid you won't be able to function at all any longer."

"That would probably serve me right," he remarked. "But I've never wanted to be with anyone more in my life than I want to be with her. I have absorbed everything about her, and now my osmosis of her is complete and beyond my will or ability to reverse. I never told her all of this directly but if she read what I wrote to her, she will understand."

"That probably *would* serve you right, if you end up incapacitated over this" she concurred. "All you've really done with her is internalize her. She's not a real person to you, but, rather, a ridiculously mythical creature like a unicorn to you now – or some circus half-woman, half-angel Nephilim Siren. She is a fantasy for you, nothing more."

"Maybe she embodies everything at the collective unconscious level that a woman should," he countered. "Maybe she's just that beautiful and powerful in every sense, physically, intellectually, spiritually and cosmically – a living, breathing goddess on earth for whom I was sent here to worship.

"Maybe she really is the masterpiece I was destined to meet so that we can merge together and complete us, whoever or whatever I am or she is."

"I don't know about the leap to goddess worship," Anima countered. "That sounds like more of a complex for you than an archetype. Besides, she actually does seem a little bit on the superficial side to me, but if that's what turns you on, it's your delusion.

"But I think it's time for you to consult with another one of your collaborators who actually did want to be with you more than anyone else in her life but never told you that or wrote about it to you."

"You're kidding me?" he muttered. "That's the last trip I need laid on me right now."

"To the contrary," she differed. "I think it's exactly what you need to hear for several reasons, with the primary one being that you had better brace yourself for what's coming if you can't summons enough of your angelic Uriel superpowers to seduce that married girlfriend of yours."

"I really don't want to have to do this," he protested. "I'd rather go back to my body now and just die if I have to die."

"Very well," she pretended to relent to him. "Close your eyes, and your wish is my command."

He closed his eyes with the expectation that he would be returned to whatever his physical condition truly was. When he opened his eyes, he blinked to try to recognize where he was in the low light of a dirt-floored, roofed enclosure and who it was seated across from him because the flesh of the ghoulish face was swollen and corroded with greenish cast to its leathery skin, as if the face had rotted then hardened.

"How are you, Jam?" asked the voice from the ghastly face. "It's been a long time."

"Brown Eggs," he gasped. "What has happened to you?"

"Don't let looks be deceiving," she voiced. "I have found my way to eternal bliss. It hasn't been easy, but it has finally happened. I had to fulfill one final pact to complete my resurrection, but my disembodied voice heard in this very well house by my own daughter has set me free, Jam."

"So that's where we are," he breathed aloud. "We are where the disembodied voices were heard after my friend's funeral."

"Yes," she confirmed. "And only those whose love was the purest for us could hear our voices."

"So that's why I heard Sirena sing and talk even though I didn't know it was her at the time," he surmised aloud.

"That's right," she replied. "And that's why only my daughter could hear me but not you or even my own sons. Her love was the purest for me."

"I'm sorry," his voice shook. "I just never felt anything like romantic or pure love toward you, I suppose."

"That's all right, Jam," she soothingly said. "You were there for me when it counted most, or rather, I should say that you will be there for me when it matters most."

"What do you mean?" he asked, perplexed by her assertion.

"I mean that you are about to undergo your first stage of transfiguration," she explained. "Your woman-angel told me before she spoke and sang to you at this very well site that for you to make your way through the Hall of Records passage to Atlantis for your transfiguration to start, you have to take me with you so that I can be resurrected.

"That will officially be your first trip back into time, then you will be with me at the end of my life, just like my children told you."

"I'm sorry, Brown Eggs, but I would have no earthly idea how to accomplish that," he admitted.

"It starts with the kiss I never got," she informed him, as her rotten face contorted to show a mouthful of yellowish brown teeth. "A kiss right on the mouth."

"Why not," he muttered as he stepped toward her and leaned forward. "I just ate a fifty-year-old egg that killed me. How much worse can it get?"

He closed his eyes before he puckered his lips to meet her open mouth. She slipped her tongue between his lips, and he met her tongue with his. He placed his hands on her shoulders and stopped breathing to lessen the stench as she gripped his forearms. The two continued to kiss until she finally pulled her tongue and mouth from his.

"I owed you at least that much," he said to her with his eyes still shut.

"Oh, that's just the start of what you're going to do for me now, Jam," she replied. "Open your eyes."

"Wow!" he exclaimed when he opened his eyes to see the Brown Eggs he remembered, full-cheeked and flush with a smirk smeared across her face. "You're back!"

"Thank you for that, Jam," she started to sob. "That just meant the world to me."

"I'm so sorry that I just left you there to die," he managed to tell her before his voice started to crack. "I never meant to make things worse for you by not being there with you when you probably needed me most."

The two then wept together as he took her hands at first then bent over her to hug her. He buried his contorted face against her neck as her chest heaved back and forth and her sobs blared. The two maintained their embrace until the floor itself started to quake. Soon, the surface gave way beneath them and they dropped, releasing each other as they screamed and plunged into unseen darkness.

At the end of their surprise plummet, the two splashed into water, instantly tumbling together through rapids that hurtled them beneath the surface. They clung to each other, their screams muffled by the churning effervescence as they sloshed through darkness.

It wasn't until he realized that the terrifying barrage wasn't going to stop that he suddenly restored calm within himself. Just as he collected her in his arms and gathered her to his chest, he felt unexpected power surge through him.

He realized now that he was with her in the underwater passage leading to the Yucatan Hall of Records. He would take her to the

Sargasso Sea as the Virginia eels shimmied past. He would lead her through the Bermuda Triangle and to the submerged site of Atlantis. He guided her through the journey that her children had described to him when he visited his friend in Virginia. He now knew that this was the passage her children said their mother had half-consciously described to them in the hospice room. He was doing now what had already happened. He had traveled back into time. He had attained his anamnesis of the archangel Uriel.

The electricity then expanded him as he shot from the water and darkness with Brown Eggs in his arms and jettisoned through kaleidoscopic light that thrummed and crackled. The light flashed rapidly before detonating into glaring heat that screeched more shrilly with each disintegrating second.

Then finally all of it stopped, and he released her to the hospital bed where her body lay. She merged into it, wide eyed as she shuddered in her reunion with her body. She then opened her real eyes and looked at him.

"Tell me," she wheezed. "That I can finally be at peace now. That the whole creation, the revelation, the salvation, all that is glorious and good lives inside of me forever."

He turned from her to observe her three children seated along the wall beside the bed. They all shifted to the edge of their chairs to listen to their mother. He understood now that his time travel had brought him where she was dying in hospice care from her cruel affliction.

"All of the afterlife mysteries are now yours," he told her. "The beauty of the angels, the courage of the saints, and the eternal life promised by belief in the resurrection religion, they are all yours now for you to finally free yourself from the bondage that has caused you such heartbreak."

"The angels, the saints, the resurrection," she repeated, smiling and staring at the ceiling above through her glazed eyes.

"This was the true wisdom kept in the Hall of Records," he continued. "This was the ancient knowledge beheld by those who came before the world we know today. The angels and the humans together in harmony until the corruption and disease of the soul led to the wrath that destroyed it all and buried it where no one will ever uncover it."

"The angels and the humans," she wheezed. "We are together again. We live."

He was now about to witness the final scene that her children told him about. Brown Eggs was about to die, but first he would sing the lyrics to his song, "Die Laughing," that Brown Eggs sang right before her last breath. He told her to repeat after him in such a manner that he half-laughed and half-sang. He vocalized each of the lines in this manner beginning with "Shaken up, but it's OK." and ending with the final line of the song – "But I know I want to die laughing."

After the two had finished the lyrics, she had mimicked the exact same laughter that he produced for her. The two of them laughed together in this way, but in the end, she died with her last gasped laugh. When her daughter had described the account of this to him in Virginia, she had beamed when she told him that her mother talked with him for several minutes prior to singing his song and dying in laughter.

But he saw for the first time what her children didn't describe: the moment of her death and the immediate aftermath for her children. With her last gasped laugh, she coughed once before her neck straightened and tightened. She shuddered one last time before a final twitch of her arms marked her departure from the world of her body. Her children jumped to her side when they saw her head slump to the side as her eyes remained open.

"No, Mama!" her daughter cried. "No! No! No! Please don't go! Don't leave us!"

"She's not leaving us," her older son managed through his tears. "She's making the way for us to follow."

As the three children sobbed and clung to the shell of their mother, he watched her spirit rise from the flesh, floating above it as though it were an entirely separate whole person. The spirit body then straightened and descended until its apparitional feet contacted the floor.

"I know there were other times when we talked here," he told her. "I will return to your past when I am fully restored to guide you again so that you can be comforted and your children can also marvel at their mother in her conversation with the angel here to help her in her death and resurrection."

"Bless you for what you've done for me, Jam," she thanked him. "Now, close your eyes and go to her. Your angel awaits you. I know she does."

"Bless you, too, Brown Eggs, for all you've done for me," he said to her before he clenched his eyes shut.

He waited to lunge from the space he had entered but nothing happened. He kept his eyes closed as he backed away from the location where he knew Brown Eggs had been standing. He crouched slightly as if to spring, but still nothing happened.

July 6, 2016
Florence, Kentucky

"NOT SO FAST," came the voice of Anima. "Sooner or later you're bound to recognize that I'm the only one who is really here, but why burst your bubble now?"

"What do you mean, you're the only one here?" he asked in return with his eyes still shut. "This has to be real enough to be true, doesn't it?"

"Open your eyes and find out for yourself," she told him.

He opened his eyes to see Anima leaning over him. He realized he was lying in a hospital bed.

"Why this?" he asked her. "Am I really in a hospital?"

"Yes, you are. Intensive care, in fact," she confirmed. "And what a stay you've had. It's been a week now, and you've been in and out of consciousness for the past few days. Congratulations for that.

"Your lovely wife already visited earlier today when you were zonked out again, but I'll let her know you're conscious again. The staff will want to have a look at you soon, too, if you can stay awake long enough."

"Don't call anyone to see me yet," he entreated her as he strained to prop himself on his elbows. "I just want to know about Sirena right now, and if I'm ready to resume my transfiguration with her so we can travel together back into time fifty years from now."

"Really now, you feel up to the sheer exertion of time travel?" she laughed. "You don't have enough strength to do any time-travelling jumping jacks just yet. Plus, you're delusionary in so many ways that you can't even imagine how messed up you really are right now."

"What are you talking about?" he snapped at her before he gave up his attempt to push himself to a seat on the bed. "I'm ready for my transfiguration."

"You know, I used to believe in something so much bigger than me," she began. "But then I entertained the notion that there's nothing conscious left after death. Nothing. Just like every other living thing on the planet. At first, this terrified me, but then I realized the beliefs that were comforting me were really holding me back from truly seeing how amazing and awesome life in the universe is without any notion of some controlling god.

"So, let me run down this little list of delusions here for you: this whole episodic afterlife sequence you've been babbling about in your drug-induced stupor is just another one of your delusions, just like the whole Hall of Records escapade with your dead author friend is, in fact, a delusion. The entirety of Christianity and all of its promises of salvation and everlasting bliss is nothing but delusion as far as I'm concerned, and even the power of your beloved writing to somehow creatively express meaning to the Biblical proportions of Revelation is nothing but delusion. "

"But what about all the truth in the book!" he tried to shout as she held her finger to her lips to quiet him. "What about the book?"

"I don't care how artful it is that you've constructed a book in the shape and guise of an egg," she began to reply. "And that you so skillfully designed the book as an egg to be eaten like the scroll provided to the Apostle John in the Book of Revelation.

"None of that changes the fact that all of what you've done and all that you think you believe is nothing but delusion. It's all delusion after delusion after delusion after delusion."

"Here we go again," he muttered toward her. "It's too real to dispute now. It has to be. She awaits me for our consummation. Sirena is the proof that it's not all delusion"

"I really don't have any qualms with your identification of Sirena as the perfect woman for you," Anima began. "But you have to understand that the act of being with her is not what's important. Your anima is sufficiently perfected just by knowing that she is your soulmate, so to speak.

"You have reached the status of masterpiece, and as the flesh and blood representative of your anima, I'm here to tell you that that's all that is truly important. The internal peace is the prize, not the external pursuit and physical acquisition."

He wanted to protest her insistence that he didn't need to pursue Sirena, but he ultimately understood her point. Over the decades he had known her, she always had a way to return him to earth much more sober and humble than he was prior to his flight from reality. He acquiesced to her logic.

"But there's more to your debacle than just your fantasyland delusions," she resumed. "You should probably know at this time that everything you've thought was real and happening to you in regard to your friend has been nothing but a carefully orchestrated hoax to deceive you for the purposes of another type of film."

"What are you saying?" he asked.

"I'm saying you've been played like an absolute fool for the entertainment of others," she answered him. "You've been framed or catfished, rather."

"What are you talking about?" he nearly yelled.

"I'm afraid you've been duped by the very person you had hoped would collaborate with your friend about the location of the Hall of Records in a book project," she revealed to him. "It seems this Trickster is involved with The Institute that you've written about. He's connected with the three men who coordinated the Salvador Dali reenactment by your friend and the fiasco of disembodied voices at the well site after your friend's funeral."

"That's impossible," he glared at her. "There's no way that could be true. This all can't be just a production to dupe me."

"The DVD that your friend sent to you wasn't recorded by your friend," she explained. "It was recorded at the direction of the Trickster and the group of men from The Institute."

"That's ludicrous," he laughed nervously. "That's just not possible."

"Au contraire," she countered. "Not only is it true, but the recording itself is an absolute fraud. I grew suspicious about it when I watched it and finally decided to have it analyzed by an amateur expert I know. It was determined just how the parts that featured you and Sirena in the edited recording were generated.

"Turns out that part of the video with you two was edited into the original, which was not even an original of the Salvador Dali performance at all, but also a copy to begin with."

"I'm just not following you," he said, shaking his head. "I don't believe what you're saying. If I understand you right, you're saying that everything I thought was true about what was happening to me is all false?"

"You're really going to need to follow this," she sternly addressed him. "This really is quite a dramatic shift from what you've accepted as reality through all of the events of the past half year or so, and actually even farther back to the time when you saw your friend's eight-millimeter film for the first time."

"How could that be?" he spewed. "I saw Sirena on that film all of those years ago!"

"I'm not so sure you did, actually," she told him. "I think what you saw was your friend's attempt to be clever with some film editing of his own. There was no woman in that room during the actual Dali performance. No woman who held a brown egg and said, 'Alpha and Omega. Your transfiguration awaits you, my love.' The original film really didn't have this other woman in it at all. She's just not there."

"You're saying my friend added her to the film after the fact?" he asked incredulously.

"I don't have that film," she replied. "But I'd have to say, yes, that it was fabricated by him, especially when you consider that the eight-millimeter film you watched had a poster with the woman on it instead of Albert Einstein like the actual Dali performance. That entire film was a fake. Your friend was never there to record anything."

"But it was Sirena!" he yelled. "It was her on that film!"

"I would bet if we did find that first film you watched all of those years ago and watched it again," she began, "you'd find that it wasn't her. The woman filmed may have resembled Sirena in some ways, but it wasn't her. You friend had undoubtedly added someone else. It really couldn't be Sirena, now could it?"

"I don't believe you," he rejected her claim. "You're just trying to alter me."

"Well, yes, I am trying to alter you back to reality," she clarified in return. "I'm actually trying to rescue you at this point. You are way in over your head this time, and the state of mind that you have induced is about to completely consume you if and when you finally do snap out of your web of delusions.

"Now that it's clear a total fraud has been committed against you, I'm afraid the truth of your situation might absolutely crush you with the weight of your own exposed vulnerability."

He stared at her as she sat forward in a chair and leaned her face to the edge of the bed. He wanted to try to sit up again but couldn't find the energy to shift his body into a position to make the attempt.

"The men who have perpetrated this hoax against you were all here to film you in this very hospital bed," she informed him. "I was just fortunate enough to observe them long enough without their knowledge of my presence. I overheard much of their conversation. I also managed to pick up a notebook one of the men dropped below a chair in the hallway lobby. What an idiot."

"Show me the book," he demanded of her.

"I read it then put it back," she said. "I stayed nearby and waited and watched. Sure enough, the man who dropped it found it where I left it. He let out one big sigh, too. There was enough written in the notebook about all of this that it added quite a bit of clarity about the overall plan to dupe you for their ulterior purpose."

"Just when I thought it was all coming together," he seethed. "And you tell me all of this. I was going to become the archangel Uriel and Sirena was about to be my half-human, half-angel hybrid goddess wife for all eternity."

"Chalk that one up to the best laid plans of mice and men instead," she said somberly. "Or best laid revelations between archangels and sirens, I guess you could say.

"Anyway, here's what has happened based upon everything I've been able to gather: First and foremost, the DVD is a fraud, like I said. The image of Sirena's face that was used is a facsimile of hers based upon images acquired through surveillance at the park where you two met to discuss writing."

"How is that possible?" he cried. "Why would anyone know where we were? I don't see how anyone could possibly coordinate something like that and then add it to a DVD that fast."

"That's exactly what they did," she confirmed. "The analysis showed that the DVD production was sophisticated. I think these people who performed this hoax have a lot of resources and financing at their disposal and quite possibly a market to sell their production if they hadn't already sold it in advance."

"You mean Sirena and I are going to wind up in a film looking like total idiots?" he asked.

"I don't know about Sirena," she chuckled. "But you most definitely would look like a really dimwitted Humpty Dumpty.

"And in the anthropomorphic scheme of things, I'd say you've got a much better chance of a transfiguration that ends with you becoming Humpty Dumpty than the archangel Uriel."

"Oh, my God," he muttered as he brought his hands to cover his face. "What have I done? How could I be this moronic and gullible?"

"Let me continue with the details about this," she interrupted him. "The sequence of Sirena holding up the egg was most likely shot from the reenactment that the daughter of Brown Eggs performed. That's why they wanted her to do the reenactment. The face of Sirena was then added to the body of Brown Egg's daughter."

"Brown Eggs' daughter was involved in this, too?" he blurted as he jerked his hands away from his face.

"Not wittingly as far as I can tell," she replied. "But she has a similar body type to Sirena and they used her to shoot that scene based upon an entry I read in the notebook I found. That's also why she was wearing the same optical-art shirt as the woman originally filmed by your friend.

"Brown Eggs' daughter was also used at the well site. You didn't know this, but they had told her that her mother would speak through a miniature in-ear headphone that she wore at the time you were in the shed with her. The Institute men had stolen the children's audio recordings of Brown Eggs for use on the playback for her daughter at the well site."

"I had no idea," he sighed. "That might explain why she heard what she did, but that doesn't explain what I heard."

"True, but this will," she said. "You were in the building with two of the men at the time your friend and then Sirena spoke to you. It was just you three. If you remember, the two sons of Brown Eggs had exited the building with one of the men and the girl before you heard your friend and then Sirena, or rather, the cobbled audio reproduction of his and then her voice based on recordings of their voices."

"You're trying to tell me I didn't actually hear Sirena?" he yelped.

"That's partly right," she said. "You heard Sirena's voice, but it wasn't the live version of her voice and it wasn't anything she actually said. All of the words and the singing were applied to the samples of voice these people had of her. That's why there was such a delay in her responses at the well site.

"And if you watch her mouth closely in the film, you'll see the words really don't quite jibe with her mouth movement when she speaks her infamous line."

"You have got to be kidding me," he groaned. "This is ridiculous. I don't see how anyone could organize something like this."

"I kid you not," she stated. "What you heard was broadcast

within the building. The two men there with you just pretended not to hear it."

"Unbelievable."

"Not really," she offered in response. "You were clearly in an altered state of mind at that time, as well as many other various parts in all of this insanity. I can see how you might have slipped up by not being too rational about what you were experiencing. You expected the unreal to happen and be real by that point."

"What about the letter from my friend and the egg?" he asked her.

"As far as I can tell," she began to explain, "the letter was definitely written as part of the conspiracy against you. I don't see how it could be any other way. I don't know if your friend actually wrote the letter or not at the behest of the conspirators, though. Either way, it really doesn't matter. That letter just sealed the deal in your mind about the authenticity of the egg and all of the other details of the ruse coordinated against you.

"And as for the egg, the staff here hasn't disclosed any of the toxicology yet, but it appears the egg was laced with an unidentified poison to cause swelling in your brain. The egg was clearly the creation of the Trickster and The Institute."

"You mean they took his egg?" he asked.

"I doubt that he ever had an actual egg," she answered. "What he showed you all those years ago was probably just some prop of his to perpetrate his own fiction, just like his revised version of the Dali film.

"But if he did actually have an egg and the folks from The Institute obtained it, they would have to figure out some way to inject the poison into his egg without breaking the egg itself. I'm pretty sure they didn't do that, but instead directly created what you received."

"You mean they really tried to kill me?"

"I suppose you could've died," she acknowledged. "You may want to pursue criminal charges against these people, but on the whole, I'd say all of this is so far-fetched that it might be difficult to get a case moved forward with any hope of trial much less a conviction."

"What about their film?" he asked. "Won't that incriminate them?"

"I would say so," she replied. "But if they never show it, then it wouldn't. They could've made their little documentary there for The Institute itself for internal use by their principals. I really don't know the answer yet to why they were making the film."

"I've really stepped in it this time," he sighed. "Does my wife know all of this yet?"

"No," she answered. "Not even any of it at all. She's just worried sick about you, though. If you had half a brain, you'd just give up all of this nonsense and go back to her and resume the life you had before you let yourself get so swept away by Sirena and all of this brown egg business. You wouldn't even have to beg her forgiveness and mercy since she doesn't have any idea what you've really been up to."

"What about Sirena?" he wanted to know. "How much does she know?"

"She has seen the DVD," she replied. "But I don't know what she thinks about it yet. I don't think she's been here to see you yet. I asked about any other visitors, but she wasn't listed."

"Please, can you find out?" he implored her. "Can you ask her to come see me and make sure my wife doesn't visit at the same time?"

"I really don't think that's such a good idea," she began before he waved her off.

"Please!" he begged her. "I have to see her and find out what she thinks about this or else I will absolutely lose what's left of my mind!"

"I know you will," she tried to placate him. "This has been very hard for you, I know. Somehow, you've managed to romantically position this woman as an ideal that you've internalized to such a degree that your projection of her informs virtually all of your conscious and unconscious activity. She's really is much more than just a muse for you at this point, I'm afraid."

"I'm in love with her," he wailed. "And without her in my life, I'm so lovesick that I'm not sure I could or would want to continue to live."

"I believe that," she voiced her sympathy. "But I believe it's a little more complicated than saying you love her. Nor is it a matter of you just only wanting to be with her in any physically intimate way."

"I would love that, though," he interjected. "I would love to consummate my love with her in every way conceivable. I'm so obsessed with her and infatuated by her that I'm not going to survive all of this."

"I understand all of that," she conveyed to him. "But this feeling you have for her is not a mutual one. I mean, there may be some possibility that she could expand her own interest in you, but I think you have to check your delusion at the door on this one, stud. Otherwise, you are headed for such a crushing fall that I would have to agree with you when you say you won't survive this."

"You mean, I'm headed for a fall anyway." he began. "Because I'm not really about to undergo a transfiguration into the archangel Uriel and she is not going be my angel hybrid of a wife. I'll be lucky if she ever agrees to even meet with me again or ever talk to me again, and if she does, it will probably be out of pity for me being such an *igmo* and not anything else."

"That sounds quite reasonable of you, Igmo, if I may call you that since it is quite fitting," she responded to him. "I think that is really the healthiest way to approach this. Don't expect the impossible or the ridiculous. Just bide your time, and we'll see what kind of meds we can get for you to help you through this time of transition."

The rap at the door was soft and quick. He looked at her as she turned her attention to the sound at the door. The latch clicked before the door slowly moved ajar into the room.

"Knock, knock," the voice came softly. "Mind if I pop in?"

The door was now open wide enough for her to show herself.

"Sirena!" his voice boomed. "Thank God you're finally here!"

"He's just finally regained consciousness, and he's still pretty fragile and groggy," Anima began before he cut her off.

"Nonsense!" he barked. "I'm fine, and I could most definitely use some change in company about now."

Sirena stepped into the room and closed the door behind her. She set her purse on the seat of the chair nearest the door. She then looked at Anima expectantly before she turned her attention toward him in his supine position on the hospital bed. He met her eyes and immediately tried to push himself up from the bed.

"Don't strain yourself," Anima ordered him. "You don't want to lapse back to where you were, do you?"

"I just want up," he groaned as he again abandoned his effort to pull and push himself up. "And I want to talk to Sirena alone, if you don't mind."

"I would actually like that, too," Sirena told Anima. "I need to talk with him alone for a few minutes."

"I have a tingling sensation about this," Anima told Sirena before she then looked at him and addressed him. "But you two do what you must. Just know, Igmo, that I will always be here when you need me to help you restore you whole again."

"Thank you for that, Anima," he acknowledged her. "And thank you for leaving us alone for now."

Anima scurried to the door then turned to face him.

"Go to the edge, my friend," she told him. "And take her with you, for what you see below you is what is truly real."

Anima then crossed the threshold, leaving the door open behind her.

Sirena stepped to the door and softly shut it. She then lunged to his side.

"I'm so sorry this happened to you," she cried as she brought her face to his and gripped his shoulders. "I feel like I've caused you so much anguish just because I was so ignorant of what was really happening to you and to us. I'm so sorry I wasn't there for you when you needed me the most."

She then buried her face into his gowned chest and cried. He curled his fingers underneath the fan of her gray-streaked brunet hair that curled and spread across his chest before he gently cradled the back of her head with his upturned hands. She lifted her face to meet his eyes.

"There's something I have to do now," she said through a stifled sob. "This is what I've decided I have to do to make you fully understood how I feel and appreciate what we mean to each other now."

Sirena leapt to her purse and reached into it. She then turned to face him and held what she removed from her purse behind her back.

"I watched the DVD," she said as she stepped toward him. "I now know what we are. I finally understand how we met ourselves. I, too, remember who we are."

He felt the nausea flood him but he repeatedly swallowed to keep himself from starting to retch. He understood what she was about to tell him, and he also knew he wouldn't keep her from saying it by informing her that everything that had happened to him and, by extension now, to her was a heart-wrenching hoax.

Sirena pulled her long-sleeved blouse over her head and flung it to the other side of the room. She revealed that she was wearing a black-and-white, optical-art patterned print shirt. The checkered squares of the print pulsated within overlapped circles as the waist of the top clung to the curve of her high hips. The long sleeves of the top tightened against her wrists.

"When I saw the op-art shirt I was wearing in the film," she nearly exclaimed, "I knew it really was me. The pattern is an exact match. It is the exact same shirt, right down to the sleeves and the neck. I just couldn't believe it.

"The film is very grainy, but I'm positive about the match. This shirt would have been chic and just emerging into style fifty years ago when the Dali surreal performance was done in New York."

"The op-art shirt is the same one?" he managed to say before he suppressed a dry heave.

"The exact same," she confirmed. "And there's no way I could have been filmed wearing this sweater more than about two weeks ago because I just bought it for ten dollars at a vintage clothing store, and this particular style of op-art print hasn't been publicly available for sale as far as I could find for a long, long time.

"I had just bought it, in fact, the day before I found you nearly dead in the park."

He felt his face burn flush and the surge of blood suddenly churn through him with power unlike anything he had ever experienced. He effortlessly managed to spin himself from the supine position in which he had just found himself too weak to overcome before now. He was surprised to find himself seated on the bed, facing her with infinite hope and a heart ready to burst from his chest. His blood tore through him now, thumping stronger and faster through every part of him, engorging his entire body with such strength that he felt as though he could levitate at will.

"Alpha and Omega," she began with a knowing smile as she revealed the brown egg hidden in her hand and held it in front of her. "Your transfiguration awaits you, my love."

The energy that surged through him virtually lifted him from the bed of its own accord. As his feet contacted the floor, the power he felt merged with the déjà vu of the scene from the film. He now knew he wasn't just going to recreate his scene with Sirena in the film from fifty years in the past: he and Sirena were about to perform the original scene despite the half-century gap in time.

Much like she had recognized her own clothing in the film, he now also knew that his scant clothing revealed in the film was in fact the very hospital gown he was wearing, revealing the glimpse of his back between halves tied by the string wrapped around his waist to keep the gown in place in the front.

Aware of his cue once he reached her and took her in his arms, he turned back to face the direction of the camera angle from the film as she continued to hold out the egg. She then leaned to the side with the egg still held in front of them both, just like the film had depicted. Both of them then detected the camera mounted on the other side of the hospital window, presumably shooting the scene that was unfolding inside.

He followed the script that he now believed without any doubt had both preceded and foretold the two of them together in the Dali film. He turned to face her, enveloping her in his arms as she brought her face in front of his. She maintained her placement of the egg between the index finger and the thumb of her right hand while she brought her other arm around his back.

He leaned over her as he cradled the back of her head in his hands. The two kissed each other, slow and deep at first. He then vigorously gripped her behind her shoulders, just like he had in the film. She brought the egg and her hand to his back as she met the intensity of his kiss and embrace.

Then with a mere twist of her wrist, she flipped the egg from her fingertip and thumb into the air before she clutched his back with both hands. The brown egg remained suspended for a moment as it spun and the two deepened their embrace.

Then the brown egg began its descent toward the floor.

Sirena's Epilogue

I COULD SEE that he had started to lurch toward me like some shit-faced ship captain cursed to smash into smithereens against the treachery that always seems to surround me. How God awful it can be to be me – the voluptuous Sirena with a voice and face that had already wrecked a thousand ships before his.

Given my apparent Nephilim nature as a Siren endowed with such power, it's hard to blame him for his deluded transfiguration into a splatter of moonstruck slop. I hardly discouraged him from falling in love with me. In fact, I admit that his pursuit titillated me, much like Bathsheba must have felt when King David hit all of the right spots for his future queen to commit adultery with his Highness. Only in my case, my adultery was with more than just some ordained king: my sin was perfected with the archangel, Uriel.

Of course, I didn't know he was such a lofty celestial entity at first. My attraction to him prefigured that revelation, and I manipulated him and our circumstances to stimulate his affection for me. Such are the wiles of woman to render man senseless in a merciless swoon.

That attraction between us, however, wouldn't have been enough to prompt me to leave a wake of devastation behind me in the way of my once-happily situated family. I'm not sure he wouldn't have left his wife and children, either, on that basis alone. We probably could've been quite content to enjoy an ongoing affair whenever it was opportune for us both to indulge.

But no turmoil for innocent loved ones, no anguish over guilt for causing such grief could have altered my destiny with him once we both understood that we loved with a passion beyond this world. I told him that I couldn't leave my husband of twenty-five years. He told me I had to leave my husband because we weren't committing adultery: we were consummating our reunion as soulmates.

The notion of soulmates is ludicrous, I know. Some of the Christian ilk may scoff at this notion based upon belief of an afterlife in which there is no husband and wife arrangement and no individual earthly love at all in heaven. Others most certainly will consider anyone who professes soulmate attraction to be pathetic in general.

But we were shown that we are far from stupidly and sloppily romantic. We really *are* soulmates. I first knew this because of the op-art shirt I wore in the Dali film fifty years ago. It was impossible for me to buy that same shirt just before Uriel was hospitalized then have it show up in his friend's film. Witnessing our embrace on the DVD flooded me with such strange tears of orgasmic joy that I felt him inside me in every way possessing my mind, my body, and my soul. I knew right then that our destiny together was a done deal. There was no stopping the two of us.

And then there's that absurd egg. How it hovered so much like the temptation in the Garden of Eden, just waiting for the two of us to savor our forbidden knowledge of each other and our angelic selves. Only it was a ridiculous egg preserved for fifty years. I still find it hard to believe that this putrid remnant of a half-century ago could conjure the magic that it did for us in its form of surreal sacrament.

Without me suddenly thrust into his life, I doubt he would have ever eaten the egg. It was a dumb thing for him to do, but I do have to give him credit for having the balls to risk everything for his seemingly impossible quest of archangel status, not to mention his unslakable craving for me.

When I first read the part of this book that was his love letter to me, I was partly appalled. I thought its content was just sheer lunacy, but soon his soaring mad love for me overwhelmed me with arousal beyond my control.

I admit I was afraid that my earthly self might not quite live up to his angelic expectations for me. He assured me that I could do no wrong in his eyes because of how pure and consuming our love for each other is.

After his release from the hospital, we went to the park but not to our spot where I found him nearly dead. No, we parked at a different place and hiked through the woods until he found the clearing where he wanted to lay down a blanket for us.

Every part of me was drenched from the thrill of epic orgy I envisioned with him, but then he surprised me.

"Stand in front of me and hold out your hands with your fists closed," he instructed me. "Say these words that will pulse within the core of your essence. They are words that are also mine, and I will say them as you say them so that these words become a vow that is ours alone.

"Then after each sentence, hold up one finger and press its tip to mine. Keep each tip pressed until we complete our union. The count of every word that follows will number us, and we will couple in the harmony of our divine love."

His dazzling, blue-eyed gaze penetrated me before the words suddenly flowed. We voiced them in unison as though his thoughts were mine and mine were his alone to guide. We then pressed a fingertip together with each line of our incantation:

"Every second of breath inside hers
Slathers him from above.
Her vines entwined around his mind.
His heart engorged at the tip of her tongue.
She is the one he is numbered by.
She buries him alive inside hers
At the fulcra where both now come,
She in her ratio of raw revival,
He in the instant he fell in love.
He is the one she is numbered by."

With the utterance of the final word and our fingertip-pressed hands now interlocked, we swirl into each other like some gear of gyrating flesh meshed together by churning hot blood. My weight on him at our opposite ends then melts me as he empties his body and soul in the gush that flows into me.

Then we are lifted and flying, faster and farther in our ecstasy until our throbbing together slows and we shake in each other's arms, standing together in a different place and a different time. He tells me why we are where we are and what we'll have to do while we are there. This is how we travel through time.

"One word by one word until we meet at 69," he breathes as he turns my head so his lips meet mine. "Our time will come over and over again until we are done."

"Alpha and Omega," I say to him on cue. "Your transfiguration awaits you, my love."

ACKNOWLEDGMENTS

Gratitude and respect for the ubiquitous Tony Acree and dynamic Stu Thaman. Thanks to both of them and Hydra Publications for bringing this novel to life.

Also, much obliged to the gracious Jamie Godby, who beta read this book and helped shape it through her vast subject matter expertise and editing skills in ways no one else could.

And lastly but mostly, an infinite string of affectionate emojis to my other, much better half, Debbie, who I adore immeasurably and humbly thank for rejoicing and suffering with me through every curve and crack of this cosmic egg.

ABOUT THE AUTHOR

Cosmic Egg Rapture is the first novel in Robb Hoff's *Eggsquisite Corpse Thriller* series of surreal psychological suspense, romance, and horror. The drafted sequel to *Cosmic Egg Rapture* hatched during National Novel Writing Month (NaNoWriMo) 2017. Robb Hoff is also author of the literary folk horror novel *Crackers For A Lycan-thrope* set mostly in the Red River Gorge region of Kentucky. Visit robbhoffauthor.com for *Eggsquisite* updates and offers.

Website: RobbHoffAuthor.com
Email: Robb@RobbHoffAuthor.com

www.ingramcontent.com/pod-product-compliance
Lightning Source LLC
Chambersburg PA
CBHW030112260626
47156CB00008B/2632